The Sara Chronicles
Book Five
The Great Unknown
and All that Lies Beneath It

Chapter One

Dying was easier than she expected; there was no pain, no lingering horrific death scene in which she realized she would never see her loved ones again, just total silence and the nagging question of what she was supposed to do next. Standing perfectly still in the nothingness, Sara thought about the events that brought her here: Vincent had just touched her, and she was gone. Gone, as not on the somewhat stable plane of the living world. Yet her limbs had feeling, the ground beneath her was hard and she was clasping two very solid hands in front of her while a cool breeze caressed her face.

Should she feel different being dead? A little angry, sad, or happy that she was beyond all the misery going on with the living? Should she stop a moment and mourn for herself? After all, she had been so young when she died. Stupid random thoughts for such a serious moment, but she couldn't seem to make them stop tumbling around her head. Everything she had ever heard about the afterlife was totally at odds with what she was at that moment feeling, like a lightning bolt waiting to burst through the clouds. Death shouldn't be this way; it was more like eternal night wasn't it, the end of it all? It was so strange to feel more alive now than she had when she was actually alive. It made absolutely no sense at all.

Sara stood in her little spot in the middle of white cotton candy-like clouds waiting for sadness and regret to overtake her but was surprised to feel happy, loved, and definitely not alone. Puzzled, she turned her head slightly and was overcome by joy at the sight of two very familiar people standing next to her, staring at the same overcast scene. Thomas and James had somehow managed to pass through the barrier to the land of the dead. How had that happened? She struggled to find a good reason for this; her brief moment of happiness shattered by the reality of what their presence here meant. For it could only mean one thing: they were dead also. As they turned pasty faces towards her, Sara fell to her knees, wailing in despair at the realization that they must have done this to stay with her. Thomas's eyes showed startlingly bright green against his pale skin as he knelt down to hug her tightly. James, his light brown skin an ashy color against the darkness of his eyes, joined him as they all huddled together. No one spoke as she cried for the sacrifice they had made to be with her.

This was not how it was supposed to be! She was the one that had to lose her life to save the others; she had been so sure that her death would mean Thomas's freedom. He would eventually get over her and go on with his life. James was meant to go with the other groups to find someone to love and grow old with after this whole thing was finished. It was the least he should be able to expect considering how left out he had been while she and Thomas were falling in love. Sara was resigned to her own loss of life because she had died to give them back theirs. They should not be here.

The three friends sat together on the misty ground, Sara trying to come to terms with what had happened to them all, and James and Thomas waiting for a sign to tell them what to do next, each lost in their own thoughts. Two happy, one sad at the turn of events.

The men didn't regret what they had done, not for one second. They shared a glance over her bowed head and smiled. Mission accomplished. When they realized that Sara was convinced that her death was necessary, and that she would use all her powers to make sure that it happened, they had done the only logical thing: followed their third into the afterlife.

They had been created to work together, not alone; staying together was the only choice as far as they were concerned. Here they were together, dead, but together, and wondering what Iam had planned for them next. Apparently, whatever they were looking for to defeat Braccus was in this place and they were anxious to get started on their mission. James sent his senses outward seeking a starting point for their new adventure, while each evaluated the effect death was having on them.

For his part, Thomas was content to rest his cheek on Sara's surprisingly solid head and inhale the wonderfully familiar scent of cinnamon from her hair. Even dead, she was the best part of his existence. Thomas couldn't have imagined making any choice than to die with her and was surprised that she would have expected him to go on in the other world without her; he wouldn't have made it. He would have given in to the darkness that Braccus had cultivated in him. If she was gone, he would no longer have had a reason to fight its call. If this was death, it was still better than the last couple of weeks of his life.

James was clinging to his friends, also puzzled at the way he was feeling. He had expected death to be far more somber, more final. The way things were now, it didn't feel like an ending, more the beginning of something. When you die, surely you aren't still making plans for the things you want to do in the future. At this point, you should be resigned to the fact that you're dead and nothing else is going to happen. It's all over. But he didn't feel over. In fact, he was already planning his next moves. Find the weapon that would kill

Braccus, hunt the creep down, end his life, and get back to the other Keepers.

It all ran in his head like a movie, making perfect sense, never once did he doubt that it was possible. The very fact that he was clinging to his two solid, yet pale companions only reinforced his belief that his thoughts had some merit. From his limited experience with scary stories, he should be a free floating white sheet with no worries in the world; he shouldn't care if one side or the other ruled the worlds. He should be aware that no matter what he did, it wouldn't make a difference one way or another, but somehow, he didn't feel that it was true. James still felt very useful and he just knew there had to be a reason for that. Besides, his family was still living back in the nightmare the worlds had become and he owed it to them to return and give his brothers and sisters a better future. Lost in their thoughts, they ignored the strange place around them for a moment. Thomas was the first to realize that they were not alone. Something or someone was very close. His alarm transmitted itself to his friends. Sara stopped crying and James began to focus on what was happening. Together they rose and looked around. They couldn't see anything beyond the fog, but felt an intense pressure that was becoming stronger by the second. The power was great here, granted. It felt a little bit weaker than it should have; death had dulled what must have once been an overwhelming surge of raw power. The visibility was poor, but it felt like whatever was putting out the energy was all around them, waiting with anticipation. Thomas was sure it was due in large part to Sara's presence. He couldn't see anything yet, but instinct drew him closer to her, while James did the same.

The three newly dead companions scanned the area in an effort to see their un-living company. They recognized what they were sharing space with: deceased Keepers were all around, watching the new arrivals with interest, but not approaching. They wanted to very much, but something was holding them back. In the stillness of the dead place, a faint echoing throb of a power itched to resurrect itself, to connect with the new arrivals. They were an accepted part of this place now, so their presence wasn't causing their hesitation; it was the other visitor the dead sensed that made them scream in protest.

James tried to use his abilities to reach out to the entities in the dead world. They were here, and very close. Faint hisses of protest sounded in his head, becoming louder and more urgent as they communicated with him. A slight tinge of darkness tainted this otherwise peacefully washed-out atmosphere, and James sensed a rising anger at its presence in their territory. The anger expressed by the deceased grew, showing itself as a bright white light shining down on the surface. Starting just above Sara, it spread outward to form a shield around the three new arrivals accompanied by a loud wailing that hurt their ears.

A small spot of darkness shied away from the area to melt into the shadows and wait for another opportunity to connect with the girl it needed to reach out to, cursing itself for forgetting to mask *It's* presence from the dead ones. Secretively, he had traveled in and out of this place many times before. But these souls had been with him from the beginning, so they knew him better than the rest, and being here required more caution then the outer worlds.

It was a little more challenging to move through this place because the dead ones weren't afraid of him and were still powerful, but in a different more subdued way. Braccus was smart enough to be cautious here, he had control of the worlds but not this place. The deceased Keepers were still not his equals, no one was, but he needed to be careful. He had things hidden in this place; things he would like to keep secret. These wasted leftover beings were a little bit too interested in his presence, and since this was the first time he had been careless enough to show himself, they were throwing a fit about it.

Watching Sara had made him forget himself, her shining soul attracted him. He had been part of her for four years, hanging out at the edge of the protective barrier Olie had put up, wanting so badly to get through and absorb all the power she possessed. The goodness he sensed in her pulled at him like a magnet. He would love to change all that goodness and watch her use her power for his purposes; it would be so much fun. *Oh, the things they could do to the worlds together, the misery, the pain...* His musings caused him to let some of the darkness out, darkness that was part of his soul. It showed up in this place like an oily stain against a lily-white tablecloth. *Oh, they saw him alright*, and it was causing quite a stir among them. Next time he would not be so careless, he would let them calm themselves, lull them into believing they had stopped him, but he would come back.

Braccus eased himself out of the area, snuffing out the darkness and quietly disappearing into the mist. There was a way to do these things, a little patience was called for here. It was okay though, she couldn't leave. She was where he wanted her, and he had plenty of time to play the game. Let her wander lost in nostalgia with the dead ones; that should be distraction enough for a while. He would be back soon enough and just like everything else, it would work out exactly the way he wanted it to. In the meantime, there were plenty of things he could be doing in the worlds. He had been so occupied with following Sara and remaining undetected that he had let the other Keepers live. Now that he was in control, he would have to work on ending their existence. He let visions of his victory over them calm him as he went back to the world where his control extended over almost everything.

Chapter Two

As Braccus sped back toward the land of the living, those that mourned Sara, Thomas, and James were involved in a drama of their own. Running for the portal to the underground, the only place left to hide, Finola stumbled through a doorway, her hand crushed tightly in Eric's. Randall, Franklin, and Alice followed after, having pushed them through so hard that they nearly collided with Maryann and Robert, who seemed to be waiting for them to pass through the door.

Randall distinctly got the impression that they had been standing and watching the opening, calmly stepping back as the four young people ran into a darkened cave. They didn't look at all surprised when Randall and Franklin slid to a stop, pushing their companions, staying just yards ahead of their pursuer. It was only after Rianna stumbled in after them that Maryann and Robert assumed a puzzled expression.

Randall didn't stop to consider why they seemed to be expecting his group; he was more concerned with keeping Alice safe, putting her as far away from Vincent as he could. At first, she resisted being pushed behind him, not wanting him to be the only one taking the risk while she stayed in the background and watched, but the panicked look on his face warned her that there wasn't time to fight over this. Alice grabbed Rianna's hand before Eric caught hold of her other one. Rianna followed without resistance, like towing a sleepwalker behind her.

In response to Randall's anxiety, Eric grabbed Alice's hand and pulled her, Finola and Rianna around behind the two adults, and then turned to face the young man following them closely through the wavering entryway. Randall and Franklin stopped immediately in front of the Keeper and his wife to throw up a field of energy, a strange combination of

11

crackling fire and snapping electrical charges merging together to form a tightly knit bubble of protection as their deadly companion, Vincent, sped in on their heels. He may be able to kill with a touch, but they were betting their lives that he could also be hurt or killed from a distance. All they had to do was throw a little danger his way.

Alice was too stunned to use her shield, which he seemed to be able to get through anyway. She stood back, sensing that Randall and Eric were having a hard time deciding the right thing to do. They were facing their third as a threat and that was not what they expected to happen. Circle members weren't supposed to be enemies, they were supposed to fight together not fight each other. As much as she wanted to help, there wasn't any immediate danger. If she had felt it the man in front of her would now be transported far from here to a very unpleasant place. Her heart went out to Randall and Eric as they struggled with this situation, but she didn't know exactly what she could or should do to help them. Seeking advice, Alice let her mind wander to a place few had access to, heeding a call that the others couldn't hear. She had to talk to Sara.

Briefly, Randall wondered what he and Franklin were doing. Did he really want to kill Vincent? Was that how this was supposed to end? If so, would they be able to do that to a fellow Keeper? From the looks of it, Vincent had purposely killed three very important members of the team. What were they supposed to do about that? How could they accept him after what he had done? Randall felt Alice's presence in his head, anxiously watching Vincent in case she was wrong about the threat he posed to them.

Eric was ready too, waiting for a sign to jump in and help the one Circle member he knew he could trust. When it came down to loyalty, there was no question in his mind; it was either him or them. He knew Randall like the back of his hand. But even so, he wasn't sure what to do about this face-off. Were they supposed to attack him? He didn't want this, any of this. To top it all off, he felt Finola standing so close to him, trying to not look back at Rianna, the visions of all that had happened on the boat still fresh in her mind. She was sacred to be near the woman and even more terrified of being left with the painful reminder of the empty husk Braccus had left behind. He was trying to give her comfort while agonizing over his own difficult situation.

The object of their fear and anger Vincent, slid to a stop in front of the small group of young people watching him with eyes burning red with hatred. He couldn't see them well, but he sure could feel the fear and rage they were putting out. The only members of his greeting committee that weren't glaring at him were the two older ones standing just beyond the deadly barricade and that poor puppet-like shell of a woman that had tagged along after Sara died.

He couldn't make the older man out very well either; what with all the interference caused by the fiery curtain that hung in the air around them. But he was tall and looked and felt like someone with power. The woman was short and felt different to the man. Vincent liked her instantly. Needing an ally, he made a decision to entrust his fate to her. There was something about her aura that was familiar to him and he yearned to connect with the kindness that flowed from her. He hadn't experienced that reaction in many years and longed to be someone's loved one again.

Vincent reached out with his mind to communicate with her. He just felt like she would be willing to listen to him, that she wouldn't see him as a monster, not like her companions. He couldn't see their faces at all now, but could still feel the fear and loathing radiating from beyond the snapping curtain they were hiding behind. She was his only hope of getting through to the others. Surely she would make them see that he had only done what he was supposed to do. He couldn't be alone anymore. There had to be a reason he had been asked to do all this. It couldn't be his destiny to remain the boy that everybody hated.

Hoping to make contact, Vincent turned in the woman's direction, dropping the protective wall he kept up in his head. Standing perfectly still, he felt a faint tingle, like another's energy was joining with his, waiting for her to say that everything was okay, that he was okay.

You killed my friends, you monster! Finola's voice exploded in his head. Vincent stumbled backward, startled that he had not connected to the person he had meant to reach. They were in his head, all of them, judging him, hating him, screaming out things he didn't really want to hear.

Why did you follow us here? Franklin's voice joined Finola's. *Are you going to kill us too?*

Vincent stepped forward, trying to find a way to get through to them. If only he could make them listen to what he had to say. But his movement was taken as a threat. In response, Randall sent a stream of electricity in his direction, seeking to stop his approach, protecting his friends without thinking of the consequences. The white arc hit an invisible shield, deflecting the charge to a pile of rocks a few feet away. Stones shattered and flew from the impact of the current; the sound quickly swallowed as Eric diminished the noise, sensing that there were people in the cavern behind them and he didn't want to alert them to this altercation. Robert helped him by crushing the stones in mid-air and scattering the dust into the tunnels. He could not allow any harm to come to the innocents nearby.

14

Both young men were so surprised by the unexpected interference that they stopped to stare at the only person who had the ability to provide this type of help. Shock and puzzlement registered on their faces as they looked to Alice for an explanation; it was her invisible barrier that had protected Vincent.

Alice stared back, green eyes pleading with Randall to understand that she was doing this for him. He could not be allowed to kill Vincent; it would be very bad for him, for all of them, if this young man died. She just wished that he wasn't looking at her like she had just broken his heart. Hurt looks turned to shock as the fiery wall of energy sizzled out, leaving them all vulnerable to the touch of the blonde man standing before them.

The protective wall had been removed with a wave of Robert's hand, forcing the group to interact despite their reluctance to do so. He knew what Alice could do, and why she was doing it. She was following instructions from those unseen, trying to make her friends understand that this wasn't betrayal but necessity.

While this drama played out, all the new Keepers were starting to assume the role of protectors. They watched Vincent carefully but were also fully aware of their surroundings. Adapting quickly to this new situation, thinking of the innocents nearby, they went into defense mode, protecting them by taking away all sight and sound of what had just happened so close to them. The group managed to isolate themselves from the refugees quietly sleeping behind them. They were becoming Keepers despite their ignorance of the matter; the natural order of things dictating that their powers react to the universal need for their services. Iam was pulling them into the game, giving them no chance to back out and become anything less than what he had intended from the beginning.

Tension crackled in the air while the collective group faced Vincent, each wanting desperately to vent their grief and anger, but holding back, being afraid to touch him and die instantly. He too wanted to make contact, yearning to find a way to redeem himself in their eyes. His first and second impressions on them had been so negative; killing their friends had pretty much soured them against him, he was sure of that. A million thoughts swam together in his head as he tried to figure out what had gone wrong and how this situation could possibly get any better.

Why did they not know what the mission was? Why did they not know what he had been shown? Why did his Circle mates not know him like they should? So many questions. He didn't know whether to cry or scream. He didn't want to show them how much all this hurt, so he just stared at them blankly; afraid to tear up, afraid to frown, too scared to show any kind of emotion at all. There was no sympathy for him, not even from the girl who had helped him. He could tell she had done what she had been told to do, but was still afraid of him and didn't trust him. He had killed her beloved friends, but maybe...

It's okay, Vincent, I will make them understand. A voice stored in his memory spoke soothingly. It was faint now, as if coming from a distance, stressing each and every word like she was trying to make herself understood before it was impossible to get through any longer. Then there was silence as he watched the four new Keepers listening to an internal message from the newly departed. He couldn't hear it, but he knew what Sara was telling them. She was telling them what they were, why things had to happen the way they had, and she was telling them goodbye.

16

While they listened and sobbed, the only one in the group to smile was Rianna. She too had turned inward to listen. Instinct had taken over and she had done what she had always done, used her mind to pick up messages sent by other Keepers. The voice she heard was coming to her like a sweet dream, a pleasant memory she longed to hold on to, then all was blank again.

Alice became very pale as she allowed Sara to pass the message along through her mind link. She had gone past the barrier in search of answers to Randall and Eric's problem. While very draining she had gone to the source, trying to prevent them from doing something they might regret. Sara was working through her to make the others listen; she stood with closed eyes as the soul of her good friend worked through her.

Finola's eyes welled with tears. She looked at Vincent while receiving the message. In fact, they were all looking at him now. Frowning, Randall, Eric, and Franklin listened to the recently deceased Sara. Alice's connection with the Land of the Dead was her link to them all. She would not be using it anymore; Sara had done what she could to make sure that she understood that she must not seek her out again.

Alice, it is too dangerous to be here right now. We are where we are meant to be. I will see to it that this link is closed to you after today. Tend to the living, they don't stand a chance without you. There are things that escaped even as we were brought here, and it is them you should be concerned about. Your gift is all that stands between these things and the people. The young woman had listened with a heavy heart and passed the other conversation to her friends.

Vincent knew when the conversation was over; the group moved slowly away, each lost in their own thoughts as Robert ushered them to a flat ledge in the cave to talk. They

17

no longer looked at Vincent, but he knew they were still very much aware of him, being careful not to let him anywhere near the group. They had stopped their attempts on his life for the moment and he knew it was because of what Sara had said to them. They still wanted him eliminated, but were no longer trying to do it themselves. He watched them fall less than gracefully onto the stone benches; faces grim while they reviewed the information their fallen friend had passed on to them. Finola buried her face into Eric's shoulder and cried as her stricken companions watched with wide eyes. The facts were hitting them hard and fast, and while it was all starting to make sense, was extremely overwhelming. They were the protectors of the land now. They had a lot to do and like it or not, their new member was part of all this too. Randall glanced at Vincent who stood perfectly still watching them from the exact same spot he'd been in when he came through the portal. If he wasn't such a deadly companion, he would have felt sorry for him but his gift kind of ruled out the giving of hugs for comfort. He just wished he could feel more than a faint acknowledgement that this guy was a part of his Circle, some familiarity would be nice. Randall was sitting next to Alice stroking her hair while her color slowly returned to normal; silently apologizing for his hasty actions earlier and all that she had gone through to keep him from making a terrible mistake.

It was Maryann's soft voice that finally broke the silence as she carefully guided Rianna to a seat. She and Robert had not expected to see Rianna ever again; they assumed she had been lost when she went after Sara. Robert had searched her mind and passed on to Maryann the sluggish state it was currently in. There was so little left of the woman he remembered. Saddened by the shape this once powerful woman was in, Maryann helped Robert heal the worst of her

18

injuries, then took a deep breath and spoke to the newcomers.

"Well, you all know what you are now and the shape the worlds are in. By now Sara has told you why Vincent had to lead you here; it is now your job to protect the people of all the worlds. Until Sara and her Circle members are able to destroy Braccus, we are all that stands between the enemy and innocent beings of all the worlds." After a brief pause, she turned toward Vincent, her soft brown eyes shining with understanding for his situation. "We will also search for your other half. I know a few things and I believe I can help you."

Chapter Three

Thomas stood frozen to Sara's side as a blinding white light shone upon them and eerie wails of protest split the air. He watched James's washed out features shift when he turned from side to side, scanning the area in attempt to make contact with the hidden source of the noise, keeping his mind open so that Thomas could hear them also. He wondered if he looked as scared as James did right now, it would be hard for him not to be. Were you supposed to be afraid when you were dead? This was his first time, so he didn't know what to expect. He almost laughed at this thought: first time! How many times did one get to die? He pulled Sara closer to him, ready to guard her with his... life?

James was beginning to pick up garbled messages thrown at him by the ancient dead ones. He had adjusted his brain to their flow and began decoding them in his head rapidly, anxious to know what was causing their extreme reaction. He wasn't worried about Sara's ability to pick up the frantic mumblings of their deceased greeting committee; the look on her face told him that she was picking up the distress signals just fine.

James could hear them clearly now, calling for caution. He passed on what he heard to Thomas, but he wasn't sure what they were supposed to be cautious about. The dead beings seemed to be warning them to move carefully, but he also felt like they were not telling them something important, like the danger they were in. The harder he listened, the less he got about the source of the danger. The deceased Keepers merely impressed on him the need to stay exactly where they were until it was taken care of. So he stood perfectly still next to his Circle mates and waited. He wasn't sure what powers he might possess here. Would their gifts go with them in death? Would they even be able to protect themselves here? Could the dead hurt them and why would they want to? Soon, the screeches and screams were joined by a tremendous amount of activity. The three new Keepers stood stiffly in the beam of light anticipating the worst.

The ground shook as if a thousand feet stomped all around them. Yet another inconsistent feature of this place: Do the dead have substance? Did their place of residence have form and texture like those of the living? Shouldn't they all be dwelling in the clouds? And weren't Keepers supposed to be in paradise with Iam? Yet they weren't, they were here; their power still lingered around them, vibrating in the air, waiting for the chance to start up again.

What kind of place was this, anyway? The afterlife was not looking too glamorous. Fog, fog, and more fog, unless this white filmy stuff around them actually was cloud material or whatever you might call it. James squinted, hoping to see beyond the bright light that hung above them, but he still couldn't make out the source of all the noise and didn't feel adventurous enough to go out and see what was happening beyond his line of sight.

Then, just as suddenly as it had started, the enraged screeching stopped. There was a muffled popping noise, like something solid had passed through a layer of plastic wrap. Then silence. Sara moved slightly away from Thomas, to reach out and grab James's hand, her other hand still tightly holding Thomas's. She had been listening to the Keepers and was aware that they had sensed the darkness; it was not a new sensation here. Faint and puzzling at first, they had restlessly sought to identify the source, but always it evaded them; teasing them with the sheltering shadow of uncertainty. But eventually they began to realize that this subtle covering could only have been put there by a very powerful being. They had watched the changes in the outer worlds and their sense of unease grew as certain forces began to take root in the formerly untouchable place. The nothingness was not immune to the disease inflicting itself everywhere else, the change they had been expecting was occurring and with it, renewed hope that they would once again be of use to the worlds.

This had been a place made of their free will and Iam did not dwell here; they were not granted his protection or given the right to rest. He had expressed his sorrow at their loss, but it seemed more of his Chosen Ones had resisted the privilege of eternal rest when it came to continuing the struggle for control of the worlds. When they had lost their lives protecting Olie, Iam's trusted leader in living form, they had joined Iam for a brief time before love and concern for their offspring had them rejecting comfort and safety for the need to reach out and share in the lives of their little ones.

It seems they could not let go of the places and people they had loved and, considering what was going on out there, the dedication they had to preserving the best of what Iam had created was too strong. So he allowed the Artregeans to guard him and let the original Keepers slip into a place just beyond the Shallow Shadows. This empty unused plane of energy had been manipulated to suit their needs and allowed them to monitor the troubling events just outside their immediate control. Most had passed their powers on to the young ones, what they'd kept was enough to maintain the integrity of this watchful place. They had been trapped here for the longest time, interested and troubled observers. Needing neither sleep nor food, the powerful deceased had nothing to do with their time except watch, endless years of watching passively for a chance to be of use again. They had dwelled there restless, waiting for what Iam had told them would occur eventually, hoping for their chance to affect the outside worlds again. They had to see that their children were safe and allowed to learn their craft. It was all happening much sooner than expected. Sara felt their frustration at being unable to do anything but stand by helplessly and watch it all unfold, still unable to help as they would have liked. Sara was their hope to change things, her arrival had given them the chance they had been waiting for; she listened and learned what they wanted her to know. They were the oldest of the old, the ones who had created life with the blessing of Iam and children formed from their eternal bonds. Keepers were destined to find true mates and bond forever. The strength of their union was unbreakable and continued after death. They had guarded the souls of their blessed offspring and manipulated the very fabric of time under Iam's direction to shelter their babies and keep them safe. The places their offspring were sent may not have been ideal. She felt the outrage their parents had experienced when they found that some of their children had not been cherished and raised in the way they wanted, but they were happy to see them find their way back to the Land of Keepers, to the place where they were meant to be.

The planes of existence were becoming more and more open to each other, and the originals were hoping that this meant that they would soon be able to rejoin the battle between good and evil, making a difference in the outcome. But this place, being accessible to the spirits of the good, was also logically accessible to evil spirits. Their powers, though diminished, were still of a threat to most things that might have entered, so the evil avoided entering altogether. But gradually, as things began to change, they had become more at risk of invasion by the harsher spirits in the worlds. At first, the faint stain on the lily-white covering of this place was so subtle they thought it might be just another attempt of minor evil to enter, with the spirit quickly moving on. But it began to happen more often. Something was going on; the power behind the entity was blocking a lot of itself, which naturally made it noticeable to them. It made enough of an impression that they began to pay more attention. Today, he had made enough of a disturbance for them to identify him. His formerly bright form was now so dark that it stood out as he stared at Sara with fascinated longing. He had become careless and forgotten to be more than a passing flutter of bad feeling.

It made sense that he would try to get in to see her. Her existence was what brought it all together. The possibilities were endless. She was either the key to ending Braccus's control in the worlds or to possibly making him much stronger than he already was. This path had several possible endings. He had just regained power and would, of course, try to keep the odds in his favor. All this she knew through them, they passed on the knowledge as they searched for Braccus, intent on driving him away from her. But, just as quickly as he was felt, he was gone and another new presence arrived, one they were happy to welcome into their company. The girl who had been given the bulk of Fraylen's gifts was here. The dead ones became quiet and allowed Alice to speak to Sara, happy that contact with the outer worlds was possible again.

Eyes closed, Sara raised her face to the sky, or whatever was above them, a small smile forming on her lips when she greeted Alice. It was nice to feel her here, even as they stood uncertainly among their lifeless companions.

Alice's greeting was short, followed by a vision of the struggle going on between her grief-stricken friends and Vincent; the boy who had just killed them. Strange that Sara could find herself thinking of that so calmly. Of course, it was what she had expected to happen to her, but not James and Thomas. Sorrow hung heavy for that event alone, and she tried to push it back and concentrate on getting the situation between the two parties in the living world under control. *Alice, I don't think I can get through to them without you. We need to make them stop fighting him. He can be hurt, but it would be very bad for everyone if he is. Help me speak to them. I don't have that ability now. I'm not even sure what I can do at this time.* She felt Alice nod and then join with her to pass on some much-needed information about the current state of things.

She used the connection with her friend to link with Franklin, Finola, Randall, and Eric, telling them that she, James, and Thomas were alright despite the fact that they were dead. Explaining that what had just happened was supposed to happen. She told them that Vincent was a necessary part of their group and they had better stop trying to hurt him because he wasn't trying to hurt them. She told them that they were now Keepers, that Robert was the only original member of the original group to have survived, and that he would guide them on their new mission, keeping the people of the worlds safe.

She said her goodbyes to each and every one of them and then closed the door on their link; a door she would not be opening again.

Chapter Four

The group of new Keepers sat and stared at each other for a moment, trying to absorb all that had just happened. It couldn't be true; they just couldn't believe that Sara and her Circle were really gone. They had been fighting Braccus and his followers all this time only to have everything go against them in the blink of an eye. There seemed to be no hope for a positive outcome when half their group was dead and the surface of the worlds were swarming with evil mutant beings. This was not what they had been led to believe would happen and, as they listened to Robert explain the events that occurred after they left, Randall and the other new Keepers had a hard time understanding it all.

"Are you telling us that this is part of what is supposed to happen?" Randall asked. Alice sat next to him, unsure of his reaction to her intervention but firmly convinced that she had done the right thing, only regretting that she had to go against him at all. He reached over and gently squeezed her hand as he waited for an answer to his question. She had done what she was supposed to do; she had kept the group together and prevented him from doing something stupid. Randall felt Alice's hand squeeze back as he listened to Robert's answer, stopping to take a second look as he felt the strength of her response was a little weaker than before. But despite being a little bit pale she seemed okay. She gave him a wide smile and he was relieved to feel her answer him clearly with a strong mental *I love you*. Encouraged by this, he turned back to hear what Robert had to say.

"Yes, I am. Braccus has control of the worlds now. His power is greater than ours and all we can do is hide and protect ourselves from his creations. Our people must survive until the tide turns in our favor again. It is your job to make sure that the ordinary people live and grow wherever they are. Your powers are all that stands between them and certain extinction."

With a wave of his hand, Robert indicated the sleeping villagers just beyond them in the large cavern. They slept soundly with his assistance; he had made sure they did not witness the struggle that had just occurred. It would not be good to see their chosen heroes fighting among themselves. They weren't going to wake up until this was resolved. Holding fast to their minds with Maryann's assistance, Robert fed them the suggestion of deep sleep.

"What you all fail to understand is that Sara cannot do what she needs to do on this level of existence. There is a bigger plan here, one that we are only a small part of and fortunately for us, her Circle mates decided to go with her. She is not alone and that is a very good thing. They did what they felt they needed to do and Vincent did what he had been prepared to do for the longest time. He was made aware of this a long time ago. Don't blame him for doing what it was his part to do." He paused as the five Keepers looked cautiously in the young man's direction. He kept his seat in a location well away from them and they were happy to have him stay there.

"Iam has a plan for us all and if it means that we have to go through some bad things before it gets better, it was all meant to be just this way. We must pull ourselves together and discuss what is to be done next. I have plenty of places I need all of you to be. We will have to use the portals to move into the other worlds and give assistance to all Iam's creations. In order to do this, I must give you a crash course on how to deal with the ones that don't even know you exist."

His audience exchanged worried glances.

"Iam created seven worlds and all of them are have been forced to hide below the surface to stay alive. Not all the inhabitants of the underground are aware of the Keepers and, given the fact that they have been forced away from their homes by all kinds of strange-looking creatures that killed their friends and neighbors; I would say they probably aren't going to welcome strangers with open arms. They don't know what's really happening, but they know they are in danger and I'm sure they will try to protect themselves. You could defend yourselves against them easily, but of course you won't. We want to help them not hurt them. We don't want to push ourselves on them, we want unconditional acceptance of our assistance and we have to find a way to make this happen."

"That's just wonderful," said Finola "How are we going to approach any of them and offer help? What's going to make them trust us?" She reached out to a few loose roots above her head and coaxed the stressed plant life into growing downward into the cave. Her instinct to save the growing things and help them adapt to this new atmosphere was taking over. It helped to occupy her mind as she struggled to deal with all the new things being thrown at it. But she still couldn't, wouldn't look at Rianna. Her guardian's body was sitting on the bench with a blank look on its face and blood all over *its* clothing. She flinched at thought of now seeing her adopted mother as an *it*; there was no Rianna present now.

Franklin helped Finola by forming two flaming orbs with the power of mini-suns and launching them upward toward the cavern's roof. Controlling the heat so that the plants, starved for the missing energy source moved toward it, glorying in the feel of it soaking into their leaves. He was glad to assist his dear friend. Soon the whole roof of the cavern was swarming with brilliant green life. Carrots and tomatoes dangled from above, shining like Christmas tree decorations. A few brightly colored flowers hung in another area, right next to clumps of strawberries, blueberries, and grapes. The variety of growth was amazing, fruits, vegetables, flowering vines; it was as if the roots of whatever that might be salvaged had managed to slink through the dirt to find the one who could bring them back to life. The plants were humming happily in her head in a language only she could understand. They were thanking her for bringing them back to life. She felt their wonderful energy from the tip of her head down to her toes.

Finola smiled at Franklin as they used their powers together, comforting each other with their close bond. Alice joined her group by putting up a filmy wall between the intense heat, the plant life, and the people beyond them, just enough to keep the leaves from catching light and the sleeping villagers from waking with sunburns. It was wonderful to act together like this again. It made them feel whole and so much stronger and Alice needed that strength right now. She drew it from them gratefully making her feel focused and firmly present in the moment.

"They will be suspicious of you all. You must find the gifted ones, the beings like Maryann who possess the second sight. They know a little more about you than the others, but still not as much as the people in the Land of the Keepers. It is up to you to prove to them what you can do, until then, when you pass through the portals you must move into the larger groups and do your best to blend in with the crowd. It may be a little bit difficult, but I know you'll find a way," Robert added, bringing to their attention that the inhabitants of each place looked a little bit different than the Keepers.

"Find the special ones and convince them. They will be the ones the others listen to. We want to do this as peacefully as possible, remember we are there to help them." Robert finished his announcement, waiting for any more questions they might have for him.

They didn't have any. He knew they were aware of the portals and had used them before to move from one place to another, once they figured out that Finola had the power to call them up. She had the ability to do this at times but that particular skill seemed to have faded away after the last battle. It looked like finding the openings would be more of a hit-and-miss task once they left the security of this place. The entryways would draw them in and offer transport to another place. Unfortunately, they would not be able to control where they went. It would be up to Alice to guide them through the exits. After that, they would be on their own.

Alice worried him. He hated to have to send her off so soon after she had started seeing the in-between places, but there was no way around it. She had to leave with the others. She had the ability to see beyond the solid world into the shadowy half worlds that existed, that harbored the bad things. Robert could see she had begun to dwell half in and half out by that slightly unfocused way she was beginning to look around her. She pulled herself back together when she joined with Franklin and Finola. He was glad they were there for her. From now on, she would be needing them and the young man Randall a lot. They would be her connection to the solid worlds.

Eventually she would master this gift, but it would take a lot of concentration to focus solely on the place she was in now. The worlds in-between were calling to her, the restless spirits dwelling were anxious to have their say; good and evil. She was strong, but it still took a lot to resist the invitations they were sending, and remain mostly where she was. Randall noticed too, her young admirer was staring at her with a concerned look on his face. He was already a part of her, Robert could sense the growing bond of lifelong partners was there and it was just as strong as the call of his Circle member's souls. It would constantly pull at him even when he was joined with his own Circle. It would be so hard to leave her when the time came to go with his Circle members, and that time would come soon enough.

Eric's instincts were that he belonged with Finola. Emotions carried over from souls that were thousands of years old, having known each other long before the bodies they now occupied. Old souls sheltered in young bodies, they needed to grow into the strong emotions they carried from past experiences. He hoped they would have the chance to make that happen. They would be fantastic together when the time was right.

Franklin, though sustained by the affectionate connection he had with his Circle, had not yet formed a bond with anyone else. He was a strong and brave young man, Robert wanted him to have the opportunity to meet someone who would give him everything he shared with his fellow Keepers and more. He was to be one of the greatest of the Keepers. Maryann had shared that she had seen him as one of the fiercer fighters, making a great difference in the struggle they currently engaged in. Beyond that brief flash of knowledge, she couldn't see more. She was limited in her sight of the futures of the Keepers, they were more powerful than her and she was not allowed to make predictions about them; Iam alone was in charge of their fates. There was a certain order to this disorder which only he understood.

Then there was Vincent, who watched them all from the outside, not having any hope of growing closer to any of them. His two fellow Circle members felt nothing beyond the knowledge that he was part of their group, his history vague and unclear to them. The faint glimpses they had of him were hardly positive; all they had seen were dead people everywhere he went. There was a part of him that was missing and until it was there again, he would remain just a token member, a scary token they had to keep at arm's length to stay alive.

Robert studied each young person wanting them close to him a while longer. It was hard to let go of the students that had meant so much to him Olie, Ferd, and Maggie, but he knew he had to send them out to other places soon. In order to get to as many of the people and other beings that Iam wanted to protect, they would have to separate into groups of two and pass through into as many portals as possible in the next few weeks. The Circles would not be called to gather together right now, so he let them choose their travel partners.

He began to talk to them again about what they were to do; Maryann would be a point of contact between the teams but contact would be limited. They would be pretty much on their own once they left the area. He spoke for an hour before finally admitting to himself that he couldn't stall any longer and prepared to let them go out on their own out into the big, bad worlds to fight the demons that were now in control, and all the while Rianna sat there quietly smiling.

Chapter Five

Swirling puffs of white fog drifted slowly upward, gradually revealing a surface that looked like a glass mirror, shiny and smooth with a faint glimmer of silver. Sara, James, and Thomas looked downward and were surprised to see not a reflection, but images of grassy hills, trees, and blue sky. Bright, clear, and clean, this land had not yet been touched by man. Animals roamed freely, plants grew tall and beautiful in neat rows ready for use. No buildings occupied space, no people walked around on the surface. It reminded them of a place they had been once before when seeking Braccus's hidden object.

They had gone back to a time before the Keepers arrived on the surface of the land that bore their name. The very first world Iam had created, untouched by anything dirty or mean, but it hadn't stayed that way for long. Even way back then, Braccus had found a way to ruin what Iam had made, killing animals and plants as he arrived to experiment on Iam's world in secret.

Unpleasant memories of that meeting with Braccus came to mind as the group stood surrounded by a place filled with nothing, but overlooking everything. That meeting had cost Thomas his freedom for a time and caused him a lot of suffering and Sara and James a lot of pain. Trying to concentrate on their current situation, Sara and her companions pushed back the incidents of a life now ended and continued to stare at the land displayed under their feet. The scene below them was filled with an explosion of lovely color but the air around them was a pale washed out white, much like the pasty muted color of their skin. Death had brought some extreme changes in their appearance.

Sara noticed that her own hand had the appearance of not ever encountering the sun. She was so pale that she was sure that Finola's new friend Eric, even as white as he was, would have appeared a shade or two darker.

As they continued to watch in fascination, the scene shifted. It was like watching the world form below them. The things they were seeing were not still like a pretty picture, they were moving. Clouds floated across the sky, and they could see people now. Human beings moved along in sturdy work clothes, farming and building, laughing and playing.

Since their view was so good, they could see for quite some distance ahead of them. it looked as if the scenes were constantly changing, time passing. The people and landscape morphed, little children grew up and older; mountains rose and wore away with the passage of time. Buildings rose and fell, trees grew and were chopped down. Events that took many years seemed to be occurring over a matter of minutes and before their very eyes.

And it wasn't just the land of the Keepers they saw, it was other places too. Exotic places with blue grass and purple skies were visible on one section of their unusual flooring, while swampy ground and deserts with orange sand occupied a section farther ahead to the left. The occupants of each section were different too; though closely resembling your average everyday person, each resident boasted the slight changes Iam had made with each new world he created.

These changes allowed their bodies to survive in the atmosphere he had made for them to live in. Some had blue skin others were pale white; still others had orange hair or green hair with features that suited the changing environments. Little differences, large muscular chests built to house bigger lung capacity, nostrils a little wider allowing them to breathe the thicker air that was part of their world. Another area revealed villagers with eyes just a tad larger than your average person, with colors that weren't seen in the normal earth type atmosphere, red, pink, and orange. Thomas guessed somehow these colors made it possible for them to see in the dense maroon fog that passed for air in their particular piece of the universe. Many more were very short in stature, with heavy legs made for keeping them grounded because the gravity of their world was not as powerful as that in the regular world. Tossing large boxes into the air as effortlessly as a piece of paper, they went about their daily routines with the ease only those born into that kind of atmosphere could. Each species was different but so beautifully made that the differences were not disturbing at all. Braccus, with all his experimenting on Iam's original works, was incapable of making living things this wonderful.

Forgetting for a moment that they were not here alone, they moved on, watching the areas below as each world progressed from the point of creation to decades later. As different as the places were, they all had something in common. At the end of all that progress they saw the same thing: the utter destruction brought upon them by Braccus. Every scene in every place they saw, seemed to undergo the same changes at the same point in time. The skies, whatever color they were, all became darker. They witnessed a terrible struggle between the braver good souls of the world and Braccus's horrible mutations.

The battles they witnessed were fierce and it was hard to watch the good people fall to the evil things they were fighting. Large numbers died on both sides, before the forces of good were forced to retreat. As the Moon Circle continued to stare helplessly, the worlds were being destroyed. They felt the pain of all those poor souls trying to survive below them, and rage at the way the worlds were being ripped apart. But all this had already happened, and they couldn't stop it, just watch helplessly while it played out again in front of them. They saw what the original Keepers had and understood what frustration and anger they must have felt because they were ineffective at preventing any of this. Still the group looked on until the last good creature disappeared into the underground, hearts heavy with the change in the fortunes of the surface dweller, wanting to help in some way, but not sure how. Being dead, they couldn't affect anything at all down there anymore. Sara, James, and Thomas stood staring until the darkness below made it difficult to make out much of anything, until hands roughly grasped their shoulders.

Chapter Six

The roof of the cavern was now covered in plant life so thick
that when one looked upward all they saw was different
shades of green. Grape vines grew from high overhead to
drape themselves like a curtain over the rocky surface, finally
ending in a puddle of big purple fruit on the sides of the large
cavern. Thick grass grew from a thin coat of dirt over the
stony surface beneath their feet to form a carpet. Every
hollowed-out area was filled with bushes so heavy with
berries of every color that they spilled onto the floor of the
cave. Finola had called over every root that still lived, and the
rope-like pieces of several different plants could be seen
winding through the central cavern to run down the twisting
corridors that branched off it. Several different types of trees
sprouted from the ground, their branches covered in so
many leaves it was hard to see the cave walls behind them.
The people, having been released from their deep sleep, had
opened their eyes to the transformation of their formerly
gloomy surroundings to find themselves right in the middle
of an underground paradise.
Many fell to their knees and touched the soft grass, crying
tears of relief to find something so beautiful and familiar to
them in the middle of all the ugliness and death they had
witnessed. Running their hands over the rough bark of solid
healthy trees and smelling the sweet wildflowers that dotted
the rocky areas, they sent silent thanks to Iam for this much-
needed assistance. Now they had life, supplies, some of their
loved ones and, of course, the Keepers. They could see that
the young ones they understood to be their next generation
of protectors, had been busy at work while they slept. This
truly meant everything was going to be alright. They would
survive this and live on; there was hope for a future.

The animals that had hidden in the distant areas of the underground passages were happily munching on the leaves and grass that had suddenly, miraculously appeared around them. Drawn by the bright lights and the smell of growing things, they stood on the edge of the large central living area eating as quickly as they could while keeping an eye on the people that stood just yards away. While naturally nervous about humans, they were far more comfortable with people than the monsters they had run away from days ago. Since they were starving, they were willing to risk their company to eat.

From every small opening they came, deer, rabbit and even a large black bear were temporarily occupying the same area as a large bobcat and none of them even considered giving into their natural instincts to either feed upon the other, or fight for the right to be here. A large rat scurried over the paw of a ragged coyote too intent on watching the activity in the cavern to react. It was enough for the moment that they were alive, eating, surrounded by creatures they recognized. There were no strange beasts here that smelled bad and set their internal alarm systems off. They could go back to being animals, with the instinct to run and hide later. Right now, they had food and a safe place to stay and that was all that mattered.

Finola had worked off quite a bit of stress coaxing the plants to grow in their new environment. She still avoided looking at or making any contact with Rianna, now seated quietly in a corner bench with that same blank glassy eyed stare and painted doll smile on her face. Her mother was gone. She didn't feel her wonderful warm loving personality anymore; this empty shell of a body was all that was left of her. Maryann had made Rianna comfortable as the newly arrived Keepers made the underground refuge more like home for the now fully awake villagers. Amid all the *oooh's* and *ahhhs* of admiration that accompanied their work, the Keepers provided what comfort they could for their people before they had to go help others.

With renewed hope, young children ran around apple trees that stood on the formerly cold stone ground gathering the juiciest red and green apples they had ever seen. Their laughter echoed off the walls to caress the bright green ferns that grew from the ground to tickle the ceiling high above. Heads turned upward, the people felt the heat from two artificial suns kiss their skin; Franklin had made them small enough to hang high above in spots specially hollowed out by Eric with low steady waves of sound to keep them in place. Robert helped the process by throwing in a special adjustment that dimmed the light every twelve hours to separate the day from the night. For her part, Alice was able to cover the area with a thin shield to protect all the things the light shone on. This place might not be as wonderful as the one Iam had created above ground for them, but it was a good substitute considering what was happening there.

It was strange that in such a short time the small group had managed to adapt to their growing abilities. Just a few weeks ago they would never have imagined that they could maintain the environment and still do more. The Keepers knew with certainty that they could move on from here and keep this place the way it was. Randall had not yet found a use for his powers; there was no one to zap right now, so he kept a watchful eye on Alice. He was concerned by the cautious, sometimes fearful look she had on her face when she stared into the dark corners beyond the well-lit area they now occupied. He hated to see her pretty eyes darken and the slight downward pull to the corner of her mouth that went with it.

Alice tried to manage a smile for Randall; she knew that he was worried about her. She was worried about the things that moved just beyond the sight of the ordinary world. They were whispering urgently to her, all trying to be heard, but she deliberately muffled the noise on her own now. Hearing them faintly but waiting for the one voice she longed to hear. Sara had put up a firm barrier to keep her from going back into the place she and her companions had gone. The portal to this part of the afterworld was sealed shut and Alice couldn't go back through. She was testing the edges of the darkness to find another way to her good friend, there had to be a path, she just couldn't see it right now.

Other things were coming through though, the dark ones mocked her, and the light ones begged for an audience, but she put them all off, pulling Randall closer to her mentally for security. It helped to have him with her, just seeing his handsome face made her forget, for just a moment, that she was now connected with a lot of scary dead things. He made her feel safe, even if she really wasn't. Eventually she would have to let them in. She realized that some of the dead ones might be able to help since they saw so much of the living worlds from their vantage point in the Shallow Shadows, but there were too many at once and not all of them were offering assistance. Some were whispering of her death and offering to kill her themselves if she entered their plane of existence. Firmly shutting them out, she listened instead to Randall's soft soothing words in her head and let him know she could handle anything they threw at her.

He talked to her quietly and tried to offer support and comfort, but despite her attempt to sound confident, he could tell she was worried about what she saw and heard. While they talked quietly amongst themselves, they listened to Maryann and Robert tell them that they had to go into the other worlds and help the people there, saying it would be safer for them to travel in pairs. Randall knew without having to think about it that he would, of course, be traveling with Alice. The time that they might have to separate into their spirit Circles to perform their duties had not yet come and he would see how he felt about it when the time came. For now, he was happy to stick as close to her as he could because he didn't know if he would be able to leave her if he were asked to.

Leaning down, he kissed as their fellow Keepers came closer, he knew Eric was in his head too and he didn't know how to explain himself to his Circle member, so he didn't even try. He knew how he was feeling and knew that Eric was having the same type of feelings for Finola; they just hadn't developed to the point as his but were quickly headed that way. He hoped they would be able to work this situation with their own Circle out when the time came because it was going to be hard to pull it all together. Eric had his loyalty and Randall knew him so well that he would jump to his side whenever needed. But beyond that, he just couldn't see her Circle as a unit yet; he certainly didn't trust Vincent. They didn't feel like a complete team.

When Randall saw the way Finola, Franklin and Alice worked together, they all made sense; they looked right, felt right, and everything went smoothly, as if it were meant to happen just the way it had. It had been the same when he briefly saw Sara, James, and Thomas. He saw the things they were dealing with personally, but they still managed to act as a team. Right to the last seconds of their lives, they had reacted instinctively to stay together. He had a feeling that wherever they were, they would be just fine as long as they remained together. He tried to put himself and Eric in that same situation in his head and he just couldn't picture it.

There was too much missing from this equation, like a whole person they couldn't trust not to kill them the way he had killed the others. It was too much to get past at this point; Vincent did not complete their circle the way he was right now.

He tried to reach into Vincent's head but couldn't connect with him, just flashes of half formed thoughts but nothing he could put together. Lots of anger though, he noticed that right away. Shaking his head in resignation, Randall turned to listen as Robert explained to the surviving villagers that the Keepers had to leave them and help other groups hidden much like their own. A statement which didn't seem to disappoint them so much now because the cavern was a much better place to be. They were given many hugs and wished well on their journey with several *come back soon's*. Small children smiled and gave them kisses on the cheek as each of the Keepers prepared to move down the darkened corridors to find a portal to travel through.

The Keepers had already paired up in groups of two: Randall stood next to Alice, still holding her hand tightly and looking over at Eric who stood with Finola at his side. An unhappy Franklin stood as far away from Vincent as he could, their forced partnership making him very nervous. Randall was about to suggest that they move in pairs of three, he was more than willing to have Franklin accompany Alice and him but, of course, that would have left Eric and Finola with Vincent and he wasn't really happy about leaving those two at risk either.

For the first time since his friends had started to have feelings for each other, Franklin felt incredibly lonely and a little bit resentful that their understood bonds left him with deadly boy as a traveling partner. The others recognized that thought before he could hide it. With apologetic smiles, they were about to suggest that perhaps Vincent would be of more use traveling on his own. After all, whatever he touched would surely die. What could possibly harm him if he went through the portals to help others? They had all but decided to suggest this to Robert and Maryann who, knowing what they were thinking, gave them disapproving glares while shaking their heads.

But what if one of the good guys accidently touches him? Finola spoke to the others, having enough compassion for Vincent to broadcast only on the familiar path shared between the other Circle members, leaving him out of it entirely. The look on his face told her that while he couldn't hear her, he had a really good idea what she was saying. It was eerie that, even as she tried to keep her communication secret, he was staring straight at her as if aware that it was she who was speaking to the others. She cast her eyes downward, momentarily shamed by her reaction to another Keeper. This was like being in high school and not picking someone for a group event because he was socially awkward, or in his case, deadly.

The small group of Keepers stood like the popular high school kids rejecting the odd boy, judging him for all that they knew about him so far. They couldn't kill him, and they couldn't leave him with others; they were siding against one of their own and yet somehow, they needed him. How was this supposed to work? Like it or not, he was part of the big picture here, whatever the picture was, but they still didn't want him to be.

Before any of them could respond to her question or respond to the angry glares from Robert and Maryann, there was another shifting in the aura around them, much like the one that had occurred when the balance had changed originally. There was suddenly a sickness of spirit that hung in the air, as if they had been collectively punched in the stomach, making them want to throw up. It was then that they suddenly realized the consequences of losing Sara were far greater than they had considered. Far above them the ground began to shake and the faint roar of a thousand voices rose together, gradually growing in volume, as those making it began to move closer to the entrance of the cavern.

Puzzled, Robert's eyes narrowed for a second, only to widen in alarm as he shared the same thought with Maryann. She had noticed it the moment Sara passed away from this world but had not thought the enemy would sense it so quickly. She hoped they would have more time to get things started before it was detected, but the shift around her told her she had been so wrong. Now that Sara was gone, the protective measures she had put in place to keep the refuges safe were gone and the things above them were suddenly aware of it. The underground places were wide open to the enemy and they were on their way to take them back.

Chapter Seven

Sara, James, and Thomas turned to face their un-living greeting committee, hands raised to unleash powers they weren't even sure they still were able to use anymore, and were amazed to find themselves facing absolutely nothing at all. They had all felt something, but there was no one behind them, just the same puffy wall of white. The only scenery, if it could be called scenery, came from beneath their feet as events unfolded, quickly becoming uglier by the second.

The worlds were mostly in darkness with a dim flickering of fire here and there to shed light on the monsters that roamed freely over the land. Occasionally they would catch sight of a few ruined structures that proved civilization had once existed. Wood and stone pieces were scattered everywhere like toys thrown around a room by a messy child. But in the middle of all that chaos, there was also activity. There seemed to be some sort of construction going on, but it was hardly an improvement on what had been there before. Large groups of ugly mutated beings were using stones pulled from the mountainsides to create a large chunky fort-like building. The structure seemed to be joined to several others by a stone wall so long it reminded James of the Great Wall of China.

Being the source of the building material, the mountain ranges now looked decimated, like broken teeth, in sunlight so weak it was like the glow from a low watt bulb. They could see enough to make them sick to their stomachs. Just when they thought nothing more could be done, the evil creatures found a way to make the surface even worse. All the worlds now had gaping holes in ground which bubbled with a thick oily green substance, making most travel impossible to all but the superbly equipped mutations that Braccus had created.

Sickened by the sight, James tried to focus on the places that skimmed along below him, hoping to see the world of the Keepers. His family was down there somewhere, and he had no way of making contact with them. He wondered if they even knew he was dead. It would be best if they didn't know. He would rather them think he was alive and fighting the enemy. In his heart, he hoped that was true somehow, that he could go back alive and well. He kept a vision of them as he remembered them - his brothers, sisters, mother and father - determined to return the balance to its former state. The thought that they might not be alive was not something he wanted to consider. His adopted father had known things, had witnessed evil's work, and would have been more prepared than anyone to protect his family; he would have seen to it that they made it to safety.

James turned toward where he thought they might be, trying to see anything familiar in the mess below, hoping that something survived the destruction. Amid all the murky rubble, in a remote section of one of the lands, he thought he caught a glimpse of something totally out of place, a large object moving along in the shadows, looking for an instant like a very big ferret carrying something in its mouth. He knelt down; still gazing intently at the animal, but it moved quickly and was out of his sight before he could identify it. James knew it was ridiculous, but for a split-second he could have sworn he knew that ferret. Shaking his head at the foolish idea, he rose up to stand next to his friends. But where were they?

Thomas was wondering the same thing. He felt James's distress as he thought of his family members down there in that mess and he wished he could help relieve his stress. While he felt bad about all those he left behind, and still very much wanted to make everything better for those still down there, he himself didn't care whether he went back or not. If Sara found a way to make it happen, then of course he would go too; his world was her, and wherever she existed that's where he would be. It was strange for him to think that way since he had been so dedicated to preserving the worlds for Iam's creations for so many years, but the longer he was with her, the more Thomas felt bound to Sara. It was more, much more than just the soul connection the three of them shared. He loved her, and she was his home now.

Smiling sadly, Sara read his mind and turned her head in his direction. They both knew this connection would cause problems later, and it would take a lot of strength to do the right thing if they had to do it separately. They were in the same Circle. It shouldn't be a problem, right? But in the past Sara had left Thomas to do what she thought she had to do alone: rid the worlds of Braccus. It had been Thomas who fought to stay with her, refusing to let her go it all alone. James was committed to fighting for their Circle too, but Thomas had been the strong connection that had bound them all together. It left a mark on him, she was so sorry for that, but would still do whatever she could to protect both him and James. Constantly at odds, she would sacrifice herself for both of them, knowing that Thomas would not allow it.

James let them talk for a moment, a small sigh escaping his lips as he tried to give them a little privacy. The mushy stuff was embarrassing, and he could tell they were trying to keep it to a minimum. Both Sara and Thomas apologized repeatedly, and he dismissed it with a short wave of his hand. He could mute things, probably most of their conversations. Half of what they said would be a steady hum in his head.

I'm sorry, James, she repeated, only to be silenced by an impatient look from her Circle member.

It's okay, just tone it down a bit, he answered, patting her hand while he continued to scan the area.

Sara reached out and connected with her Circle mates, using their connection to its fullest extent, pooling their powers, especially James's powers of persuasion, hoping that it would draw someone, or something to them. Collectively holding their breaths, they tried to locate the occupants of this lonely place.

Eventually, their combined efforts were rewarded by a slight shifting in the atmosphere; white puffy air drifted past their faces, but they still couldn't see any better than before. Then millions of twinkling lights appeared, sparkling just above their heads and in a straight line for quite some distance. Red, white, silver, green and blue in color they twinkled merrily in the sky like multicolored stars lighting the way to something exciting and special.

Chapter Eight

As soon they were aware of what was happening, the group reacted immediately, like they had rehearsed it a million times. Splitting up into the three groups they had formed earlier, the Keepers raced for each of the three corridors branching off the large central cavern, hoping to prevent the enemy from getting to the people gathered there. Maryann and Robert remained with the refugees, ready to defend them against anything that managed to access the tunnels, because something was sure to get through soon.

Loud triumphant screeches erupted from the throats of the mutant army, now aware that the doorways leading to their enemies were open and unguarded. Nightmarish creatures rushed toward the darkened entrances, looking eagerly for the prize that waited inside; the chance to kill off the rest of the good creatures hiding there. The horrifying sounds they made bounced off the hollowed out underground tunnels, terrifying the human beings huddled together in a circle waiting for the approach of a force more than willing to tear them to pieces. Mothers lay crouched over small crying children, shaking uncontrollably at the thought of anything touching a hair on their precious heads. Fathers and brothers, the few that were left, readied to give their lives to defend their loved ones. The memory of friends and family members whose violent deaths they had witnessed still fresh in their hearts and minds made their blood run cold.

Robert stayed in touch with the Keepers, watching their activity as they relayed what they saw around them. Portals, seen and unseen, shimmered in their heads as Alice guided her fellow Keepers to the many entryways. Making it to the ones they could, sharp snaps of electricity created by Randall blocked the others. Parts of legs and arms fell into the cave as the monster's approach was stopped with a combination of the strong electrical currents and Alice's force fields breaking off and burning anything that crossed through their path. Racing past the now fortified openings, the Keepers moved in pairs, anxious to see what had managed to pass through before they had contained the situation.

At one entry, Eric passed thick grey fingers, the decapitated torso and head of an Ornose, its six pairs of eyes looking upward, unmoving, as they faced the ceiling of the caverns. Skirting gingerly by it, Finola's hand still grasped firmly in his own, he moved down the dimly lit tunnel, heart beating so hard it hurt. He was glad they were in the caves where he had the advantage; all that time he had lived in darkness made him able to see every surface in detail. Yellow eyes focusing on everything in the area, Eric shared his enhanced eyesight with Finola, helping her to make her way closely behind him.

Bunnies, snakes, and rats skittered into deeper holes, getting out of their way, but it was the bigger things about the concerned him; both Iam-created and the other deadly ugly things made by Braccus, things that could, and would kill, the things he needed to protect her from. The object of his concern gave him a mental thump, warning him not to be so caveman-like, but she didn't understand how important it was that she be okay. He had to keep her safe until they were able to regroup and win this thing, because they were going to win.

You bet we are, Finola piped up in his head, *but I feel just as strongly about your safety, so be careful,* she shared this even as they both scanned the area for the creepy things that could attack them at any second. She was being incredibly brave, he knew she hated dark places, bugs and rats especially, but despite a slight shiver as they moved in the semi-darkness, she did her best to hide her discomfort. Moist cold cave walls were all they saw but danger was also very much present. They could feel it hanging in the air. Knowing they couldn't hide it from each other, Finola and Eric shared their fear and let it guide them away from the darker places where evil might hide. In a battle, instinct was everything, and they were going to use it to keep them alive.

A hurried message from Maryann told them that they were going to have to stay close together because once this place was locked down, they would have to exit though one of the doorways quickly. If they were under attack then other refuges were also. This meant that they were going to have to leave as soon as possible to move into the other worlds. With a warning to be careful sounding loudly in their heads, the Keepers stayed in their intended pairings and went in search of invaders.

Hurrying past the doors that appeared as blue, green, sometimes black, glowing holes in the cavern walls, the group checked out the areas beyond each of them. At each entry they found yet more pieces of Braccus's ugly creatures. Thumbs, legs, and charred skulls slowed their progress in the shifting shadows.

In one passageway, Franklin, moving as fast as he could, tried to maintain a safe distance from his deadly companion. Just his luck, he was with the one person that could kill anything he encountered, including the people close to him. He tried not to sweat too much as he raced down the thin, twisting, badly lit passage occupied by hideous, evil things while concentrating on every move his traveling companion made. What if Vincent stopped too quickly and Franklin ran into him; that would be instant death, wouldn't it? What a way to go! The possibility of death by accident caused him to erupt in flames as he moved behind the blonde guy in front of him.

Forget being visible to the enemy, that was the least of his worries; he was going to ensure that Vincent kept his distance.

Vincent was well aware of what Franklin was thinking; it was probably a good idea that he was on fire at this moment. It had occurred to him that, in the heat of battle, he might turn and bump into one of his allies. He wasn't exactly an experienced soldier, not having to really learn to fight, his obvious advantage putting him at least risk to his enemies. He had others with him now, kind of, and even if none of them liked or trusted him, there was still the slight chance that the situation might change, and he didn't want to accidentally kill them before that happened.

In another part of the caves, Alice and Randall moved into the darkness. Senses reaching outward while she maintained her force shields and traveled down a narrow corridor, Alice ran, passing a large black bear that shrank into the shadows. She moved away quickly; it was a wild animal, after all, and not above killing to protect itself. Turning, she almost slipped on the twisted remains of a rabbit; its body so badly decapitated as to be almost unrecognizable. The animal's remains were scattered all over and she gagged at the sight of it.

As he followed closely behind, Randall urged her to slow down. Rays from the artificial suns shone over his shoulder, putting out enough light to see the stone beneath him. But there was still a lot he couldn't see. Shadows formed in the deep corners of the passageway, making it hard to determine what they were facing. He too had seen the dead animal and had a bad feeling about the way it looked. If the bear had killed it, it would have taken whatever it hadn't eaten with it. But this thing was just pulled apart, mashed into the ground as if whatever had killed it had done it just for the fun of it.

He had a feeling that whatever it was had to be somewhere in the tunnel with them.

Stop, he said, pulling hard on Alice's hand. They froze together and listened carefully for any signs of an intruder. It was so quiet now that even their breathing sounded loud, amplified, no doubt, by their fear. It almost masked the sound of the padding footsteps of something very big and heavy. At first, she thought it might be the bear, but she could still see it out of the corner of her eye, cowering in a recess of the tunnel. Its big hairy body curled up as if it was trying to move away from the source of the noise. There was only one reason a large and normally ferocious animal might be afraid of something and that's if the something was bigger and scarier than it was.

Alice scanned the area using her extra sense, the one that let her see the dead, evil things that lurked on the edge of the civilized worlds. All she could see were shadows and the stone walls of the winding tunnel; nothing that might cause the animal to cower in fear. In fact, the darker patches were becoming more predominant. That didn't make sense when she was convinced that something had slipped in one of the doors when they were open. They had heard movement, so what...

A movement caught Randall's eye. He screamed and lunged at Alice as the thing sprang from the shadows. A thick arm swiped the air whistling past Randall's head, catching his cheek with the force of the blow. The young man flew backward into the tunnel, hitting the hard surface upon impact. Alice was lying where he had pushed her.

Temporarily stunned, she gathered her wits about her while she stared at the lumpy rock-encrusted beast jumping from the shadows. Facing the fallen young man on the ground, it shuffled over on thick legs that marked the ground. The bulky monster raised a heavy arm to deliver a fatal blow to Randall's head, only to find itself burying its hand into the fleshy face of an Ornose hovering outside one of the blocked entrances where Alice sent it. There was a fierce struggle between the two evil things before both died from their wounds, their lifeless bodies littering the ground on the other side of the barrier.

Alice moved to Randall, tugging his arm to pull him toward her. He responded groggily, watching her two blurry faces swim into view as she touched his head and soothed away the bruising on his brain. He smiled with relief when her face came into focus and he just saw one of her smiling at him. A small relieved laugh escaped his lips just before she disappeared from view and he was holding a pair of thin stick-like arms and looking at the dry ugly hag-like face of a Hateress.

Chapter Nine

Sara, James, and Thomas moved along, watching the lights, like three airplanes guided by bright beacons to a safe landing spot. With each step they took the clouds became a bit thinner and Thomas was sure he saw the faint outline of buildings becoming more definite by the second. *What would dead people need with buildings?* he thought for a second before his attention was drawn once again to what was under his feet. The scenery was changing bit by bit. The violent scenes they had seen before were fading away to be replaced by a white surface resembling a concrete sidewalk; smooth slabs of material formed a straight path that disappeared into the mist in front of them.

The paved walkway was soon surrounded by a thick layer of well-maintained green grass and brown wooden slats of a few short fences formed a border of sorts around three or four hazy structures looming in the background. A few more steps down the road and they saw patches of blue sky above their heads as the stuff surrounding them drifted farther and farther apart to reveal a pale-yellow sun shining down on their heads. After moving a short distance more, they could see tree branches hanging low over the grey shingles of several buildings that looked solid enough to be real.

Unsure what they were walking into, the young Keepers all stopped and watched as the last of the white, whatever it was, drifted upward to settle in the sky. They could now see that they were in the middle of what appeared to be a small neighborhood. Twenty houses dotted the area around them; each place a small masterpiece constructed of wood, stone and brick, carefully tended versions of the ideal home landscaped to perfection. Since they were in a dead place it was rather surprising to find this little piece of civilization appearing in front of them. What did this mean exactly? Was the afterlife really just a move to a nicer block on a different level of existence? If so, where were the other dead people? Facing outward in a half circle they kept their senses wide open, ready to address any threat that came their way, wondering when they would receive another message from their hosts.

 They soon got an answer.

They heard them before they saw them; faint whispers to announce their arrival, letting them know that it was now safe here. The voices were excited and slightly nervous. Sara and her companions could sense them smiling when they returned the mental messages, but they still could not see any sign of a physical presence.

The path they were following branched off in three different directions about a hundred yards ahead. Each individual stopped and picked a direction to watch and waited for the welcome wagon to come into view. James spotted them first, putting a hand on his companion's arms to bring their attention back to the center path. Six anxious figures, three men and three women, walked in pairs on the thin sidewalk, pale faces wearing trembling smiles as they approached.

Sara and Thomas turned and gave them their full attention s. The dead ones' souls were firmly attached, showing as beautiful swirls of red and blue swimming in the air around them. Colors made brighter by the paleness of their skin.

The first in line was a blonde-haired couple, their brilliant blue eyes fastened on Sara, pride and love showing on faces that closely resembled her own. James could tell that they were holding themselves back, trying not to run right over and gather her in a big bear-hug. Behind them, stood two other couples, one with dark hair and caramel-colored skin, and the last pair with olive skin and dark straight hair; both had the same looks on their faces as they stared at him and Thomas. It was obvious by the resemblance the couples had to each of the young people and the way they felt as they got closer, that they were about to meet their parents. What did one say at this type of occasion?

They were facing people they had never seen but knew immediately and felt a part of. It was a strangely wonderful moment, all this emotion packed inside. They were too stunned to do anything but look at each other across the distance separating them. It took a few minutes to process the situation, each of the newer Keepers trying to come up with a something important to say at this time.

"Hello," was the only word that broke the silence, it came from Thomas's lips because his two companions were stuck to say another; their mouths gaping open with nothing impressive coming out of them. That one word was enough to set it all in motion. Groups split into three, as parents sought their child, holding them tightly and then pulling away to admire the lovely creatures they had sent away long ago. Words like: "They're so grown up!" and "Aren't they beautiful?" tumbled out of the older Keepers' mouths as they enjoyed the first contact they had had with their children since they gave them human form, and handed them over to Salius to hide among strangers. Sara felt the regret her parents felt over how she had grown up, their rage at how they had not been able to protect her from the Finklestein's and had to watch their cruelty from a distance. She touched her mother's face and held her father's hand as she let herself feel whole for the first time in her life. Death wasn't so bad, now was it?

They shared each other's thoughts. All those years coming together in a matter of seconds. She, hearing what they knew of current world events, which, because they had

decided not to separate themselves from the outside worlds
for long, was pretty much close to what she knew. They were
proud of all she had done to help and very worried about all
that still needed to be done. Their emotions were conflicted.
As they both mourned her death and rejoiced at the fact that
they could connect with her at last. As far as Sara could tell,
the washed-out condition of their skin was the only thing
that set them apart from a living person. For they were quite
warm to the touch and every bit as solid as she, Thomas, and
James were.

Thomas looked over at Sara even as he shared his thoughts
with his family, his mind still connected firmly to her and
James. The lonely years of living with that horrible
psychopath that had replaced his adoptive parents was well
known to his real parents. They too had watched while he
lived in fear every day of his life. Every one of those days was
a nightmare for them because they wanted to be with him so
badly. And in a way, they had. When he had felt like giving
up, Thomas had a feeling that he had to be strong and wait
for his chance to escape. That feeling had been sent to him
by his loved ones. It was all that they could do for him at the
time but it had kept him going. They had been so happy to
see James and Sara arrive at his home giving Thomas a
chance to fight back, someone to fight for. All his triumphs
afterwards, even to the moment when he had battled
Braccus and kept him from taking his soul, had been
observed and caused both distress and immense pride, for
they were loved by all the older Keepers and were the hope
for the future.

James held his parents' hands as they talked and shared their
joy at his good fortune at having found his adoptive parents.
They had shared the other Keepers anger and sadness at the
way their children's lives had gone and they were so grateful

that their son had been spared that fate. They had acted with the other Keepers to keep their children strong, trying just as hard as their friends had to keep all of them from giving up. They had mourned with James when he avoided Sara during her long sleep, offering what comfort his living family could not, and had given him strength and knowledge in battle that had not come from his earthly teachers. They, like the other parents, had been there as much as they could for their children, even if the children were not aware of their presence.

It was all happening as they had been told to expect; the Circles were meeting. Still it was many years before they were able to find all the Circle members and more time after that to become good fighters. But all they had witnessed, had led to this moment and, though it had been hard to wait and even harder to watch what they knew had to happen to bring their children here, it was the start of a new chapter of the struggle for the worlds. A struggle that was their children's responsibility to undertake. They just hoped that they would be allowed to contribute to it in some way.

After a few precious moments of holding their children close, the beings that each Keeper knew only as mom and dad, moved back slightly, still unwilling to let go of their hands, and introduced themselves. Sara's father spoke first, "My name is Daniel and this is my wife Maura." He drew Sara's mother closer to his side, gazing at her with adoring eyes before turning to look at Sara with the same. "This is Janika and Havis," he said, nodding in Thomas's parent's direction. "And this is Levi and Cloette." James's parents nodded back as they were introduced to the group.

"Your arrival has caused much excitement among the people here. We have waited a long time for this to begin. Please do not be alarmed by this place, all is not what it seems and neither are your deaths. We have a lot to explain to you but there is something that we, as your parents, feel that we owe you and would be pleased if you would let us do this one thing for you."

James turned and exchanged a puzzled look with Sara and Thomas as the world around them flashed a blinding white and they quickly lost sight of both their parents and each other.

Chapter Ten

Shaking his head vigorously failed to clear the vision of the Hateress, Randall tried to convince himself that what he was seeing was a result of hitting his head so hard. But the fact that his arms were burning uncomfortably where sharp twig-like fingers were digging into them, helped him decide that what he was seeing in front of him was very real. The Hateress' face was very close to his own, her mouth open and spewing a grainy grey substance as she bent to take a bite out his neck. Randall felt the razor-sharp tip of one of her teeth scrape against his skin, felt something sticky and wet as she drew blood. He was hitting her with all the strength he could muster, scraping his hands on her thick hide, but the only effect his struggles had was to have her raise her head to laugh as she watched the trail of red drip on his shirt. He sent jolts of electricity from his fingers into the hag's body trying to break her hold, but her grip stayed strong and her lips opened wider as she bent to take another bite. Before her mouth could make contact again, she jerked backwards and fell to the ground in a heap.

The next thing he knew, Alice was in his arms, crushing him in a fearfully tight grip and planting kisses on his face. He didn't mind this part at all, but he was bit puzzled as to how it had happened. Looking over his companion's shoulder, he noticed the Hateress lying on the ground. A short distance past her body, he saw the bodies of a Garren and two Kreel. This was not how Alice fought and he was surprised that she had not just set up a shield or transported the enemy from the area. A movement to the left of one of the Kreel's bodies gave him the answer to the unspoken question as to what had caused their deaths.

A pair of sneakered feet moved out of the shadows where Vincent shifted uncomfortably as he tried to step away from Franklin's still flaming body; his presence giving a pretty clear indication as to how they died. Both young men's eyes locked as Alice looked back and greeted Franklin, her arm still holding tightly to his own. She glanced at Vincent and knew what he had done also. She didn't know quite what to make of it, but she had a good feeling about this situation. She nodded her head slightly before turning back to look at Randall to check on him.

Extinguishing his flames, Franklin moved forward, noticing a large bruise on Alice's head and the steady dripping of blood from Randall's neck. Without saying a word, the three friends linked hands and combined their powers to start the healing process. Vincent, still very much on the outside, looked on, feeling lonely and left out. Head bowed, he was about to throw up his hands and head for the nearest door, ready to try his luck in one of the other worlds. He might find at least one person out there who didn't think he was a monster and maybe, just maybe, he'd find his other half.

Vincent managed a few steps down the corridor before his departure was halted by a strong compulsion to look up again. When he did, he found Randall looking right at him. Instead of suspicion in his eyes, there was a thoughtful, almost respectful air about the way he studied him. If he didn't know any better he could have sworn the man's lips almost made it to the smile position. Then remarkably, for just a second, Randall was in his head and they shared a thought.

Vincent couldn't have explained why he had stopped running down the pathway he and Franklin had been in, and doubled back until he found Randall and Alice's corridor. There had not been any real connection between him Eric and Randall when they met, so he wasn't sure what to make of the chilling alarm bells that sounded in his head. He just knew that for some reason he was needed here at this spot, and had run blindly down the semi-dark cavern with Franklin's brightly flaming body in hot pursuit (he had to stifle a snicker at his choice of words). When he arrived, he had found Alice fighting off a large rock thing, a grey monster, some tall skinny pale guy and two ugly little monkey-looking men, while Randall was backed into a corner with some haggy thing trying to munch on his neck.

He got to Alice first. She had managed to make two of her enemies disappear somehow, but the tall skinny guy had gotten close enough to hit her on the head with a rock, leaving an opening for the monkey men to jump on her back. Reacting quickly, Vincent reached out for the pale man first, touching him before he was even aware he had company. In an instant, he was lying face up on the ground quite dead. The monkey men had seen him next, and foolishly ran at him. Letting them come right up to him, he didn't move at all. Sharp nails dug into his arms as they latched on, ready to do serious harm. In an instant, they died with surprised looks on their faces; bodies already stiff when they fell to the stony floor. After that, he moved directly to the wooden-bodied thing holding onto Randall while electricity crackled through both of them and received a nasty shock that burned his hand. Despite the pain, he didn't pull away; Vincent held on and let his gift work. His touch did what the electricity could not; the wood-witch was dead in a second. Vincent moved back to hold his injured hand and watch the others comfort each other; still the person on the outside.

It took Randall a minute to realize what had happened. He was getting information from two sources: Franklin and Vincent. He and Franklin had been way on the other side of the main cavern, already moving toward an open doorway almost two miles in the opposite direction. Most of the information came to him from Franklin. They had almost reached the exit, ready to follow Alice, while keeping an eye out for anything that might be waiting in the shadows, when Vincent got a funny look on his face and turned and ran faster than Franklin would have thought possible. Franklin had been forced to cling to the side of the corridor to prevent touching, *tag and you're dead, boy*. When Vincent didn't slow his pace, curiosity, and determination to not be left behind made him follow. It wasn't until a few seconds later that he felt Alice's distress and was able to see that she was engaged in a struggle with several bad guys and trying to make her way to Randall.

Before Franklin could make it to his friend's side, Vincent was there. Randall saw what Franklin had seen. He saw Vincent reach out and kill all of Alice's attackers and then touch the Hateress. He also saw that Vincent had been injured, and compassion had him trying harder than he had since he met him to get through the barrier that was keeping them from communicating as they should. It must be possible to get through because something had made Vincent aware that they were in trouble in the first place. Thoughts of despair sounded in his head as he made a tentative connection. He knew that Vincent was aware of him and that he felt what his other Circle member was feeling, for a split-second at least. They couldn't touch him to help with healing, but Randall couldn't see not helping him; he had been hurt saving first Alice and then him. Vincent had run to help without being asked, using a connection that had not existed before today, and neither of them had intentionally reached for the other. He still didn't know him the way he knew Eric, who was sending messages in a panicked tone asking what was wrong and moving closer to him by the second, but some kind of bond, loose as it was, had been made. Randall turned and made his friends aware of what he now knew about their companion, letting them feel what he knew Vincent was feeling. He also told them that, even though they couldn't make physical contact to help heal his wounds, that they needed to find a way to fix the damage done in rescuing them.

The subject of their conversation listened, too stunned to open his mouth or even share his thoughts. He held them closely, not wanting to look too much like a wimp when all he wanted to do was cry in relief. They still hadn't accepted him the way he had hoped but at least they weren't letting him stand alone and suffer. They were going to help him, they were almost treating him as if he mattered. It wasn't as much as he hoped, but at least it was a start.

Chapter Eleven

One minute, Sara had been standing next to her parents, holding tightly to their hands; overwhelmed by the intense love and sense of belonging they had given her, the next she was standing in a room that she would have designed herself if she had a lot of money. Looking very much like a scene from an old movie, the room was richly decorated with satiny fabrics of soft pastel colors mixed with fine white linen. Two overstuffed chairs with high backs and a large couch occupied an entire corner of a room which had a large picture window. There was a row of other windows on the opposite side of the room with short stretches of wall space in-between. This arrangement let in lots of sunshine to the main seating area and a wooden king-sized four-poster bed that occupied a corner cut only slightly larger than the bed itself. Sara was sure that the bed was only for show, as she was sure that dead people had no need for sleep or houses in particular. What would they do there? Of course, so far, throughout her newly dead experience, nothing had been what she expected. Maybe she was wrong about this too. Walking carefully around the room, she studied it to try and find meaning in this new environment. The walls were decorated with posters of different sizes, one of which had a picture of a dark-haired young man dressed in a white shirt with a high collar made of some kind of hard, stiff material. He also wore a brightly colored vest that reminded her of something she had seen in a used clothing shop once; it was a style from the nineteen sixties or seventies, a time long before she was born. Large colored letters beneath the handsome smiling face proudly proclaimed his name to be David Cassidy. She didn't recognize the name; maybe he was famous here in the dead place. Could dead people be fans of other dead people? Sara was still thinking this over as she went to look at the next poster.

This poster showed the same smiling young man and five other people - a pretty blonde woman, two small blonde children, a brown-haired girl and a chunky red-headed boy - all standing in front of a brightly painted bus. The words *The Partridge Family* were written underneath the image in the same large print that was on the other poster. Who were they, and why were they on the walls of what she assumed was supposed to be her room? Were these pictures of Keepers or people from one of the other worlds that she should be aware of as celebrities of some kind?

Other printed pictures plastered the walls, each bearing the faces of yet more handsome boys in fancy clothing. Young men posing with instruments or microphones and with names she had never heard of occupied space next to scenes of running horses and cute kittens. The furniture, she could have maybe understood whose mind that had come from, but what was it with all the posters? She turned and walked slowly to the bed, sitting at the foot of it as she continued to stare puzzled at her new surroundings. She reached out for Thomas and James but received no reply, no visions, no voices, nothing. Should she feel scared? There was nothing threatening about this place. It just didn't make any sense and she didn't feel that her parents would have sent her here without a good reason.

Her puzzled thoughts were interrupted by a knocking sound coming from the only door in the room. Narrow and painted a light cream color, it had the words *Sara's Room* written in big blocks letters across the middle, totally taking the guesswork out of where she was now.

"Come in," she called out hesitantly, unsure of what to expect next. A second later, the door opened, and her parents walked in with big smiles on their faces. She could feel that they were waiting for her reaction to this gift and she didn't want to disappoint. She smiled and gestured at the large room.

"It's beautiful, thank you so much, Mom and Dad." Mom and Dad, the words sounded so strange; she had never called anyone that before. They beamed with pride at her words, wanting so badly for her to have this place, this moment. Like so many parents, they wanted the best for their child and, after having seen what her earlier childhood had been like, were anxious to offer her something they had watched other parents give their children: a happy home.

Having had years to watch the activities of the worlds from afar, Daniel and Maura had observed families going through the daily acts of building a life in all the seven worlds. They paid special attention to the ordinary dimension most humans occupied, because this was where Sara was. They had watched her but could not get much information about what an ordinary child would like; she hadn't had that kind of life. So, they picked up what they could from different sources, which, of course, meant they got their information from dead people that had once lived there.

Time passed here differently than in other places, so they had no real concept of it, or of when the people they were talking to had come from. They tried to get some information from a teenager who had passed through their dimension several years back, that's when they first heard about this David Cassidy boy. They were sure he must be really popular with kids Sara's age. The girl they had spoken to had quite a crush on him and so naturally, they had picked this boy's image from her head and used it to decorate their daughter's walls in the hope that this would make the room look more like a typical teenager's room. What they didn't realize was that their guest had passed through over thirty years before, and a lot had changed in the outside worlds since then. Sara's parents desperately wanted to give their daughter what they had never been able to give her. For just one day, they wanted her to experience life with them as a normal family. This would be their only chance before she had to go out again and face the ugliness that she was supposed to protect everyone else from.

"Do you really like it?" Maura asked, scanning her daughter's thoughts for her reaction. If there was anything that she could change to make this place better for Sara, anything at all, then she would do it. When she read Sara's mind, she found only gratitude and sincere pleasure. She squeezed Daniel's hand to share her excitement. They had gotten it right! It was exactly as the girl had said; their daughter loved the musical family and especially this David Cassidy boy. Not as much as she loved Janika and Havis's son Thomas, but a crush was an acceptable thing for a young girl to feel for a celebrity, they had been told.

So, he was a celebrity. Sara picked up her parents' thoughts and the reason for the posters was suddenly made clear. Relieved that she had managed to carefully hide her puzzlement about the strange pictures displayed in the room, she smiled. It would have been a shame to ruin the moment by having them explain themselves, when the moment was all they were going to have together. If they wanted to give her this one day, then she was going to enjoy it as much as she could. With this in mind, she let them lead her out of the lovely bedroom and give her a tour of the rest of their amazing home; the one they had created just an hour before.

In another lovely home, James was walking around a space decorated from a carpenter's dream. He knew this came from inside his head; he was surrounded by things only he would know about. His parents knew that his adopted father had taught him the woodworking trade and that he loved to create things of beauty. The very large room had several finely carved pieces of furniture in it. He smiled when he recognized the storage chest, bed, and large mahogany chair as copies of work he had done for customers when he was alive. Having worked for his adopted father before he had to leave full time to fight the enemy, he had made beautiful things for other people, things he would have liked to make for himself one day when life was more peaceful and settled. That had always been his wish, to settle down with his family, making wonderful things but somehow, he never really believed that it would happen for him; that wasn't his destiny.

"No, it's not," his father said as the door to his room opened and both he and his strikingly beautiful mother walked in to show him all that they had made for him to enjoy. Walking with him, they showed him each expertly made item of furniture, the carved knick-knacks sitting on top of one of the many tables filling every spare inch of floor in a bedroom that was much larger than he had seen in any one person's home, including the rich people he had been hired to make things for. It was a heartbreakingly bittersweet moment. All this stuff was almost too much, especially when he shared the thought from his parents that this was all that they could offer him. If they had gone a little bit overboard, it was because they had never had the chance to give him what they had seen him have with his adoptive family. They were showing their love by bringing everything he had made and enjoyed during his brief life to this place so that they could share it together.

Even though Levi and Cloette knew they had done the right thing by giving their lives to save Olie and the other inhabitants of the worlds, it was still so hard to have sacrificed their time with James. Knowing he too had been created to serve as protector to Iam's creations had been both a blessing and a curse because they knew it would bring him so much pain along with the joy of using his gifts as they had been intended.

"We have this one day to live a life we never had together," his mother said as they walked toward the door of the room. "I'm so sorry it can't be more."

Her deep brown eyes were swimming with moisture as he turned to place a kiss on her cheek. "Then let's make the most of it," he said, walking out into the bright sunshine of his make-believe life.

Chapter Twelve

Having raced from a corridor on the opposite side of the large central cavern, Finola and Eric moved to join the other Keepers, automatically taking positions beside their friends at Randall's request. Then the five people facing Vincent began doing something they had never done before, also at Randall's request: reaching out and healing another person from a safe distance. And it was working. It had been a little bit difficult for the others to find a connection to the injured young man, but with Randall's help they managed to find their way through to him. Once they had started, it began to work very well. From what Randall could see in the light provided by Franklin's fire, Vincent's burned hands had lost their charred appearance; the skin a pinkish white color once again, the nerves repaired in a way he couldn't explain but could definitely feel.

Randall saw the look of relief on the young man's face as the power of their combined spirits took away the pain and mended his injuries. He was very glad they had been able to do this. The others felt his satisfaction; they took a moment to share a pat on the back with each other for a job well done.

They still might not want to be around Vincent, but now it was mostly because he could kill them without really trying to. One accidental move in the wrong direction, bumping into him when they were fighting together, would be a serious concern for them all. How should they deal with that on top of everything else they had experienced with Vincent so far?

They were not buddy, buddy with him by any means, but Eric, Finola, Franklin, Alice and Randall were now all aware that something significant had happened between Randall and Vincent. A connection had been made and it had saved both his and Alice's lives. It didn't erase the last thing he had done but, like it or not, he was the reason they were currently a group of six live people, not just four.

Finola shared a glance with Alice now that Eric and Randall's third, or part of it, was healed and was saddened to see how shaken she was. She knew Alice felt terrible about letting the Hateress get to Randall; she should have been able to feel that evil thing with her new abilities as the darkness detector. But she hadn't felt or seen a thing that indicated anything was there. The things that had attacked them were obviously evil, so why didn't they put out an energy she could see? Could something have blocked her ability? Randall could have been killed. The whole group could have been killed and she would have been responsible, all because she didn't know how to use this new toy she had been given.

She was looking at Finola and sending out all this confused energy and guilt while her friend tried to calm her down and offer comfort. At first, she and Franklin had tried to gently reassure her, but Alice's mind was a confusing swirl of contempt for herself and Finola had had her fill of listening to it. Finally, in frustration at not being able to get her to listen, she sent what was equal to a sharp mental slap on the arm back to Alice, causing the girl to step back for a minute and shoot her a puzzled look.

What did you do that for? Alice asked her friend. All the anguish she had been feeling just a second before was forgotten as Finola sent angry messages to her on a private connection. Worried for Alice after all he had heard her going through, Randall started to move toward the two girls as they simply stood staring at each other; one with an angry look on her face, the other with first an anguished look that turned to surprise then hurt.

He wanted to get into her head, be part of the conversation. He had to make her feel better; let her know he cared, that it wasn't her fault. His advance was stopped by Eric and Franklin who sensed that there was something about the exchange that made them hesitate to interfere and they were telling him to stay out of it too.

Stop doing that! Alice said as Finola told her exactly what she was feeling about the self-pitying little episode she was having.

No, you stop doing that! Finola fired back. *I don't know exactly what made them undetectable to you but get a grip and fine tune this new thing you've got, because we are counting on you to get us through these doorways and help all those people. Randall is okay now, but if you expect to travel through one of the portals with him and help keep him that way, I suggest you quit freaking out and pull yourself together.* She said this in an angry tone, but her eyes were full of compassion as she changed Alice's focus from a sniveling mess of doubt and self-contempt to a very angry young woman.

As quickly as it started, the whole episode was over. Alice, upon looking at Finola's stern face, saw something else besides anger. She saw satisfaction at having distracted her from the whole beating herself up thing; making her just angry enough to stop and focus on what was important. It was a wake-up call to get her moving in the right direction again. Her approach may have been a little less than soft, but it certainly was effective, and she loved Finola so much for bringing her to her senses.

The startled young men watched puzzled as Alice grabbed Finola and hugged her while crying on her shoulder. Finola had snapped her out of it, focusing on what could have made those things slide under her radar. They must have had some help and she was going to have to get past whatever had been blocking her connection with the Dead Ones.

Following the dark trail that was visible only to her, she grabbed onto the filmy slime surrounding the dead bodies of the Garren, the two Kreel and the dry, brittle Hateress. The ugly evil spirits still hovered in the area, not knowing where to go to because they were trapped in the cave. They were not allowed to move to the peaceful place that Iam allowed most souls to go to. the other place, the in-between place that the old Keepers had made, was a little bit iffy now. Death had not robbed those good souls of all their powers. They were still very much in control of the Shallow Shadows. The evil spirits had been told that their kind was sometimes allowed to move around the bright ones in the place that they had made, if they just stayed on the outer edges. But now the good souls were watching evil closely and could do some bad things to a dead soul if they chose to, and now they chose to. It took a minute or two of intense arguing between the four filthy souls of Braccus's followers for them to come up with a decision. Should they stay here staring at their own lifeless husks, or take a chance and enter the afterworld?

Desperate to escape the sight of their own battered corpses, the dead enemy tried to enter the Shallow Shadows, willing to risk whatever the dead Keepers could throw at them in the hopes that they could meet up with their own kind. Surging toward the thin barrier that only the dead could see, they tried to enter, only to find the door was blocked to them. With shrieks of frustration, they were forced back to linger over their own bodies, having no other place to go. Trapped next to their stiff corpses, they were forced to watch as the man that had killed them was being healed. He stood among the other Keepers, all of whom were looking at their carcasses with satisfaction.

Alice took hold of the oily black and brown lines that bound her enemies to their dead shells with little effort, because whatever had kept her from sensing them before was no longer there. She grabbed hold of Franklin and Finola's hands and used the connection to keep centered. It helped a lot. Alice had control now and she was going to get some answers.

Alice had a whole bunch of questions to ask these horrid spirits but didn't have time to mess with the attitude they were throwing her way. She could feel their rage at not being able to move on, and having to deal with her invasion of their very limited space was making them angrier by the second. Loud hissing and screaming noises emanated. They did not want to tell her what she wanted to know. But with a little persuasion, in the form of a promise to get them out of this place, she was able to get them to give up their benefactor; Braccus was back. Back? Where had he gone? She pushed harder to get the answer.

Snapping and snarling, the wicked creature's spirits tried to resist answering her questions, but she kept asking, and the more she asked, the angrier they got. *You will answer me,* she insisted.

More spitting and cursing followed, but she was forcing them to answer and they did not like it at all. The harder she pushed, the brighter her spirit glowed, causing the darkness in them to shriek in pain. Unable to endure the agony any longer, they had to tell her what she wanted to know. Braccus had gone into another dimension following something he considered to be very important but had suddenly come back with a renewed eagerness to help his armies fight. Throwing his power in to aid their cause, he helped them hide from Alice while they snuck into the unguarded doorways.

Her spine tingled uncomfortably at the news, and now that they could no longer offer her any more information, she sent their bodies back up to the surface, forcing their spirits to follow.

You're getting just what I promised you, she told the angry evil souls, *I am letting you leave here.* They left, cursing her for not setting them free as they moved with the fleshy anchors that would slowly rot while they watched; unable to leave even after they crumbled to dust.

Sharing an open channel with her companions, Alice relayed all that she had learned. Grabbing hold of Randall's hand, she gave him a big kiss on his cheek and sent her friends instructions on their exit points. Then she did something that she wasn't aware she could do until now, she sent her energy toward all the doorways forming a thin shield at each point of entry, enough to prevent invasion for a short time. It wouldn't last forever but it would be good enough for the time being.

"We have to leave now," she said, as they separated once again down the various corridors to travel to the different worlds, trying not to share the fear they all felt at traveling into the unknown.

Chapter Thirteen

Thomas sat next to Sara in a movie theater unlike any he had ever seen. Okay, he had never been to a movie theater before, but he had seen pictures of them, and this was very impressive. The size of a large field, the theater had deep red curtains surrounding a large white screen with ornately carved white marble cherubs of various sizes set high up on the wall beside it. The chunky little angels, frozen in positions of mid-flight, hung close to the ceiling looking down on the center of the theater. The floor was covered in thick red carpet and rows of blue velvet covered seats occupied by people he didn't recognize.

You'd have thought that after all the people he had fought with had died, he'd know at least a few of these dead people but he didn't. He wasn't even sure if these people were real. True, they sat there laughing and watching the movie; but they were more like part of the scenery than interactive characters. The theater was packed with these people all hanging out in the background, like extras in another movie; pale faces staring at the screen and nowhere else. The laughter they heard was like a sound recording, and their expressions shifted only slightly as they watched the action in front of them. It was as if the Keepers had set up a movie set of their own and placed Sara and him into it.

Growing up in the country, in a land that was a little bit technologically behind the rest of the lands, he never really had the opportunity to go to a movie. Even when he was able to travel from world to world, being that it was for the purpose of fighting horrible creatures that were there to terrorize and kill the inhabitants, he never seemed to find the time to go looking for entertainment. Today was different, though. Today, he had been to the movies roughly fifty times. All on dates with Sara. Not that he was complaining; if he had his way this day would go on forever. Ever since he and Sara had acknowledged their feelings for another, there had not been time for them to enjoy just being together. Their parents had been thrilled to see them falling in love from their perches high above the worlds and they wanted to give them time to be together, a day that seemed to go on forever.

Time passed very slowly in this place created by the original Keepers. One day could seem like several months; it was their way of giving their children some of what they had seen other's experience. The Keepers had lived among many of Iam's creations and had gotten to know them quite well, but they had never actually been one of them. Keepers had been given human forms by Iam, bonded with his creations, and grown to love them, but they had to learn what and who they were from close observation; the human condition had not come naturally to them.

The Keepers had never been children or teenagers; anything they may have learned about growing up as a person had been passed on to them by those they'd watched through the years and the dead youngsters that passed through this place from time to time. They hated to see them that way, people should not die young, but when they did, they were a great source of popular culture for their time. It comforted the young people to talk with them and it gave the ancient ones' valuable insight into the world they no longer occupied.

Armed with the information given to them by the young and departed, they had sent Sara and Thomas on about three months' worth of dates to all kinds of places like this. They had been to dinners they could not eat because they were dead, sporting events in which pale athletes had played all kinds of games from basketball to football with incredible skill, and long romantic walks in some of the most beautiful parks they had ever seen. They had talked for hours, even though they knew so much about each other through their soul connection; it was nice to communicate like this, laughing and forgetting that they carried the weight of the worlds on their shoulders. Their parents could not have given them a better gift than this.

It was after their third date that Sara and Thomas shared their first kiss. It was everything he had always imagined it would be, a magical moment; one that he hoped would also never end. Soft lips smiling at him, beautiful blue eyes staring into his; it happened during one of their many movie dates. Her lips were just as soft as they looked, he could kiss her forever and never have the need to fight again. The rest of the world didn't matter. He just wanted the here and now; even if the here and now was in the afterlife. Thomas knew that eventually he would have to help the outside worlds but he wanted to be selfish just a little bit longer and pretend that this was real. He had never been so happy.

Despite this, he still worried about James who said he was fine, placed in the position of third wheel in their group again, even in death. Thomas checked in frequently with James, and Sara let them have their private connection, feeling awful that she could be the cause of any problems between them. She wanted James to be happy too.

Someone must have been thinking the same thing because the third time Thomas spoke with James, the young man's thoughts changed, going from depressed to curious and then very happy. It seemed that their parents were sensitive to their situation and had brought a very special soul to meet James; he shared this information with both members of his circle and they were thrilled to feel what he was feeling.

The special soul, a young woman about twenty years of age named Diandra, had died just hours before they had. Like them, she had no idea where she was or how she got there. Whatever had happened had happened suddenly; she had no time to prepare for being this way. A lovely girl with golden red hair and purple eyes, Diandra's last day had been spent walking quickly down the street in her world of Glendt trying to convince the people around her that they needed to go underground to be safe from some very bad things. At first, they just laughed at her. They did that a lot, so she was used to it. But then word started spreading about horrible events in several small towns on the edge of their world. Tales of ugly beasts coming out of the darkness and killing people, destroying entire towns and the surrounding land caused a rising panic in those around her. When survivors, and there were very few of those, had begun to show up on the doorsteps of her little town, they knew she was right once again and they hated her for it.

Diandra was just that slightly odd girl who seemed to know things before they happened. When the things did eventually happen, most put it down to coincidence, a few tried to lay the blame at her feet if it was bad. Others just avoided her or tried to use her for their own selfish purposes; asking about winning lottery numbers and the future success of businesses and other ventures. She never told them what they wanted to hear, it was always something that they would rather not know. Bad weather coming, the need to stop doing something that would harm themselves or someone else. Her visions were an inconvenience to most people and it wasn't appreciated.

She had been telling them of unwelcome visitors, doom and death for months before it started, but it wasn't until trouble started in their own neighborhoods and they could no longer deny it, that they finally acknowledged that she might be able to help them escape the coming nightmare. Well, some of the people did, anyway. For others, it was too late.

She had seen the monsters in her head just before she saw a young blonde woman who began to urge her to warn her people. *Get them underground, that is the only place they will be safe,* was the message she had received. She had done as she was asked, running around her town telling everyone what she had been told. The people who listened followed her toward the entrance to the lower part of her world. Diandra had found the opening following instructions that a woman who identified herself as Sara had put in her head. She was still trying to get more people to follow her when she saw one of the monsters close up; it was one of the last things she had seen in life. The tall thin man with the shockingly white face was running at her as fast as he could. Then there was a bright flash of light and she was here.

It had taken James several hours to convince her that she was actually dead; it was kind of hard on her since she couldn't remember having been injured much less killed. But after seeing where she was and speaking with both James and the other Keepers, she had come to terms with her new situation. It wasn't all bad, because after a life of not fitting in with living people; she finally felt at peace, not dead, but at peace. And then there was this handsome young man standing in front of her. He had been there to greet her when the bright lights faded away. Diandra was comfortable where she was after she saw him. It wasn't just that he was so good-looking; it was the way he made her feel when she glanced at him, like she had just met her soul mate. He was here, and that suddenly made this the perfect place to be.

For his part, James was suddenly no longer lonely. He remembered standing with Sara and Thomas shortly after they came back from their private reunions, and they were talking about what they should do next. Things were happening so quickly. They had not received any information from their parents, had not even had the opportunity to ask, because one minute they were in their homes in the Land of the Dead, and the next they were standing next to each other in front of a park bench. Puzzled by the change, they stared at each other and waited for some kind of clue as to what was happening now. Should they just stand there and wait, not really being sure what they were waiting for, or should they take this as a sign to move on and do what they were meant to do?

They had begun to consider moving off on their own and looking for signs of Braccus's presence here. Only for things to change once more. Their parents had appeared again, excitement evident in their eyes as they shared their plan to give James, Thomas, and Sara the best day of their lives. It was shortly after this that Thomas and Sara had been going out on a lot of dates, and although James had accepted his place in this group and still loved them both, he was very much alone. The optimistic feeling he had originally felt just after death was beginning to leave him and he started seeing himself as a lonely wanderer destined to remain here forever, helpless and hopeless.

That feeling lasted for a whole twenty minutes, because his parents had pulled him aside and brought him to a place with a glowing white door. It was while he was standing in front of this door that Diandra had appeared, and whatever feelings he had for Sara were suddenly reduced to a childish crush. When he saw this girl, it was love at first sight. As Sara and Thomas went on all these dates, he was spending precious time with Diandra. The first day of their death was absolutely wonderful but, of course, too good to last.

Chapter Fourteen

Franklin and Vincent walked toward a green door that glowed brightly from the end of the dark corridor. They had separated from the others thirty minutes earlier to go where Alice had told them. *The doorway that you will be entering leads to the world of Marrik. This world is made completely of stone, there is not a green thing growing anywhere in this place. Definitely not a place for Finola to be, her powers would be useless here. You and Vincent will do well, though.* Alice spoke to them while guiding them through the darkness to the exit door. Wishing them well, she told them she would see them later, like it was a promise she meant to keep. Saying goodbye would be too final, an admission that they might not ever be together again and that wasn't going to happen. It might be difficult to reconnect, but they definitely would. Alice's voice faded out and Franklin missed her terribly.

Franklin wasn't too sure how he felt about traveling with Vincent to a place far away from his friends. He was torn between being very mad about having the last pick of travel buddies, and glad that he was in the company of someone that the enemy couldn't touch at all. Would this be a good thing? Could he count on this guy to help him out? Could he trust him? Thirty minutes ago, he would have said absolutely not. But then he saw what Vincent had done for Randall and Alice and he hoped that this was something he could count on happening all the time.

The scene played out in front of him again like a movie. Vincent turning suddenly, changing direction without warning so that Franklin had to flatten himself against the cave wall to avoid touching him. Then he took off running so fast that Franklin had difficulty keeping up with him. The lighting in the caves had been poor and most of it he had seen from behind Vincent, but he was receiving distress signals from Alice and he knew something bad was happening with her and Randall. After that, Franklin had picked up his pace, ashamed that Vincent, who had never shared anything with his circle before, had sensed the danger before he had.

If Randall's group was beginning to form a connection with Vincent, then it must mean that they were getting closer to becoming a complete unit. It gave him the feeling that maybe this situation wasn't hopeless, after all, maybe there was a way out of this for all of them. It was this thought that made him put aside his prejudices and follow Vincent slowly through the doorway to the land of Marrik.

For his part, Vincent was breathing a little bit easier as Franklin willingly followed him to the doorway. For a second there he was sure the man would refuse to go with him, and maybe he wouldn't if he had known that Vincent had received a short message from Sara that Randall and Alice were in trouble. He wasn't joined with his group the way he should have been yet, but her help had put him in their good graces, allowing him to save the day. While he still wasn't officially one of the gang, he was no longer considered the enemy, and as such he would be tolerated, if not totally accepted. It was a start and he could live with that for now, it gave him hope that things could get better. They had to. He could no longer sense Sara and he had a feeling that her last message was literally her last message to him.

With a renewed sense of purpose, Vincent crossed through the doorway in front of Franklin. It would be safer for him to go through first. If there was an enemy force waiting on the other side, all he would have to do was let them touch him and they would die instantly. Franklin could protect himself from anything that managed to get past him. With a nervous nod to his companion, Vincent walked into the blurry light and into the unknown.

As soon as did so, things almost got seriously messed up. Vincent was forced to stop suddenly, his passage blocked by a large boulder a few feet in front of the door. Franklin had been following more closely than he realized and almost ran into him. As he struggled to avoid contact with his deadly companion, Franklin burst into flames while Vincent did an odd sidestep, both to keep from being burned and killing his partner.

Startled by what almost happened, both let out muffled squeals of alarm before moving away from each other. Each held their hands in the air, showing the universal sign of *hey, I'm harmless*, as they backed away from each other. With lips clamped together, they fell silent as they realized that they might attract a lot of attention making all that noise. Since they didn't know exactly what they were walking into, it seemed better not to announce that they were coming.

The large boulder stood next to several other large boulders to form a wall which provided the perfect cover for their undetected arrival. But, while it was wonderful to not be seen, the wall, which extended to about two feet above them and roughly twenty feet on either side, was also blocking their view of everything around them. Movement on the other side of the wall, muffled grunts and grumbling in a foreign language, told them that they were not alone, that there was a large group of some kind on the other side. Since all that was good had been driven from the surface, it was safe to assume that there wasn't a large friendly group. Franklin looked at his companion and nodded as they both shared the same thought: they could not stay here forever. Moving past the wall and into the middle of an enemy gathering was the only way out of this spot. If only they could see past this barrier to figure out exactly what kind of creatures and how many they had to fight. Just because Vincent had the ability to kill whatever he touched and whatever touched him, did not mean he couldn't be hurt or killed from a distance. A lot of care had to be taken before they went running out into trouble; which, of course, they would have to do soon.

Vincent was also thinking that it would be nice to have an idea where they would have to run like crazy to get to. The good people of this world were hiding beneath the surface. It was their job to protect or rescue them. But where were the entrances located? Did this ever get any easier?

Where do we start? Vincent sent a message to Franklin, who though he still stood as far away from him as possible, was at least sending some vibes that he had decided to trust him. In fact, he had turned to look at him in response to his question with a look of we're in this together on his face. So, he waited for an additional positive sign.

Let's start walking that way. Franklin's voice sounded softly in his head as if, even in this mode of conversation, he could be overheard by the evil things on the other side of the wall. His body no longer glowed with his internal fire, but his face was flushed either from nervous excitement or terror, as he turned toward his left and extended his arm to indicate the way they should go.

Vincent nodded his head. *I guess we should find out what's out there sooner or later.*

Chapter Fifteen

Sara and Thomas were on a park bench directly across from James and his new constant companion Diandra. They had double-dated several times and Sara liked her a lot; the girl had a different aura around her. Her soul, which still hung close to her body, was brilliant with a lovely green tint to it and it felt clean.

Shortly before she died, Sara had started to see the souls of everyone around her. They hung close to bodies like shadows varying in color. The Keepers had the brightest sharpest blue tones and regular people's being a dim muted pink. But this girl had the same color around her that she had seen so far with only one person: Robert's wife Maryann.

Diandra wasn't a Keeper so she must have the ability to see and feel certain things, just like Maryann. Sara had known there was something different about Maryann when she had first seen her. After watching her carefully and doing a little snooping in her head, she had learned what the woman was really capable of long before she herself was fully aware of what she could do.

Diandra was just like her. Well, mostly her aura was a brighter green color than Maryann's but that probably just meant that she was more aware of what she could do and had used her gifts longer. Sara had a feeling that these two women were not alone in the worlds; there were more like them. While they did not have powers like the Keepers and their lifespan not as long, they were created to help Iam's creations in some way, just like the Keepers.

These special people were connected to the Keepers and it must be why Diandra seemed to be perfectly suited to James.

When Sara looked at the two of them together, she saw a beautiful purple glow that made her smile. He looked so happy; both of them did. It was a shame that James had to die before he found someone to share his life with, so to speak.

On this particular date, as much as they didn't want it to end, they had the feeling that it was time to leave this place. It was the main topic of their conversation as they wandered through the beautiful park, finally settling on this bench to discuss their next move. Part of what they were looking for was nearby, Sara could feel an unpleasant energy radiating from somewhere to the west of them. It hung on the edge of her inner eyesight like an unpleasant odor in one of those trash bag commercials; a brown mist of dirty air that told the audience how foul it smelled. At first, Thomas and James hadn't noticed it, but Diandra had. While the group sat and talked, Sara noticed the girl sitting up straighter and looking to the west with a frown on her face. Diandra couldn't see it but she certainly felt it and that's what got her attention. Diandra had turned to look at Sara after she felt it; she knew the trail was there, felt its nasty lingering effect. Sara was impressed by this because the older Keepers themselves had failed to notice it; she had been in their heads and pulled out many things with little effort. Sara had done this out of necessity, not to disrespect them. There were certain things she needed to know; three months' worth of dates, while enjoyable, was more than enough for now, and her group needed to know where to start their journey. She had to find out how much their parents knew about why they were here and what they were looking for.

Sara let out a small sigh; she was going to miss the time she spent with her parents. Since they hadn't needed to take time out to sleep, Thomas, James and Sara were able to spend what little time they weren't on a date with their family. Sharing what they had seen and experienced throughout the centuries, the birth of the worlds and the struggle to keep evil in its place, had been wonderful. The older Keepers had a lot to say about the evil ones. There were more varieties of Braccus's mutations than they realized, and they were made aware of a few protective measures that might be employed against them. It made Sara wonder why they should care about this, since they were dead. Maybe they could use this information to help the living in some way.

It was strange that their parents had felt Braccus when he followed them here, but they hadn't noticed the residue he had left behind on a previous visit. The trail she saw was years old but hung in the air to be detected only by Diandra and herself. Its presence only confirmed what she already knew; it was time to end the dates and the fairy tale family time. This was not their reality, even in death. They had a purpose and it wasn't to hang out and have a great time. The trail was just a reminder that all this had to end quickly. A great big wake-up call hanging in mid-air, urging them to follow where it led.

Braccus liked games, but for some reason she didn't think this was one he was playing. She felt very strongly that he didn't want her to find what he had been here to hide, because hiding was the whole point behind this. He had entered after them to watch and had only left after the Keepers detected him. But she knew he'd be back; he needed to for some reason.

Sara was watching her new friend closely as all these thoughts ran through her head. A familiar vibration in the air caught her attention and she turned to greet the parents, who she was sure were here to say goodbye. But who were the two extra people she had sensed in their company, a faint shimmering in the air revealing their arrival? She was about to speak when her attention was divided by the need for her presence elsewhere, so she sent a little bit of herself away, and waited for them to come to her.

Chapter Sixteen

Finola held Eric's hand tightly to still the shaking of her own as they walked through a hazy grey doorway and into a barren brown field. They could see the faint blurry shapes of thin figures standing alongside shorter bulky ones, like they were looking at everything through a filmy barrier. This barrier hadn't come from Alice, the soul connection was different, familiar, but different. She felt love and a longing for the connection that was just strong enough to make her miss the person that sent it. There was still so much to be said between them and she was sad that it couldn't be said now.

They hadn't expected help from beyond, but Finola knew it was Sara who she remembered had specifically told Alice the door to the other side was closed. Maybe that didn't go both ways, Sara was still meddling in their business and she loved her for it. The kind of power she had been given was strong enough to seep through into their world. She was still trying to help them out from beyond the grave. Alice had been able to lead them to the exits only, her ability to assist them ended there. Once they had moved back onto the surface, they were on their own.

Wherever she was now, Sara had felt their need and, like always, sent some of herself to her friends. Her sister's spirit was here. This girl, related to her only by the time they had spent with Rianna, was as close as she had come to a family with the exception of her Circle mates. She could no longer feel Rianna, and that hurt so much, but she could still feel Sara; that had to mean something. It had to mean that she was still within reach somehow. It had to mean it would be possible to find her again.

It had to be possible to find her again, because this amazing woman had done so much that no one else could have. Power like hers, power that could move beyond the veil of death was too strong to be gone forever. Her sister was giving them just enough cover to help them get their bearings and make a run for it to the underground places. Finola had no idea how long this gift of secrecy would last, so she decided to make good use of the time they had been granted.

Finola studied the area in front of her; the dirt surface was pitted with many holes from which the plant life had been brutally ripped and trampled. It hurt her to see the land this way; it was so damaged that she had to reach deep into the soil to find something to work with. It took a few precious minutes to locate anything that she could use; the plants weren't responding. She had to try harder. The misty covering in front of them began to waver as their protected time wore out. The soil was hiding what little assets it had left; the seeds and roots were buried so far down in the ground that they didn't want to come out of their safe hiding-spots.

Finola, honey, I hate to put pressure on you, Eric said softly in her head. *But we need to do something soon; we won't have this cover for long. If you could just bring up something to get tangled around their feet, I will come out making so much noise, they won't be able to get themselves free.*

Dark curls bobbed as Finola gave him a tense nod. She was trying not to choke under the pressure and just concentrate on finding something she could work with. She searched even deeper into the soil and put all she had into grabbing the few tangled roots she could find and coaxing them toward the surface. Sweat was dripping from her forehead as she drew them upward against their will. After all the damage that had been done, it was much harder to get anything to even want to go back up to the horrible place the surface had become. Finola had to command the plants to go back to what had once been their natural habitat, a fact she regretted terribly because she was going to have to sacrifice a lot of them to the enemy.

Thorny bushes and weeds, about the only thing that would be sturdy enough to break the unfriendly environment, crawled along the underside of its hard shell, gathering strength to burst back topside again. Finola prepared to unleash them, having directed them into place beneath the monsters who now occupied their former territory. But what was the plan after that?

Once or twice in the past, Finola had been able to visualize portals and make them open, but this talent seemed to have faded even as her current gift with the growing of things became stronger. She was clueless about where to look for the escape route, so she turned to Eric for some help.

Eric, where are we going? The question popped into his head, while her big brown eyes looked at him pleading for a reasonable answer. She was ready to act and fully prepared to run like crazy once their temporary protection disappeared, but she was going to need to know what direction she was headed before she could direct the plants to cover them. Eric seemed so confident that they could do this; he had to know something, like where to go when they announced their presence to the enemy. Finola was disturbed to enter his thoughts and find that he didn't seem to know any more than she did.

Surely that couldn't be right, one of them had to have a clue and he had been so strong for her lately. She had just seen enough to know that he was scared for them both and trying hard not to show it. *Eric?* Her heart thumped in her chest as she divided her attention between preparing for attack and opening a doorway somewhere, trying to get back the skill that had saved their lives once before. Why was it that nothing happened consistently in this darn place?

The wall of thicker air in front of them was beginning to thin out. In fact, it was getting so thin that a Garren on the edge of the group had turned and was looking in their direction with interest. Eyes narrowed as he squinted at the grey mass that had been hiding Finola and Eric from view, its appearance had changed enough times so that it was more than just a blurry part of the background, more like a blanket with holes in it. The two people behind it could now see the barren land in front of them quite clearly in spots and, judging by the slow smile that was forming on the evil brute's face, he had noticed it also.

The super skinny man barred his teeth in a smile that looked more like a painful grimace and nudged the grey-skinned Ornose standing next to him. Finola ducked down a little as one of the holes appearing in front of her widened, revealing the glowing doorway behind them. They were not visible yet, but she had a feeling that the Garren knew there was something nearby that was not evil; something that they would have a really good time tearing apart.

Eric knelt on the ground next to Finola, turning his head slightly at the sickening sound of the portal snapping and popping as it grew smaller. Those stupid openings had a habit of closing with very little warning, and they still had no idea where they were supposed to go as it closed completely, leaving them frantically scanning the area for another way out.

Finola sent her plants bursting through the soil as the last of the thinning veil in front of them disappeared. They were standing out in the open, clearly visible now, staring in dismay at their unfriendly greeting committee. Five enemy soldiers, three Garren and two Ornose began to run in their direction, intent on catching their newly arrived victims. Vines covered with thick thorns pushed out of the hard soil wrapping around the ankles of two of the Ornose while the rest of the plants formed a wall of green which turned brittle and brown at the touch of one of the Garren behind it. The enemy was busy breaking the plants apart, causing Finola wince with the growing things were experiencing, feeling everything that they did.

Trying to save her some of the pain, and of course to buy them time to escape; Eric blasted the air with waves of high-pitched sound, making the beasts back off for a minute. Hands over their ears, a grayish-yellow substance oozing from between them, they screamed in pain.

"Run," Eric yelled at Finola, her hand still firmly gripped in his. Their direction of travel was still unsure, so he simply turned to his right and pulled her along behind him. Two pairs of sneakered feet pounded the hard ground as they ran for their lives. Eric was still sending out sound waves which were slowing, but not stopping the pursuing beasts who continued to stumble along behind them.

Finola continued to send her beloved plants to keep the enemy back, tears dripping steadily down her cheeks as she felt them destroyed almost as fast as she could grow them. She was still looking back at her diminishing wall of green when Eric tugged at her hand and pointed to a small pink door glowing brightly in the dim greyness; drawing their attention like a firecracker on a dark night.

Hope renewed somewhat, they turned toward it and ran at full speed, knowing that passing through it was just the beginning of their struggle rather than the end. It wasn't a safe haven for them; they still faced a group of suspicious strangers that may not welcome them with open arms, but at least they stood a better chance of surviving down there than up here. Knowing things would get worse before they got better, Eric felt compelled to say something important to Finola before they moved into another very stressful situation.

I love you. Even though it had been understood, he had never said it before, and it was just something that he needed to tell her before they went underground.

Finola wanted to turn and give him a big hug, but running for her life took up all her energy. They knew so much about each other and had only recently begun to remember that they had been acquainted for hundreds of years. Many memories of their past existence were slowly trickling through to them each day. They had years of shared experiences from a time before they even possessed a body. If they had to start all over again in these forms that was fine, but she was not going to let those ugly brutes kill them and cut short what was sure to be a wonderful renewal of their relationship. Determined to get out of this nightmare, Finola put all her residual energy, what little she had left, to bringing up even more brambles and weeds. They were thicker and filled with razor-sharp spikes designed specifically to inflict maximum injury. She directed the plants to the arms, legs, and torsos of their pursuers, understanding that it would do little but buy them a few minutes.

Finola was running so fast now that her lungs ached, but she let out a small satisfied chuckle as she heard the screams of pain from the enemy's throats, felt their blood run down the length of the plants and soak into the ground. It was a small, short-lived victory as she felt another unfriendly force moving in from their other side to help their pursuers.

Frustrated growls and shrieks sounded from behind them and the ground shook with the force of the struggle that the Ornose were putting up as they ripped plants from the ground with renewed vigor. The sky crackled overhead with bright green lightning as the monsters behind them began to receive a little assistance with their struggle from another powerful entity. One of the lightning bolts struck the plants and the accompanying boom of thunder helped to diminish the effect of Eric's sound disturbance. As a result, he was forced to raise the volume and stall them a little longer. The piercing squeals were now so intense that he and Finola would have died from a brain injury if he hadn't been able to mute his own gift. Trying to tone down his panic, Eric looked straight ahead and was relieved to see their exit door getting closer with each advancing step. Several more leaping bounds brought them right up to the way out of this particular nightmare.

The warm light of the underground entrance made their cheeks pink as they paused outside it. *I love you too,* Finola put the thought into his head, hoping that they would have time to grow and catch up with their hearts. Squeezing his hand; she spared him one quick glance before the sound of approaching footsteps spurred them into entering the doorway.

Chapter Seventeen

Sara snapped back into her body, or whatever her soul currently occupied, so quickly that her head flew backwards. Thomas reached out and steadied her with a cry of concern. What was going on? One minute she was helping her friends, the next she was thrown out of the place Finola and Eric were running through and back into her lifeless shell. She had tried to hide them from the enemy while they attempted to locate one of the underground entrances. They were struggling to get their bearings in the strange place they found themselves in and she had felt their need for assistance. She couldn't just watch from a distance while the enemy closed in on her friends, she had to help.

Sara knew Finola sensed her there providing assistance and she wanted to talk to her so badly, wanted to apologize once again for all that had happened in the last few weeks of her life, but she couldn't seem to do that. Her connection to that side was becoming thinner and thinner. Sara tried to force the issue and push her way past the ever-thickening wall that was keeping her from traveling effortlessly back and forth between the living and dead, but someone was pushing just as hard to keep her where she was.

Brief glimpses of Vincent and Franklin moving somewhere with a very rocky landscape and Alice and Randall creeping slowly across a wet, humid field played in her head. She struggled to be where they were and give them what protection she could while doing what was required of her in this place. But it wasn't working like it should and she couldn't figure out why. She had always been able to move around effortlessly before, but she had been alive then. When she told Alice that she could not use her gifts to cross the barrier to contact her, Sara had just assumed the door was closed only to Alice, she never dreamed that it would be closed to her also. She hadn't wanted to make it any more difficult for Alice to do what she needed to down there, but she hadn't thought it would go both ways.

This was so frustrating. She needed to make sure they were safe, looking passively at the events that rolled by underneath her was not enough. Sara wanted to be with her friends, fighting alongside them or, helping them from a distance if that's all she could manage. It was awful to lose her grip on the other world entirely. The reality of her death had finally hit her.

Thomas and James both stood closer and quietly offered their support. They knew what she had been trying to do, and even though they had a bad feeling about it, done nothing to stop her. She would have tried to do it anyway and while she refused to acknowledge it, they weren't supposed to interfere with the living now. Not being able to participate in the affairs of the outside world somehow made all this final and they knew she was finally realizing it. She hadn't seen it that way until now because she still figured she would be able to do everything she had always done before. Well, she figured wrong. Iam had just given her a reminder of her promise to leave that place and come here. Thomas wiped the tears from her eyes, placed a kiss on her cheek and made her return her full attention to the people now standing in front of them. *It's not over. It's just beginning,* he reminded her gently.

Sara's parents watched her closely. They knew what she had been trying to do; they had done the same thing years after they had died with the same result. It was painful to see her go through this, but there was still so much she didn't know about her situation, things she wasn't meant to know yet. Sara's mother Maura broke the awkward silence, bringing her daughter's attention back to the two figures standing next to her. They had given up eternal rest to be here like the others and had been so excited to hear of Sara's arrival.

"They will be fine; they are Keepers now, fully aware of what they can do, even if they haven't developed their powers to the highest level yet. They will learn to adapt to stay alive, trust them to be able to do this for themselves." She sounded stern but there was compassion in eyes so much like her own Sara had to look away to regain her composure. It was then that she noticed the short red-haired woman and tall dark-haired man waiting anxiously for their chance to greet her and her companions. She pushed her panic and sadness aside.

"Maggie!" Sara cried, reaching eagerly for one of the first Keepers she had ever met. This little woman, along with her constant companion and fellow Keeper Ferd, had greeted her shortly after her arrival in the Land of the Keepers and had made her aware of her part in the mission to rescue Olie. She had helped to train Sara and the other children to fight Braccus and his forces; they would have never survived or gotten as far as they had without her help. The little lady returned her hug enthusiastically, while they both expressed joy at seeing each other again. Tears in her eyes, Sara pulled away and looked at the man next to Maggie as she came to terms with her total withdrawal from the ordinary world. Playtime here was at an end. She had a job to do here so she'd better pay attention to what was going on around her. The Garren that stood in front of her really looked no different than when he had been alive; they were already so pale in life that his ashy skin was a close match to his regular color. The difference between this Garren and the evil live ones was his warm smile and the clean feel to his soul. The fact that he had a soul was a miracle because. As a rule, the

Garren had no soul. Braccus had created them, after all, and he was incapable of providing them with that particular spiritual attachment.

This Garren's soul was a gift from Iam because he had accepted what Iam offered, a chance to live life as something real and solid in the service of a greater good. Few of his kin had willingly done this and it had made him an enemy to his own kind. She recognized this Garren from a time when she was training with Olie, Rianna, Maggie and Ferd. His name was Milo and he had been very helpful advising them on how to defeat his own species. She hadn't exactly greeted him with open arms then, and still looked at all Garren with a suspicious eye, but he had helped them a lot and she hadn't forgotten that. He deserved the respect and gratitude of all the Keepers for his assistance.

Thomas and James recognized him too; they had fought beside this man and had admired his courage in battle. Last time Thomas had seen Milo, he was lying dead in a field, beaten so badly that he wouldn't have recognized him. The Garren, though originally without emotion, had evolved to develop a new feeling: pure hatred. They had unleashed it on Milo, a traitor to his own kind, until he was trampled and torn into a bloody pulp. Thomas was glad to see that this man's sacrifice had not been in vain. Milo's presence here meant that he had once been with Iam and, like the others here, had chosen to leave and find a way to watch over the worlds.

Both young men grasped Milo's hand and shook it enthusiastically. This man; because that's what he had become when he got his soul, a true man; had embraced his new life and had been a good friend. They were happy to see him with the Keepers. Sara hadn't been there for all this, but she saw it in the minds of her group and that, with her memories of his help years earlier, prompted her to shake his hand too. She was looking at him as they saw him, as a fallen hero, someone Iam had felt worthy enough to allow into his inner circle and whom the Keepers trusted enough to be in the place they had created.

James and Sara pulled Diandra forward at the same time, introducing her to the two people that had just arrived. Sara had a feeling that it wasn't quite necessary though, as the girl seemed to be well aware who both were. Diandra's face showed no surprise at their arrival and a scan of her thoughts showed that she had seen this meeting before it happened. Her presence here was all part of this somehow, but her knowledge only went so far. Other than vague impressions of the trouble down below before they happened, most of Diandra's visions seemed more spur of the moment and not far into the future.

The young woman looked back at Sara with an apologetic smile, as if to say she was sorry she couldn't give her more. Sara knew Diandra was here for James and it was very important that she stay with him. She nodded to show her support and received a bright smile from both.

When all the hugging and handshaking was finished, they moved toward a few conveniently located benches to hear what the Keepers had to say to them before they said goodbye to this nice imitation of life and moved on to something less pleasant.

Chapter Eighteen

Alice and Randall stumbled through a doorway right into a rainstorm that was falling so heavily, it was like buckets of water were being thrown at them by a thousand angry angels. They were wet within seconds of slipping into the portal. It had snapped shut as soon as Randall's foot cleared it and he stumbled forward as the electric force behind the closing door pushed against his own internal energy. Alice steadied him and they both knelt on the ground in the pitch darkness surrounding them, huddling together for a few moments, trying to get an idea of where they were. Alice knew this to be the world of Yalder; she learned it from Maryann who had been sending messages until the connection had been cut by passing through the portal. This place had once been mostly water with a few isolated islands scattered about to provide housing for its small inhabitants. Alice got an image of graceful athletic beings with bright red hair and strong physiques adapted for an active life. They had been peaceful, unused to having to protect themselves from evil because it rarely showed itself here. Except for a few isolated incidents of violent behavior exhibited by the strange-looking animals that had begun to appear out of the water recently, they had not needed to defend themselves from anything. Then one day the sea just exploded, water gushed upward, literally vomiting up a large number of thick rock-covered creatures and ugly grayish-black beasts. These beasts crawled up on shore and proceeded to kill everyone not fast enough to escape their deadly blows.

A few Yalderites escaped harm by jumping into their main mode of transportation, thin boats made of reed that they used to move from island to island. But the enemy seemed to anticipate this and the sea around them began to drift upward as if the sky were taking a huge drink, draining the water away, leaving the survivors stranded on a soupy sandy surface. Dead sea-creatures lay all around them as they stumbled out of their boats and ran for their lives. Iam's creations would have been completely wiped out if it had not been for a certain dead person with blonde hair who made the earth buckle with the assistance of her two strong male companions. Then she made the way below visible in the form of a shiny silver door, bright enough to get their attention. The doorway emitted a signal so soothing to the Yalderites that it drew them to it, promising safety from the enemy.

The rain that now fell upon Alice and Randall was the contents of the sea being returned to its original holding area. Alice knew that in a day or two the water would be quite deep. The mini-movie in her head explained a lot, especially why they needed to find the underground place before this area was covered by ocean again. The connection between her and Maryann had been flickering and distant as if something was attempting to cut it off altogether. Just before she had lost touch completely; Maryann had urged them to be very careful, Alice especially, but she was gone from her head before she could explain why.

Trying not to dwell too much on the warning, Alice put a barrier up around her and Randall which, thankfully, stopped the rain from coming down upon them any longer. Randall rested his head against hers while they conversed silently, looking around, afraid to move before they knew where to go. Both Keepers were sitting in a puddle, shivering from cold, fully aware that they could not stay still for long. Randall patted ineffectively at Alice's wet back, wishing he had Franklin's powers so that he could generate a little bit of heat to dry her off and warm her up. As it was, he could only keep her company, hugging her and shivering alongside her. He was afraid that if the enemy did find them here, his own gift would be a curse; using it in this wet place could electrocute his girlfriend.

Is that what I am? she said with a small smile, absurd to feel happy at a time like this, but she couldn't help it.

If we're not at a serious relationship after all we've been through, I'd be really disappointed, he said, leaning over to kiss her. A small spark jumped from his lips to hers, it didn't hurt; just felt warm and tingly. The moment should have lasted forever but, of course, it didn't. Alice was just enjoying kissing him back when a shifting in the wind reminded them that they were not alone. The air carried the strong smell of decay directly toward them. There were dead things here and, as far as Alice and Randall could tell, they were the only living things with souls hanging around.

Bad news: they weren't alone. Whatever was here was alive but didn't have redeeming sprits. They felt something moving closer; foul, rotting pieces of moving meat that generated living energy so dark it hurt their heads. The ground around them vibrated with the footsteps of a large group of evil beings about two miles away, neither was sure where that estimate came from, they just knew it to be true. They were safe for the time being beneath her protective shield, but they had to leave soon; they had people to protect, themselves included.

Alice pulled back reluctantly, smoothing his wet hair back from his face, stalling for just a little longer in hopes that she wouldn't have to move out into the darkness but knowing, of course, that they would. She was more aware of what was in the places others couldn't see and it was far worse than the twisted mutants that had tried to kill them so far. True, there were good souls out there wandering in and out of the space between the worlds, but like everywhere else, the evil ones were beginning to outnumber them. She ignored them just a little longer to concentrate on her handsome boyfriend. Boyfriend. The word made her so happy.

Okay, so we're going steady, but it would be great if you'd take me somewhere nice for a change. They sat and stared at each other for a few minutes longer. It was strange that they couldn't see much of anything around them in this light, but they could see each other quite clearly. They sure did look great together. Shaking her head to refocus, the smile still plastered on her face, she took his hand as he helped her up and pulled her forward. Alice tried using her inner sense to find the doorway to the underground place they were headed for, but for some reason it was not making itself known. Finding the way to safety was obviously not going to be easy.

Shadows shifted around them in the murky darkness, but Alice sensed that Randall didn't notice them; becoming aware of them only after she let him see what she was seeing. To be able to see darkness in the darkness was a unique talent. The darkness that defined the dead things appeared like an orange glow to Alice, making them very visible to her. She focused on them and was distressed to see how many of them roamed around the area. She was seeing more of the fluorescent beings skulking around the edges of her shield, studying the defensive bubble she had put up with great interest.

Making his mind up that he really didn't like this situation, Randall held Alice's hand tightly. He was moving slowly, noting through her eyes that the dead watchers paused to look intently at them as they changed position. As he turned to look at his companion he saw Alice staring at what, to his naked eye, was empty darkness. When he switched back to their shared channel of communication, he saw what she saw, and what she saw scared him to death.

Whatever they were, they moved fast, zipping around the jagged remains of tree stumps that littered the landscape like broken teeth in an infected jaw. Stringy masses of dark stuff grew from their scalps, sticking up like mini-Mohawks on the top of heads. Their fearful faces sported mouths gaping open in silent screams with a dark gritty substance oozing from the side of them; wide eyes dripping the same black stuff as they stared at his dark-haired girlfriend. Randall pulled Alice's slight form closer and urged her to walk forward; he could tell that she was thinking about answering the whispers he was beginning to hear from inside her head and this bothered him a lot.

"We can find it without them," he said, tensely, as he turned to look at her. "We don't need their help," he repeated, as she started to open her mouth to tell him why she thought it might be a good idea to use them to find their way to the portal.

Maybe they were the reason she hadn't been able to see it and if she just talked to them, maybe she would learn something about what the living things were. She knew they were drawn to other beings like moths were drawn to light and, since they could move through other doorways with little difficulty, they must know where the good beings were hidden. If she could convince them that they would somehow benefit from helping the creatures that still had blood pumping through their veins, maybe they would show them the way out. She thought frantically about what she could offer them in return for their cooperation. Somehow she knew they wouldn't do this selflessly, it had to be because they could benefit somehow. Innocent beings were now at risk of being destroyed, not to mention the fact that she and Randall were in danger of drowning if they weren't able to find the way down. Maybe she could appeal to them in some way and work out a deal.

Randall listened to Alice's rambling thoughts for a second before jerking her around to face him. His actions earned him a shocked look. He was sorry to have to do that but at least he got her attention, and for a minute the voices that had gotten her thinking this crazy way were silent.

"Alice, we don't need them to show us the way out. Please let's start walking and I'm sure we will find it. You have the ability to locate the way below. Come on now, we haven't been here that long, and we haven't really tried to look. I don't think we can trust them; stop letting them mess with you!"

Reaching up to touch his face reassuringly, Alice took a deep breath, nodded, and together they moved toward a large open area on their right. Walking quickly, their eyes scanned the horizon for a sign that they were going in the right direction. Valiantly trudging onward, she tried to show Randall that she was willing to try this his way, but she kept hearing the whispers in the back of her head as the dead things followed them at a distance, and it was getting harder and harder to push them back.

Chapter Nineteen

Sara listened to her parents, Maggie, and Milo, with half an ear. Her mind was wandering, restlessly seeking a way to make this all work the way she needed it to. Instead of accepting what was pointed out to her by her total removal from the outer world, she still had to believe she could be of some use to her friends. It was making her sick to her stomach to feel so out of touch with her loved ones, so she refused to accept the limits she was given. This was so hard! She suddenly realized that this must be what their parents had been going through since they had died, and the full impact of their pain hit her. She was crying inside while she listened to their explanations of why this place was being invaded more often by evil. The original Keepers were trying to explain to their children why it had taken them so long to sense Braccus's presence here, and why they still had no idea where his secret might be hidden.

Sara's began thinking back to a time when she had held one of Braccus's possessions in her hand, a barbed spear with a letter *B* carved into it. Salius, a former Keeper, turned traitor to his people had helped her find it. He had died helping her get it, earning himself redemption and saving her life in the process. Sadly, she had lost track of it before she had also died and had no idea where it was now. How could it have been lost so easily?

That spear had Braccus's blood on it, she remembered that quite clearly. If it had been used to hurt him, it meant that he had a weak side; a part of him that he would never admit to having. It was why he had gone to such lengths to hide the object yet was still afraid to destroy it. Though she sensed he had promised himself he would. Whatever it was that made him keep these things made them something that could be used against him and Sara definitely planned to do that.

She wondered what had happened to the spear, and what her chances were of getting it back. It wasn't the object that would lead to Braccus's destruction, but it was connected to it in some way and that made it important. With all the confusion that followed Salius's death, it had disappeared, and she couldn't seem to remember exactly when it happened. Her parents didn't seem to know either. This bothered them a great deal because it was another indication that they were losing more of their gifts. They were worried about their ability to use what was left of their powers on the enemy to keep this place safe.

Even though sheer will and a deep abiding love for all they had left behind had given them strength to eventually create this place, it too had developed many different layers and they had begun to lose control over parts of it. Braccus's secret place could be many different places and they would not be able to help them find whatever he had hidden. It was a painful for them to confess their weakness to their children; that they were not what they used to be. They had given up most of their power in death, parts having passed on to the future generations to carry on their works. The rest was just enough to maintain this area; the closest that they could get to the worlds, watching always but being unable to affect them in any way. They had been strong enough to scare Braccus off earlier, but they weren't so sure how long that would last since the change had begun.

The original Keepers could feel the effects of the change in the balance between good and evil, could feel when the darkness became stronger and began spreading to their refuge. Evil had gradually seeped in until there were several grayish places dotted throughout the afterworld. The originals had begun to centralize, pulling out of the outer edges to get ready for the arrival of the new Keepers, and trying to find a way to reach out to the world they had watched from a distance for so long.

Sara, Thomas, and James, were here to move out into those lost outer edges and retrieve whatever it was that had been placed out of their parent's reach. But the older Keepers also saw that the wavering line that separated the dimensions was weakening and decided to use it to their advantage. If the evil things could wander in from out there, maybe they could use what was left of their powers to move through too. Ideas now began to form about a way out. They had an opportunity to help the living and were going to take it. While their children were charged with finding the object that would help end Braccus's control over the worlds, perhaps his very existence, they were going to try and find a way to break the restrictive bonds that held them here. This meeting was their last chance to see their children before they attempted to get past the barriers between the dimensions and rejoin the fight. They had come to say goodbye and escort the young ones toward the outer limits of the afterworld to begin what they were intended to do.

Milo had come along to help find the way out. He was anxious to rid the world of his own kind; it was the one reason he had not stayed with Iam. He had never felt worthy of the honor this great being had bestowed upon him and was still anxious to prove he could help restore the balance in favor of good. One side effect of having a soul was that he now felt shame for all the things he had done before he realized what he was doing was wrong. Iam had never asked him to make up for any of his previous cruelties and had urged him to stay. But Milo made the choice to do what he could, and give up the brief time he spent in total love and acceptance to fight for Iam's worlds.

As for Maggie, who had died thinking her usefulness in this world was over; she found herself unable to accept the rest that she was offered. She had watched with horror as Ferd and Olie had been torn apart, willing sacrifices to the change they had been expecting to occur for hundreds of years now. She had felt tremendous pride in Ferd's courage and resolve to protect their beloved students that all she could think of now was wandering the worlds with him and Olie. Forever was not too much of a sacrifice for her if it meant she was going to be with those precious souls again.

Maggie had begged Iam to allow her return and he agreed to let her come as far as this place and that was alright, for now. At least she got to see Maura and the others again; she had missed them so much. When she arrived to find that Sara and her Circle members would be coming soon, she waited with her loved ones for the fight for the worlds to begin.

Sara's parents Maura and Daniel wanted to be with their daughter through all of this, but they also realized that they couldn't do anymore for her then she could for herself. She hadn't realized it yet, but she was already twice as strong as they were. Other than their need to be with her as much as they could, they could not offer her as much as they could Iam's other creations. It was a big risk, but leaving Iam and giving up the rest he offered them had been a big risk also. They were moving further and further from their creator, all in the hopes of offering themselves to the world again. They had served as guardians to the worlds too long to let them fall to evil.

Iam watched all this with both sadness and great pride. Free will is one thing he had always offered his people, and he understood why they were doing all this, but he wasn't going

118

to make it easy for them. If they were determined to move back into the fight, they would have to find a way to do it on their own; they would get no help from him. In order for this to count for something, many sacrifices had to be made and defiance, though well-intended, had its consequences.

The original Keepers didn't consider their actions as defiance, more desperation; one last bid to help those still in the fight, including Olie, their leader on earth for hundreds of years. It had been difficult to watch as he and Ferd had been killed. They knew why those two let themselves die, fully aware they wouldn't be going with Iam or even arriving here. Their devoted family would certainly have welcomed them with open arms but if they were both going to stay out there, then that too was a sign that it was time for Maura, Daniel, Janika, Havis, Levi, Cloette, Maggie and Milo to find a way to join them. Their intentions were being loudly broadcast to the young people standing in front of them, and their children not only approved but were very proud of them for it. Thomas and James were paying close attention to the directions being given them as their parents passed on images of the place between the worlds they had made. It was interesting to note that, while the center was bright and beautiful, the edges had a gray cast to them. The gray areas were hard to see inside with the murky air getting thicker and thicker by the minute. These darker areas were where the three of them would have to look; it was what their parents had come here to show them. What they could make out in the foggy gloom was hardly encouraging; jagged rotting pieces of unidentified material shared space with slimy puddles that were calm and slick one minute, and full of restless movement the next. James saw a twisted gray arm shoot up from the nasty wetness and grasp ineffectually at the air above it for a second before jerking back downward

119

as if pulled by something stronger. Shadows shifted, occasionally revealing things with faces so terrifying it made their blood run cold; it seemed that there were things to be afraid of even after death.

While he registered all he saw, Thomas held Sara's hand, squeezing it to bring her out of her tumbling thoughts. He felt her resolve to get back into the worlds and reminded her that, for now, she was needed here. His unspoken tone was a little sharp, forcing her to look up at him with wide blue eyes. She saw the concern and love there which pulled her back to him and the conversation that was occurring.

Next to them, James looked to the girl at his side. Diandra was listening carefully to what the originals were saying, lips tightly set together to hide her fear. He was already so attached to her he didn't see how he could leave her behind, especially when the power that created this place was going to be diminished further by the loss of several of its powerful guardians. But he was also afraid of what they would be walking into. He could sense that a few less powerful Keepers were willing to remain here to keep a place open for clean souls to move through, but they would be more vulnerable to the growing tide of evil that was moving in on their territory. Even so, this place would still be safer than the darker edges. Maybe she should stay here. Diandra turned and gave him an angry look as he thought this. Was it the expression on his face, or was she reading his mind in some way?

"I'm going with you," she whispered into his ear, lacing her fingers with his as if tying them together forever. He was about to argue with her, concern for her safety prompting him to keep her far away from what they were about to go into. Whatever she was; she wasn't a regular girl, but she wasn't a Keeper either. Was she even supposed to go with

120

them? Maybe she would be allowed to go to wherever Iam was. Surely that place was safer, completely closed off from the evil that was beginning to wander through here ever more frequently.

You'd be safer somewhere else, I can come back for you later. I promise… He had begun communicating with her through a personal path, suddenly sure that she would be able to hear him this way. Confirming that she was no ordinary girl, she stopped him mid-sentence with another angry look.

I will be going with you, she answered him firmly, not letting him say anything else. *I'm supposed to go with you.* She looked at him with lips pursed in irritation.

Of course she is, Sara piped in while they continued to listen to the instructions they were given. She knew without a shadow of a doubt that this young woman was here to help James in some way. Diandra was so strongly connected to him that Sara could only see them as a unit. There was a reason for this and she intended to keep them together. This girl was going to stay with them all the way until she figured out exactly what her part in this was. Sara broadcast her thoughts clearly to James, who gave her an angry glare. He couldn't argue with her, he sensed that she was right, even though he didn't want her to be.

James could feel her certainty and knew it came from a source far more knowledgeable than anyone here; it was all part of her spooky, *now you see it, now you don't* powers, which had intensified after death. So Diandra would stay with them for now but he was upset with her and Sara for bringing that fact to his attention.

Chapter Twenty

Franklin was getting very tired of looking at rocks, they were all that he had seen for an hour. Whenever he thought they were about to come to the end of the wall, there seemed to be more of it. When they first arrived here they had assumed that the wall was an intervention that had been created for their safety. This barrier had been conveniently located in front of their entry portal to hide them from the enemy, so it had to be for their benefit. After traveling along the length of it for quite some time, his opinion on that matter had changed. He now believed the barrier had been created by Braccus as a way to keep them from reaching the people they needed to help. This had his power signature written all over it. He just couldn't figure out why they weren't just attacked as soon as they crossed through the doorway. Why keep them hidden from what sounded like a large group of deadly beings waiting on the other side? Wouldn't it have just been easier to let them walk into the middle of an ambush and get it over with?

Franklin almost reached up and smacked his own forehead. Of course, it was in Braccus's best interest to keep Vincent away from his army; he would have reduced their numbers significantly minutes after appearing on their turf. Franklin would have lasted a little while, but Vincent would have been the last one standing in this match-up. By keeping Vincent and him traveling blindly around this new world, the evil army would have time to move underground and kill all those taking refuge there.

It would be very satisfying for Braccus to have them arrive to find that those they had come to help were either dead or dying. He would, of course, let a few of the gifted ones live long enough to see that their heroes had failed to reach them in time. He could read the intent in the air as surely as if Braccus had spoken to him personally and, as scared as he was of the prospect of seeing that evil scumbag again, he was determined not to project any fear for that beast to detect and feed on.

Even though he hadn't said it, Vincent had come to the same conclusion and he looked more mad than scared. Of course, he had always been the scary one and whoever this Braccus guy was, he wasn't going to get the better of him. He had never met him, but Vincent knew that he was the reason that he had lost his other half, and someday, he would meet this guy, not just the monsters he sent out ahead of him. In the end, it was Sara's task to bring an end to Braccus's control of the worlds, but he hoped to at least get to see him and have a hand in his removal.

Franklin heard these thoughts and nodded; he felt the same way. The one good thing about spending this time with Vincent is that he was beginning to learn a lot about his travel buddy, and he could now hear his thoughts quite clearly. The more he learned, the less he felt that he got the short end of the stick when they were put together on this mission. He was beginning to feel exactly the opposite: that he had gotten incredibly lucky. With little else to do while they walked aimlessly onward, they had begun to talk, and despite the fear that Vincent's gift inspired in those that were aware of it, he found himself not hating him as he had when he first met him.

This guy had been through more than he realized; when Vincent spoke of losing the important connection to his childhood companion, Franklin could hear the pain and longing in his voice. For thirty minutes, Vincent had been trying to give him a description of a person that was basically a phantom to him. A bare whisper of a memory that, even though he couldn't tell his reluctant partner if this memory was of a man or woman, didn't know the eye, hair color or age of said person; every fiber of his being was telling him he had to see this person again. This total stranger that Vincent called his other, the better part of him that would somehow make his power more of a gift than a curse, would be the one to officially bind him to his circle members. After a lifetime of living without relationships, all he wanted to do was make as many connections as he possibly could, and so he talked to Franklin, telling him everything. The tone in his voice had Franklin convinced of his sincerity and he found himself promising to do everything in his power to help find this person for Vincent, if they survived.

Vincent also learned a lot about Franklin, listening to his stories of training with Olie and the others. His experiences with Sara and the Keepers during their initial battle with Braccus had Vincent looking at the teenager with admiration and gave him insight into the close bond that all the original trainees shared.

He also felt Franklin's sorrow over his inability to help Sara, his guilt over how he had given up on her when she needed him the most; his joy when she returned, and rage when he lost her the second time along with Thomas and James.

Vincent tried not to flinch when he heard it said again aloud. He was the one that had killed them with his touch. This would always be an issue. How could it not? He couldn't change it, couldn't explain why he knew he needed to do this for the greater good. He would never be able to make any of them understand. When Vincent started to turn away and continue walking, Franklin's voice stopped him.

"But I do understand now, or at least I began to after the shift started and we became Keepers. Sara tried to tell us all that this was coming. She knew it was something that had to

125

happen in order to help restore the balance of the worlds. We just didn't want to hear it, none of us did. When it happened anyway, we all hated you so much, but she didn't. Even after she was gone, she told us to forgive you and let you into the group, that it wasn't your fault; it was your duty to do what you did. Well, I want to tell you right now, I do forgive you."

Vincent tried not to look shocked by Franklin's statement, but he was sure that he did anyway. "Thank you. You don't know how much that means to me."

"Okay, then; we're good. I won't be sharing any hugs with you anytime soon, but I will work with you." Franklin smiled slightly. "We will be fighting a really rough crowd soon, and if we happen to find the hidden refugees of this place we need to work together. I just wanted you to know that I've got your back."

They both had their strengths; Vincent knew he would be covering Franklin quite a bit on the way to the underground entrance, but he had a feeling after they found Iam's creations, Franklin would be the one to deal with the people there. His own interpersonal interaction left a lot to be desired.

Bonding conversation finished, both men nodded; an awkward pause followed as each shared the same thought, this wandering had to end. They were going to have to find a way to get past this wall and face the things beyond it head on. Vincent had no problem going through a large number of monsters, but he couldn't budge this thick stone wall; it was too high to jump over and asking Franklin to boost him over was not an option for obvious reasons. So what to do now? They had stopped to consider their options, resting their backs against the smooth stacked rock that kept them from seeing anything past it. With time to sit, they looked at the landscape and saw what they had seen for quite some time: nothing. It was as if this world's border stopped just beyond the wall. On one side of them was wall and the other was black sky littered with thousands of stars.

It was a strange sight to see the rough rocky terrain they were standing on suddenly drop off into outer space. Yes, outer space, like they were looking at the sky up close from the window of some kind spacecraft, without the protection it provided. There were stars twinkling brightly in the blackness of never ending night that existed beyond the planet's boundaries, and Vincent caught occasional glimpses of a few things that looked like large flaming rocks speeding past.

The fiery projectiles burned brightly against the dark sky, flames changing from dull red to blinding white before the objects blew apart completely. Pieces of rock scattering around the black void in a slow spiraling motion before drifting gradually out of view. Vincent and Franklin watched the destructive show in fascination while struggling to come up with a way past the wall they were leaning against.

Another blast of meteoric material, this time closer than the last, had thrown a few chunks of the floating rock onto the surface they were resting on, reminding them that they really needed to move, yet neither did, still stuck in *how to get past the wall* mode.

The thump of rock landing on rock jarred them out of their thoughts, each considering what might be happening while they sat here totally useless and out of touch with the others. Vincent hadn't been able to connect with them anyway, other than a few flashes of insight and the ability to answer their internal communication when they chose to let him. But Franklin felt them struggling, involved in their own situations. They were alive, but couldn't do anything to solve his problem. He needed to get it together and rely on his current traveling partner to help him out here. Another explosion had both men scrambling hastily to their feet with a new resolve to get moving.

Vincent looked at Franklin's hands which were now a dull red color. His expression became thoughtful as the same idea went through both their heads. "How hot would that rock have to get before it would explode like that?" Vincent asked his companion.

"I don't know, at least over eight hundred degrees. I'm just guessing, though. I've never done anything like that before." He didn't ask why Vincent asked him that question; he had already figured that out as he looked at the wall thoughtfully. Would he be able to blast away some of the stone that was separating them from what was undoubtedly the way to they needed to go?

That's a lot of heat. Franklin switched over to mental communication in case the enemy was listening. *I can't build up that much fire; I would have to draw from something really hot,* he said, trying to explain the way his gift worked. Every time he used his ability, he had to draw from a natural source. That source was usually the planet's core or the sun above their heads. Unfortunately, due to the current state the worlds were in, both sources were compromised. His powers still worked, but he didn't know if he could generate the intensity required to do what they were thinking.

Franklin's doubts were pushed aside by another explosion on the space side of their narrow pathway. Grinning, he closed his eyes and reached for the fire just miles away from their location, it was just close enough to connect with now.

It took a little more effort than usual, and he really had to concentrate to reach the source of the heat. At first, to his surprise, Franklin felt his body cooling off to the point where he felt goose bumps rise up on his arms. What was happening? Was he losing his power? He had never been this cold before, literally never, even at night when the sun wasn't shining on him. He must have looked confused because Vincent offered words of encouragement.

Space is cold. You must be picking up that temperature like you pick up the heat. Push it out and reach for the heat source.

That made sense, so he tried again, reaching outward for the flaming chunks of rock still floating past them. This time he was rewarded with a slight tingle and a spark of flame just about big enough to light a birthday candle coming from the end of his finger.

Vincent snorted as he looked at the less than impressive results of Franklin's efforts. He hadn't meant to do that really, but this was not what he expected. He had been watching his companion's face shift; nose scrunching, lips curled as if he were pushing himself to the limit to generate this impressive burst of flame and this little presentation was such a let-down. He clamped his lips together after realizing that the sound had actually escaped, muttering a quick "I'm sorry," before adding "No, really, please try one more time." *It was just nerves, I won't do that again,* he said by way of apology.

He got a terse nod from Franklin before the Keeper with the fiery gift turned to face the darkness to see another rocky projectile burst into flames. He was annoyed with Vincent, but his annoyance made him push harder to get an impressive result. He absorbed every bit of heat he could from the flaming rocks and felt his fingertips tingle pleasantly. Warmth traveled up his arms and soaked into his skin. Small flickering flames moved through his nerve endings building and building until he had quite an intense, almost painful sensation that signaled he needed to release the heat from his body. Then just seconds later, with a *move quickly* warning thrown at the man standing near him, Franklin whipped around and directed a white-hot wave of fire toward the wall.

This time his efforts were very effective, thick chunks of wall crumbled and flew outward, directed purposefully forward both to inflict injury upon any enemy that might still be behind it, and to keep Franklin and Vincent from harm. A few muffled shrieks of pain and protest sounded as stone fragments met enemy flesh. Vincent stepped in front of Franklin as they moved out onto the field of battle.

Chapter Twenty-One

Wow, so this is what a nightmare looks like, James thought as he and his friends moved into the darkened area just beyond one of the last few safe places left in- or outside the worlds. They had known the minute they left the protected area that there was a sickness hanging in the air that they had not felt until now. Just two feet behind them they had felt so happy and complete with their parents, but a few footsteps away from the spot where they said their tearful farewells, was a bleak and terror-filled land. It wasn't anything in particular they feared, only unlike their previous location, it felt like death here was a final and hopeless situation. Diandra stood next to him gripping his hand tightly, sharing his fear, trying not to let him see how scared she was. He loved her so much for that. Pulling her closer to his side, he tried to locate the cause of all their unease.

In this dreary place, there was a lot to be uneasy about. What they had seen from the safe side of the afterworld had been disturbing, but when paired with the heavy sickness of spirit that hung in the air, it was ten times worse. The thick, foul air nearly chocked the Keepers. If they had been lesser spirits, they would have been unable to move into this place any further. Something watched them with great interest. The feeling of lots and lots of eyes staring at them was so real it was like being poked repeatedly with hundreds of sharp pointy fingernails. The Watchers were not happy to see them here. When they came out of hiding, it was doubtful that they would give out hugs and kisses. Pain and fear was the name of the game here.

Diandra shared James's thoughts as they both sensed the intent of the evil things hidden here. His new girlfriend's wide violet eyes scanned the darkness as every hair on the back of

131

her neck stood on end. She thought once you were dead you no longer had anything to fear. Death was a safe haven, and they should all be beyond worry, but then she felt the hatred directed toward them, James especially, and she felt so afraid. She wanted to just grab his hand and run back the few feet that separated pleasant death from this permanent horror. But he had to stay with his circle and she, of course, had to stay with him. Diandra clamped down on her fear, tightened her grip on his hand, turned, and prepared to follow Sara and Thomas as they moved further into the night. Pale grey mists floated past big hulking black objects. They were not alone though, shadows shifted around them, visible even in this dim, dreary lighting because the evil that created them was darker than anything around it. Empty and deep, the rotten beings that wandered here had the group's senses screaming all kinds of warnings.

James also felt voids where the ugliness hid. Whatever moved around in here was most assuredly dead, but he doubted it had ever been human. There was a distinct difference between one of Iam's souls and the things that Braccus had thrown together and zapped energy into. Granted, they had moved around, walked and talked, but inside they were as insubstantial as plastic toys.

When Iam's creations had killed these evil beings, they simply passed from one plane to another, empty husks restlessly moving, driven only by the anger Braccus had fed them. Without an outlet for all this rage, they paced about, eager to affect anything they could. Trouble was, they were formless, unable to connect with the living world and had only been able to watch the changes the worlds were experiencing from above. Now they saw four very appealing targets. One of whom was getting right into their heads, reading their thoughts. The evil shadows desperately wanted to hurt him for that, but were afraid to do so. The power he put out, though dimmed by death, was still more than enough to keep them in check.

This is where his mind control paid off. James was able to get into their heads and convince them that he was bigger and badder than the one they feared most: Braccus. They figured he had to be, for no one else had ever been able to latch onto their twisted mental path before and make them stay hidden like he was doing. He was broadcasting a warning so loudly that they were forced to stay away. Images of light and the pain, of being seen by the creator of the true living things, kept them from moving any closer. Iam was their enemy, having the ability to destroy darkness with his presence, and this one seemed to have a strong connection with him, so they had to be careful.

As James's repelled them, the girl standing in front of him drew them in. They needed to get close to her; it was programmed into their brains from the moment they were killed and sucked back into this place. Here they had waited for years with the understanding that this particular girl would arrive, and it would be their duty to drive her from this place. They could not kill her because she was already dead, but they could destroy the spirit that remained. If they couldn't do it now, they would follow and wait for an opportunity. The way things worked around here, time was in their favor, and so much could be done in as little as a day. With both pride and regret, the parents of the first Circle members watched them cross over to the evil plagued section of the afterlife. In the past, they would have been the first ones to attack the ugliness that had taken over but they knew their children were better equipped to do so. They had another mission now, diminished as they had become, they still had enough power to cause the enemy trouble in the other plane of existence. If they could just find the way out, they would be able to offer some assistance to those hidden from the enemy. It was time.

Milo was the key to their exodus from the Dead Place. He planned to use his connection with the corrupt souls by accessing the part that remembered what he had been. By tuning into the evil energy they put out, he hoped to follow the dead ones to the portal they had been using to pass in and out of the in-between place. The shift in power had made it much easier for the bad things to travel, so latching onto them had to be the way out.

Daniel took a second to look back at his daughter once last time before he became a thin white mist. She was so lovely, just like her mother, and he loved her so much. A quick movement of his lips sent a message to her across the barrier. He knew she heard what he had to say by the slight nod of her head, but she didn't look back. The message was for her alone and given in such a way that no one else would detect it, not even her mother, who he had never hidden things from before. But this was something he needed Sara to know; her mother would not have approved of the risk that following his advice would bring.

Having found the key to his return to the worlds, Daniel thought it only fair that she be aware that she might find her own way back there as well. She just had to know what to look for when the time was right. It would be hard, and it would be painful, but if she really wanted it, she would find the way. She needed to be given the choice and knowledge that it was possible. Once he had said what he needed to say, Daniel turned to follow Milo's trail with the others.

Sara felt them leaving, her father's gentle whisper lingering in her ear. She pushed back the pain that she felt at the loss of a family she had just gotten to know, and moved forward,

134

not looking back. As usual, there was no time to mourn another lost loved one. There was still so much for her to do and she didn't have the luxury of giving in to the sadness. If she did that, it would take her down and she might never be able to get back up again.

Sara stored away the information he gave her, along with the love that came with it, and moved forward with Thomas close beside her. Concentrating on the vacant spots in the air, she knew something was watching but chose to ignore it for now. Another energy source was calling to her from a distance ahead, a faint teasing glow that she needed to get closer to. Whatever she was supposed to find was here, or part of it anyway, and she needed to go and find it.

Without saying anything to the others, she did what she was supposed to do and led them onward. As she moved on a random memory of kissing Thomas popped into her head. *Strange thought for such a stressful moment*, but a nice one, too. He sent her this memory to remind her of all they had shared and what he still wanted to share with her. He wanted to replace all the sadness in her with one of his favorite memories of their time together.

"We will have a future together," he promised quietly as the scene around them changed in the blink of an eye, and they were walking down a dark rain-soaked street littered with trash and strewn with dead things. The evil ones had decided to start playing games, and they could manipulate this area just as well as the older Keepers had in their little section of the afterworld. It would do for now, until they could figure out how to get past the one that was in their head. Then all bets were off, and they would destroy what was left of these intruders.

Chapter Twenty-Two

Randall had to prompt Alice to move faster. She had
managed to get a bearing on the direction they needed to go
to find Iam's hidden people, but it felt like they were running
out of time. He hated to push her so hard, but they were
moving a little slowly for two people in a hurry to get
somewhere. She started out so fast when she first got the
image of the way out, but once they moved into this ruined
world, she hesitated from time to time, as if unsure how to
proceed. She had shared with him a picture of the entrance
to the lower places as it materialized in her head; it was gold
and green and five miles to the west of their current location.
But even as she moved in the direction, she had initially
insisted was right, she wavered a bit with each step they
made; sometimes stopping altogether. When he asked what
was going on, she simply shook her head and moved forward
again with a confident smile on her face; a smile that did not
reflect in her eyes. She was doing her best to look like she
knew exactly what she was doing but he knew this part of
her gift, the whole ability to see the unseen was still very
new and she wasn't used to it yet.

Judging by what she had shown him, there was much evil
here, and he was very afraid for her; something was not
quite right about the way she was acting, she wasn't telling
him everything. This bothered him for many reasons,
primarily because he loved and trusted her so much. She
should be able to tell him if she were scared and needed
help. He watched her with concern as they picked up the
pace once again, rushing toward the location outlined in her
head.

Randall had, of course, been correct in his thinking. What
Alice had failed to mention was the fact that, along with the

image of the exit, came the voice of a child prompting her to move toward the doorway. Soft and sweet, the voice urged her on as she managed to convince Randall that what she was seeing came only from her ability to visualize the unseen places, the ones Iam had allowed Sara to open for the safety of his beloved creations. Her child-like assistant also promised to protect her from the other things that roamed in and out of this world. It said that the bad things had not yet discovered the doorway she was being shown, and that it could guarantee that she and Randall would be the first ones through it. When she asked why it was helping in this way, the voice simply said it would tell her when they reached their destination.

Alice hated to deceive Randall, but she was also afraid that it would take too long for her to get past the mind-block she was experiencing; she had not seen the doorway before the voice offered her help. The water was already coming down so fast it was up to their ankles. At this rate, they would be swimming in an hour or two. She was trying not to show him that she was risking their lives by trusting the voices he told her not to listen to in the first place. Feelings of guilt and doubt were what made her hesitate as she moved closer to where she was being led.

Alice needed help and Sara was no longer able to give it to her. She had to rely on her abilities and use the connection she had with the dead to lead her to the openings. She knew the dead things weren't all good, she wasn't stupid enough to believe they were out to help her, but for all evil ones that roamed the land, there were a few bright spots still visible in the darkness. Something clean and pure was lurking at the edges. She had become increasingly aware of them over the past hour or so. Somehow a few good souls had managed to break through a barrier and make their way out into a world that had been dominated by the worst of beings. True, they did not hold enough power to push past the dominant foul beings, but they were there, nonetheless, and while she wasn't quite sure which type of soul was guiding her toward the entrance below; she was desperate enough to risk following it and lying to Randall about what she was doing. The spirit that was guiding her noted her reluctance, the slowing of her steps and the brief pauses as she got nearer to what it had assured her was the way to the refugees' hidden place. It addressed her quietly as if aware that Randall must not overhear their conversation.

Don't you trust me? the girlish voice asked with a slight tremor. A chilly breeze ruffled Alice's hair, giving her goosebumps.

I'm going where you told me to, aren't I? she answered, with a quick sideways glance at Randall to see how well she was covering her conversation with the dead thing. He merely smiled at her encouragingly as she pulled him closer to the opening now visible several hundred yards in front of them. His supportive behavior was making her feel even more guilt about what she was doing.

Alice moved forward, allowing Randall to lead the way even as she continued to listen to what her unseen guide was saying.

That's true, you are, said the little girl in her head as they got close enough for Randall to see the door without Alice's help. But the voice didn't sound any happier when she acknowledged it once again, the tone got lower, hesitating for a second as if unsure what to say to her next. The silence stretched out as Alice studied the door now so close to them she could feel warm air flowing from it.

Nestled in-between two piles of pink and white coral, the only covering available in what had once been seabed, the portal beckoned to them with a promise of accomplishing their goal. So pretty, it practically invited them to enter, the light coming from it that lovely golden green color that reminded her of a nightlight she had as a little girl. The nightlight had been shaped like a small castle with little windows generating just enough illumination to keep the darkness at bay. Too bad this didn't do the same; she had a feeling that it would draw in the bad things rather than keeping them away.

Alice had placed a thin protective shield over the doorway as soon as she saw it, but dealing with this entity was really messing up her concentration, she felt her control wavering and had a feeling this thing that guided her was sensing that. She had a bad feeling that was getting worse by the second. So now they were here, and they needed to get in and close this opening up tight in order to keep the evil ones out. Once they did so, she and Randall could begin their mission to preserve the good that was left in the world. They were so close. Maybe, whatever they were called to do would lead to the end of this all. When they were safely off the surface, she could apologize to Randall who was beginning to throw out an angry vibe in her direction. His anger was broadcasting itself very clearly now through the barrier she had created to try and hide her weakness. Reaching up to push away the tears that were welling up in the corners of her eyes, she looked hopefully at the way to the underworld, determined to think only of getting inside and finding the special ones who would know why they were there.

A shadow shifted in the small space between Alice, Randall, and the doorway as the girlish voice suddenly became sharp, sounding loud in her head.

Not so fast, Alice, the voice was hissing at her now, all pretension of friendly helpfulness gone. *I would hope you aren't thinking of leaving without returning the favor I so graciously granted you.*

A wispy puff of dark smoke settled firmly in front of the door. *You got here awfully fast despite Braccus blocking your vision, and I was the reason. I would hope you would be willing to return my kindness.* The voice was still that of a little girl but now it sounded pouty, demanding and very threatening.

"What do you want?" Alice asked aloud, abandoning all attempts at hiding the conversation from Randall. He could already tell from the look on her face that something was definitely wrong. When he reached into their connection, he saw the black cloud hanging right in front of her face. Whatever that thing was, it wasn't friendly, and was blocking the entrance to the underground places.

A strong current of energy flew from Randall's fingertips and made brief blinding contact with the entity. The electricity was enough to break the cloud apart into swirly puffs of blackness but wasn't enough to make it stay that way. The darkness reformed quickly and flew toward Randall, settling into his body before he could protect himself. The unwelcome visitor made itself at home, changing Randall's eyes from his normal pretty gray to a strange yellow, and rearranging his handsome features into an unpleasant grimace. The young man then turned to Alice, his tall frame standing so close to her that she caught the faint whiff of decay accompanying the evil thing that had taken over his body.

"Never mind, I don't need you now," it said, using Randall's voice to speak to her. "I have got a body to go through the opening with. That's what I needed this whole time. This is the only place we have not been able to get through; the dead cannot pass through these doors, we are forbidden for now. My allies, the Garren are still about one hundred miles away. They are supposed to let us use the bodies of the captives they took with them from the last battle to make it through the door. I was going to wait for them, but you were kind enough to come and follow me straight here." The thing that occupied her handsome boyfriend laughed at her stricken look as he pushed her aside and moved closer to the glowing entryway.

"I should be able to kill a lot of the hidden ones before help arrives. I'm sure Braccus will be very pleased with me when I greet the troops with the heads of his enemies in my hands and let them in to finish killing the rest."

Alice moved around her possessed boyfriend, re-enforcing her protective shield in front of the portal to prevent his entry. The evil thing followed her every move and, while it didn't quite know what she was up to, it knew she was trying to keep him from getting where it wanted to be. Intent on making contact with the girl now that it had a solid form, the entity walked right into the invisible barrier she had put up between them, bumping Randall's face against it as if he had just run into a wooden door. Rubbing his nose in surprise, Randall's body turned to look at her while she tried to think of him as anything but her boyfriend. Randall was in there somewhere, but she wasn't dealing with him now, she was dealing with the thing inside of him.

Yellow eyes glowing, the creature swung at Alice, testing the strength of her barrier, dipping inward enough to make her dive toward the ground in response to her shifting shield. An enraged bellow sounded inside her head as Randall protested the creature's use of his body to lash out at her. As mad as he had been at her for getting them into this situation, he loved her too much to let himself be used against her. He was going to fight against his own body to prevent that.

A shocked look appeared on the young man's face as his body jerked violently and fell to the ground. Randall's internal defenses had kicked in and he was releasing electricity to push the unwelcome visitor out of his body. It tried to hang on to its host, causing pain by stabbing at the young man's brain with waves of negative energy, but Randall fought back just as hard. He let down the internal barriers that normally protected him from his own gift. Sending jolt after jolt of electricity through his own body, he did his best to make himself an unfriendly host for his unwanted hitchhiker. Razor sharp claws dug at his insides as it tried to make him stop, but he hung on and kept shocking himself.

Being a Keeper, he was somewhat protected from his own gift, in that it couldn't be used to kill him, but it sure did hurt a lot to be electrocuted. White hot pain sliced through his entire body and he didn't bother to put a damper on it. He didn't want to dull the agony of his burning nerve ends because he wanted the thing inside him to feel it too. He didn't want it to want to stay; he wanted it to leave as soon as possible.

Randall could hear the shadowy creature in his head, screaming in protest at the pain he was causing them both. It shouted for him to stop, slapping at him from the inside, ripping at his lungs, but it still could not match the pain he was inflicting upon himself. After several minutes of intense struggle, the evil inside the young man gave up and left the body it had tried to use as its own.

Randall sat up; cloudy blackness still swirling around his head, red hair standing on end where the current had passed along with the entity he had evicted. He stared at Alice with

143

concern; he knew that this wasn't over. That thing that had been inside him was not going to give up and now it was madder than ever at having been pushed out of its host. He could tell by the way the darkness moved toward Alice that it was planning to use the connection it had established with her to get through her barrier somehow.

Alice also sensed that the dead thing was going to try and break through her shield and either take control of her or put her out of commission. She took a second to look at Randall to make sure he was alright before she closed her eyes and did what she suddenly knew she could do. They didn't have time for this; she needed to do something to get rid of that thing. Alice wasn't going to allow it to stall them until its allies arrived, and it wasn't going to use either her or Randall to get through the doorway. She had to end this struggle right now.

Without trying to figure out if it was possible or whether she had the ability to get past that slim barrier she could hear and see into, she reached out toward the swimming darkness. Her body shimmered out of view and slipped into that in-between place she now had access to, the place the thing in front of her dwelled. She was determined to see what she had been dealing with this entire time and face it head on. They were now occupying the same area; the blackness was shifting, attempting to form a definable shape so it could confront her.

What she saw greeting her with that same childish voice, was the ugliest being she had ever seen. A thin column of wavering blackness stood before her, yellow eyes glowing from the center of it. She was able to make out a gnarly, pitted face with lips so thin they were more like slits at the bottom of its head. Sharp, gray teeth stuck out of the mouth at odd angles; some pointing outward and some pointing in so that they struck the creature's thick black tongue, slicing deep tears in the muscle when it tried to speak. It was a terrifying thing to see, bearable only because it shifted so often, unable to maintain its shape for more than a second or two before it rolled around in a confused state once again. She wasn't sure if the unstable nature of its appearance was due to Randall zapping it or because the dead thing didn't have enough strength to stay in one piece. Either way, she was glad to take advantage of this weakness, it had just enough time to utter its last words, "They'll be here soon, and you'll die like all the rest of them."

Alice's eyes widened in panic as she quickly threw up a protective barrier between the thing and her and Randall. The yellow orbs in its head flared in triumph when it sensed how afraid she was at this moment. This was her first true encounter with an evil spirit and it wasn't exactly in awe of the fact that she was a Keeper.

Somehow, she thought that her new abilities would come with a neon sign that flashed *I am a powerful being, fear and respect me.* Well, they didn't. Apparently, she was supposed to do something impressive to get his attention and establish her reputation as someone to be reckoned with. The creepy thing laughed at her. The sound sent chills down her spine as it tried to find a way through her internal defenses and make itself at home inside her body.

Determined to ignore the panic she felt as it pushed aggressively at the thin shield covering her, she looked straight into the dead thing's eyes and did the last thing it would have expected her to do. Instead of turning and running from the beastly thing, she let her shield fall and reached into its filmy center. This time she felt something solid, wet and gooey like a hard-boiled egg wrapped in spaghetti. For a split-second, she was reminded of one of

145

those games you played as a kid when you reached into a bag and tried to guess what the object inside was, usually some kind of gross food combination placed there to get your fingers all messy.

She was pretty sure that what she held wasn't an egg and she was also sure that she didn't want to stop and look at it. Instead, she clamped her fingers down tightly and pulled, freeing the object, which she then threw behind her as far as she could. Whatever she had removed from the dead thing made it fizzle out of shape and disappear.

Randall could still see her; he had always been able to see her in invisible mode and he followed her movements as he sat on the ground trying to recover from the encounter with the evil spirit. It had taken a lot of energy to push that thing out of him; it certainly had not wanted to leave, but he had gotten encouragement in his efforts to remove the hitchhiker. It came in the form of a strong male voice, one that he felt sure he should know, especially since it had called him son. The communication was faint but distinct and made him increase his efforts until he had successfully completed the task. He felt a sense of satisfaction at the sound of approval his father made before becoming silent once again, it was a short but meaningful moment for him with a parent he had never known while walking in this body.

The original Keepers were not close, but he could tell they were watching, cheering them on in their small victory here, joined to the two of them by Alice's connection with the dead places. When the black slimy thing she had ripped from the shadow's chest flew through the air, he helped by zapping it with a strong current of electricity until it disappeared in a puff of smoke.

Alice moved back into the solid plain of existence once again, running back to fall on her knees at his side. The words, "I'm sorry, I'm sorry, I'm so sorry," falling from her lips as she gave him a fierce hug; a hug which he returned before allowing her to help him to his feet and move toward the portal once again.

"Apology accepted," he said, trying to regain his composure and dismiss his hurt feelings. Love for her helped him do this, but he felt this gesture allowed him to throw in a condition for his forgiveness.

"But I stay in your head all the way from now on, and we do this together, no secrets that can get us possessed." Alice's last words of agreement were swallowed by their entrance to the underworld and the barrier that went up soon after.

Chapter Twenty-Three

Vincent calmly stepped over a line of dead enemy bodies. The ones that had been too scared to come near him had been fried to a crisp by Franklin who had been following close behind him working clean up on their greeting committee, which consisted of several big lumpy rock creatures, about fifty Ornose and a few ratty little Kreel. The troops had been lined up in front of the wall in such a way as to look impressive and threatening to the two young men who had broken through it, but both knew it was merely another lame attempt to slow them down.

The creatures that had been waiting for them were just there for show, placed there as sacrifices to delay the Keepers arrival at the door to the safe places below. Both young men had managed to move through the ranks of enemy fighters quickly despite a concentrated effort by several of the rock things to take out Vincent by sneaking up on him. Franklin watched amused as the thick bulky beasts moved in a mass behind his companion, their heavy footsteps creating craters in the crispy soil in what he guessed was a quiet approach for them, but still sounded like a herd of stampeding buffalo in the otherwise silent landscape. Hard shelled arms reached out to clamp down on Vincent's shoulder. When they made contact, the dumb things fell instantly dead to the ground and Vincent simply turned around and shook his head. Apparently, they thought he needed to do the touching to kill. Boy, where they wrong. He was just one big no-no when it came to contact of any kind.

"Guess that's where they got the expression, dumb as a box of rocks," his fellow Keeper said with a smirk on his face. They were both getting a little bit cocky from their success at diminishing the enemy ranks and the superhero comment just flew out of his mouth; they felt invincible. Franklin shot a wall of flames from both arms at those who sought to bypass the deadlier Keeper and come after him; they weren't even fortunate enough to get close, being turned into piles of ashes that blew easily away with the wind that was picking up around them. *Wow*, he was getting equally as impressive as his companion. He had never felt quite this powerful before. It was amazing and scary at the same time. At this point, there was a danger in overconfidence that could cost them a lot if they let it override their better senses.

Franklin had managed to fine tune his ability to draw from the flaming comets at his back. As a result, the white-hot flames he was now producing burned whatever he aimed at in a matter of seconds. He and Vincent were shaping up to be a pretty good team. At this rate, they would be at the underground entrance in no time; if they just knew where it was, that is.

There's a few more lines of them in front of us, which direction should we take? Vincent spoke inside his head, mirroring his own concern as they looked at the enemy forces spreading out in front of them.

Can you talk to her? I don't think she is open to letting me in her head. We need to know where we're supposed to go. Vincent passed on his request as he turned his head to check out the constant movement around them. He should have been amused by the way they hung back, made cautious by the death of so many comrades, but instead he felt more than a little worried. Braccus's power had grown and it would be foolish to believe that they would get out of this so easily; the sooner they pushed past this roadblock the better.

Alice, Franklin reached for the special connection they shared, only to receive a jumbled mass of thoughts; she was afraid. Wherever she was, it was pretty intense at the moment, and she couldn't spare any words for him. She had just gotten her own sense of direction; her escape door had just become visible, but she had to get past an enemy to enter. She searched for the signal her barrier put out and found their doorway. With no time for a *hello, how are you doing*, she simply sent him an image of the direction he and Vincent should be heading and then was gone again.

Take care, Franklin said, pulling back to keep from distracting her further than he already had. She was alive and still fighting. It was an important fact that he had to hold on to as he couldn't help her or handle anything else. Randall was with her and had to trust that he would keep her safe. Franklin tried not to let his feelings of anxiety for her leak through into their connection as he gratefully turned to the right and followed Vincent who had received the directions via their new link.

They moved forward, walking into a suddenly very determined enemy line. Angry Ornose rose up and dashed right past Vincent, determined to cause harm to the more vulnerable person in the area: Franklin. They ran at him like they meant business, but quite a few of them became heavy piles of ash before they made it anywhere close. Still, they were persistent and gradually moved closer. Vincent called for Franklin to stop and then placed himself directly in front of his new friend.

Keep up the fireworks, he said as he walked deliberately into everything that came their way, so that soon they were through the crowd and what was left of their attackers had begun to slink off toward a thick cloud that seemed to descend and act as a cover for the last of them to escape. Vincent and Franklin watched the enemy move off to a safe distance, waiting to follow them to the underground refuge. This activity bought a smile to both men's faces; this was

151

what they had been waiting for, the mutations that had been in their way were suddenly just were they needed to be: out of the way. The stupid lugs were thinking of following them straight to the portal, but it wasn't where they thought it was.

Franklin raised his hands and channeled every bit of energy he could from the flaming comets. Then, directing them downward, let loose a tremendous burst of white hot flame at the ground. Both Keepers fell straight down into the broken earth, following the flaming path to the underground city they both sought. As the enemy rushed to follow them, realizing too late that they had let their prey get away, the ground miraculously sealed itself on the surface to cover their escape route.

Chapter Twenty-Four

They were all underground now, Maryann noted with satisfaction, she could see the young Keepers passing through the portals. Each pair slipped into the darkness of the underground tunnels hoping to blend in with the large number of people gathered in small groups throughout the caverns. She couldn't speak to any of them, only watch from a distance, hoping to see them connect with the gifted ones soon. The success of their mission depended on the help of the special people who would recognize them as Keepers and help them gain the trust of the other refugees.

Eric and Finola passed through their doorway to slide behind a pile of loose boulders and watch the group in front of them, who had apparently accepted the fact that they would be down here for a while, and were settling in. Buildings were being constructed from materials that had mysteriously appeared at several locations in the tunnels. Wooden one-story structures, simple but sturdy looking, some complete, others in various stages of construction, stood in neat rows along the walls of the caves.

Makeshift neighborhoods were forming in the largest part of the caverns, narrow lanes with alleyways created in the spaces between the houses. Common storehouses, which were little more than simple wooden frames lined with shelves, stood at the end of the street where the cave walls became too high and jagged to build into. These half buildings held extra supplies to be used by the entire community. There was no need to secure the provisions as the spirit of cooperation was still high at this point; they were still being provided for down here as they had above ground and had no reason to expect it would stop now.

Maryann knew this had all been made possible by Robert's daring visits to the surface to salvage whatever was left after the enemy took control of the upper worlds. Fearlessly delivering all this stuff to each world by shoving them in the doorways and scuttling off in his altered form to find more things. She was both proud of the risks he had taken for the people and relieved that such efforts on his part were no longer possible. There was nothing useful left up there, the enemy had long since destroyed it all, a fact that none of the refugees was aware of.

She watched Robert move among the people he had worked so hard to protect and her heart pounded with love for him. Returning his puzzled smile, she turned inward once again to see the visions she was receiving from the young Keepers. Maryann was pleased to note that Finola was slowly but surely adding to the dense foliage in this cave. Even though she wasn't actually here, she was able to call up whatever growing thing she could find to come and make itself at home in the weak light shining down from a few slim openings in the cavern roof. The holes must have been too small for the evil ones to gain entry, at least for now, and the brave sunlight managed get past the spells blocking it, giving enough pale misty light to make the people hidden here yearn for more. The plants felt it too. Tender green shoots moved upward along the stone, trying to get closer to the warmth it promised. This place was well provided for and she hoped it would only be a matter of time before they were all this way.

People of various ages milled about building and interacting with each other, she saw another scene just like it through Alice and Randall eyes. In another cave, another group of Iam's hidden creations roamed about making the underground tunnels suitable for a long stay. The two

Keepers moved slowly out of the shadows but only Randall was visible, they had decided it was less obvious that way. One new person moving into the large group that seemed to be coming in from various places in the cave wouldn't raise alarm bells, two might. Besides, he would fit right in with the red-headed people here.

The shaken populace was seeking comfort in each other's company and introductions were being made, it was the perfect time for Randall to move in and become one of them. Alice tagged along beside him, visible only to him and at the same time throwing part of her energy into protecting the portals both here and in the other refuges. It was very difficult to divide her powers in this way, but she was managing for the time being. Randall was helping by pouring all the energy he could into her force fields and trying to become a trusted member of this new society at the same time. Just an ordinary guy, down here with all the rest. An ordinary guy stretched in many directions at the same time, using his powers to help keep these people safe and worried sick about protecting his girlfriend. No stress here, then!

In their little section of the underworld, Vincent and Franklin were seeing several people moving around below them. They were perched up on a stone ledge watching people with heads a little bit bigger than the people they were used to seeing. They had all the same features: eyes, nose, ears, arms, legs, and hair in all the same places. Men, women, and children were present, young, and old with various skin colors, just like in any other place in the worlds. It was just that their foreheads bulged out a little more. There must be something about the larger heads that gave them an advantage over the other worlds. These people had managed to create something a little bit more than the images of the primitive dwellings that were being sent to them from the other Keepers.

While the other worlds were camping out in their makeshift buildings, these people were creating an underground city using mostly materials at hand. Houses chiseled directly into the rock walls of the cave extended upwards four or five stories with access to each floor provided by stone staircases carved out at each end of the structure. In addition to being sturdy, the houses were also beautiful, with incredibly detailed pictures of angels and animals carved into the posts supporting each individual level of the building.

Franklin counted at least two of these impressive housing units with work being started on two more. This group had accomplished quite a bit in a few weeks and they showed no signs of slowing down now. Everyone here was busy. In fact, Vincent was getting tired just watching them carving, lifting, and carrying things. This activity was easy to see because, in addition to all they were doing, someone here had discovered a light source that wasn't fire-related. From each level of the building a steady warm bluish-white glow lit the area up so well, most of the central area was visible with very little being hidden in darkness. The spot they observed from was one of the few areas not directly lit by this system, a fact that they appreciated, but it was going to be hard to sneak in and mix when they could be seen from everyone here. Not to mention the fact that it was going to take some powerful mind control to convince these people that they looked even remotely like them.

They are obviously advanced beyond the level of the other worlds. How are we going to get them to trust us? Vincent addressed Franklin silently, as a worried look passed between them. People as sophisticated as this would certainly take a lot of work to get through to; they weren't so simple as to be impressed by a few showy tricks.

Maybe they're not very smart, Franklin answered. *Maybe they just have big heads.* Even as those words flew out of his mind he knew he had made a stupid statement. Vincent's raised eyebrows and the nodding of his head in the direction of the wonder city below only reinforced this assessment.

I don't think it will be that easy to get through to them, Vincent repeated, as Franklin passed on a plan to try and use his gift of persuasion on the refugees here.

Oh, you'd be surprised at how easy it might be, came the reply, only it wasn't Franklin's voice in his head. They turned around to find a small group of people standing on a narrow ledge just yards away from theirs, watching them intently. Franklin stood quickly, anxious to keep Vincent from moving toward the group; they certainly didn't need any deaths to occur right now. They were here to help these people not create enemies.

"Hello, Franklin and Vincent, we have been expecting you," this greeting, spoken aloud, came from a figure standing in front of the four others in the group. He was the smallest of the five and totally unlike the others. The others were the big-headed people they had seen below, but this guy was small. His other features were quite different, too. Built like a child with soft pink skin, purple hair and the pinkest eyes Franklin's had ever seen. In fact, the only pink eyes he had ever seen. This little man seemed to be the one getting into their heads; he was doing all the talking for the group and it was his voice telling them to get up and move quickly and without resistance exactly where he told them to.

Maryann's vision blinked out of focus just a second after she saw Franklin and Vincent rise and walk forward, guided by the five beings behind them, but she couldn't see them again. By then, she lost vision for a minute or two. When she was able to use her eyes again, she was surprised to find herself back in her own cave. The people around her had stopped what they were doing to stare at her curiously. She hadn't realized Robert had come toward her until she felt his hand gently grip hers. He had seen what she had seen and, knowing that it had begun, was more concerned now with keeping his wife and the people around them safe. There was nothing they could do for the young Keepers, they were on their own now and would do what they were meant to do, take care of Iam's creations.

Robert helped Maryann to her feet, carefully guiding her to a seat across from Rianna who simply sat on the stone ledge and stared at the wall behind them with a vacant smile on her face. The couple began a silent conversation about what to tell their people about the state of the worlds, when Rianna startled them both by uttering four words so softly, they were almost convinced that they had misheard. Her expression had not changed, and she still stared straight ahead without blinking. But then she said it again and their blood ran cold at the callous singsong tone that she used, "I'll kill them all."

The last words to escape her lips weren't even hers; Braccus had used his distant connection with the Keeper to throw some fear into the hidden people. She was lost in her own head, but the part that was still in his control was forced to respond, passing on his message was the last act of her life. Snapping back, she pushed him out for the very last time, using the little part of herself that was still hidden away. It took everything she had left. Rianna's eyes focused for a moment on the two people in front of her, the last that she would ever see.

The ancient soul that she was became aware of Robert and Maryann for the first time since she arrived here. Tears dripped slowly from Rianna's eyes before the woman Robert had known since he was created, ceased to exist. All that she had been was gone, no breath passed her lips and her heart stuttered a few last beats before stopping altogether.
Robert's heart broke as the last of his immediate family left him for good, making him feel so empty, lost, and completely overwhelmed by the world he occupied.

Chapter Twenty-Five

Milo had found the way out. Drawing on the ugliness he remembered from his former life, he was able to see the doorway. It was hazy and very hard to make out, but memories of his darker side began to filter in, and the doorway grew sharper and more distinct as he concentrated on it. It was just the very place that souls as good as the Keepers would be unable to pass through unaided. In fact, it had been hard for them to get close to the exit without Milo's assistance; it hurt them to feel all the ugliness of those that had passed through before them. It hurt Milo too, but he was determined to find what he needed within himself to make this work.

Anger and hatred hung in the air around the exit, left behind like the foul stench of a garbage dump site. It made them gag, but they had do go through somehow. Milo himself was having a hard time dealing with all the negative emotions that had once defined what he was, but he pushed on anyway. These souls had not been intended to leave the afterlife, but they were challenging that rule; stretching the limit of Iam's patience in order to reach out to the people they loved.

They would pay for their disobedience. If they crossed through this door they would be doomed to roam the ruined worlds without rest. They could not return to Iam's land and they couldn't go back to the place they created either. Love's patience could only be stretched so far. They understood this and were willing to accept the terms of their escape. Following Milo, they passed through the door without looking back. It was difficult; they felt like pieces of rope being stretched beyond breaking point. They moved on, pushing past their uncomfortable feelings. Taking on a misty appearance, visible one minute and invisible the next, the originals raced to do what they could to affect the worlds once again. Moving into the darkened doorway had made them feel wasted and joyless as if they had never been the first of Iam's perfect souls.

The group flew past corridors that glowed so brightly it hurt their eyes. The light came from places beyond the worlds that Iam had created in the solid reality of the living; alternate dimensions in which all his imaginings came into being. These were places that evil would never be allowed to enter and it hurt to see them knowing they too would be denied entry into the beyond. They would remain creatures of light, but they were now tainted and unworthy of these perfect places. It was to the darkness they were now drawn and that's where they would stay to help the living.

There were other doorways visible too, entrances that showed the ruined worlds up close. It was horrible to see so clearly what they had been watching from above for a while now. Braccus's troops had been busy reorganizing the surface to suit their needs. Along the debris littered landscape several hulking structures had gone up like acne on the formerly beautiful surfaces that Iam had created. There was nothing left topside of Iam's handiwork, all had been laid to waste and replaced with constructions made of what appeared to be human and animal bones set into charred wood and stone.

Just ahead of them in one of the battered worlds, Maura could see Jason and Chandra's child Alice in the distance fighting a dark spirit. She and the others shimmered helplessly in their spot wishing they had the ability to jump right in there and help her and Randall out. They were not allowed. Iam had conceded their right to help his creations,

162

but the new Keepers were in the worlds to battle the enemy, it was what he had created them for.

As it was, the originals could only combine their energy and reach out to the parents of both these Keepers. The two young people were very capable of getting themselves out of this position, they just had to know this for sure, had to believe they could defeat these spirits. Their only weakness was in the uncertainty they were feeling. The best thing the former Keepers could do was give them the inner strength needed to survive and make it to their destination.

Jason and Chandra, Alice's parents, had gone on before the other Keepers. Having seen their daughter doing so well, going to college, and living a somewhat normal life, they were happy and had no thoughts of interfering with the way things were going with her. They had remained blissfully ignorant of all that had happened since then, content that her life was on track. But things had begun to change in the order of the world and, despite Iam's calm assurance that all would work out, began to worry about their child. They had been good obedient souls, holding fast to their loyalty, and had not left with the others; choosing to stay in the perfect rest they had been given.

Sara's father Daniel respected their wishes. In honor of their memory, he chose to do something for his friends, gathering the collective energy of his fellow rebels and pouring it into a growing certainty, a knowledge he passed on to Alice. He could tell that she felt the change, her posture going from one of quivering fear to steely determination. She moved toward the demonic thing in front of her and took control of it.

The thing she faced was a dark spirit formed from the first of Braccus's evil thoughts. The seeds planted in the foul air of hatred and discontent he had spewed out from the beginning of time, had given birth to these bitter, rage-filled shadows hellbent on destroying all living things in hopes of occupying the bodies they left behind. They wanted these bodies badly, hoping it would give them something they had never truly had: life. Armed with the certainty they had sent to her, Alice managed to remove the only thing that gave this filmy bundle of bad air any substance. Removing the pits of its discontent, she threw it back into the darkness it had been born from. It was wonderful to see her rise and gain the advantage this way, they were so proud of the way she stood up against this abomination, destroying it as only a true Keeper could.

Randall too, had benefited from their intense concentration; the brief message contributed by his father Zian had been enough to remove the unwelcome inhabitant from his body, reminding him that they were not victims in this battle but strong forces to be reckoned with. It was so good to see them both recover and pass through the door to the underworld.

Full of pride and hope, Daniel and his companions stood on the edge of the darkness, watching the new Keepers disappear from view, their faint glowing presence causing a rising anger from the spirits all around them. The air vibrated with loud hissing noises from the evil souls far outnumbering them. The small group glided onward, narrowly escaping the swarming mass of darkness closely following them in a world where they no longer had home advantage.

Rather than feeling alarm, they felt encouraged. They had affected Alice and Randall's situation in a positive way and helped them triumph. If they could do this for the others, it would be worth all they had given up to be here. Slipping into yet another dark entryway, they went in search of the other Keepers, hoping to get through to them in some way.

Chapter Twenty-Six

Sara walked the shadowy streets in a place hastily constructed by evil spirits that followed her every move with great interest. Thomas gripped her pale hand, steadying her as they navigated the cobblestone paving loosely laid beneath them. It was slow going, both because of the lumpy surface and the fact that they were forced to step around the dead remains of several creatures scattered around in careless piles.

The body parts they passed seemed to be a mixture of human and a few other species, or mutations, whatever you chose to call them. The pieces were all mangled and jagged as if they had been ripped from their owners by something very strong and ruthless. Twisted, malformed limbs of different colors and shapes lay on the ground as if carelessly tossed around; a hand here, a torso there. A few steps further had them passing some dark-colored, strangely shaped fingers. Thin and stringy, with nails that grew to a sharp tip, the severed digits were scattered on the ground at intervals like some sloppy eater had dropped a pile of burnt French fries as they walked along.

Something horrible had happened here and, being as this world was no longer a happy and gentle place, the carnage was left right out in the open as proof of what they were facing: a cruel and unmerciful enemy. It was no longer necessary to hide murder; this place was without law, order, or even common decency. The dead, good and bad, were left to rot alongside one another while other nightmares continued to contaminate whatever civilized elements remained here.

As they walked along, structures started to appear on either side of them, shimmering into view from thin air. Sara was aware that they were not real; nothing was real here. The houses were as the evil ones made them appear. Stage dressing for whatever they were planning to do next. She was also aware that the plan of this place's inhabitants was to kill her; or whatever about her that was still alive: her soul. She didn't intend to let them.

One-story buildings of wood and stone lined either side of the makeshift street. Unimaginative and ugly, the thick rocks were piled together and joined by roughhewn logs with a plain wooden door thrown haphazardly onto the front of each. There were at least ten of these structures that Sara could see now, with more popping into view as they moved forward. Thick straw roofs formed the top of the buildings. Stray pieces of the primitive material swayed in a strong breeze that carried the foul stench of death. Several small windows set in rows along the front of each construction spilled out a soft yellow light barely bright enough to push away the darkness swimming all around them. It had been enough to illuminate the bodies on the street, but that was intentional, adding to the creepy factor of the place.

As they continued forward, trying to ignore the horror movie-like setting that was being created around them, Sara felt a pull of power, like an invisible cord attached to her body. It pulled her onward even as the shadows around her screamed warnings for her to stop. She got closer to it with every step she took and was so focused on following the trail that she barely noticed the activity around her. The formerly empty void was filling up fast, shadows shifted in the spaces between the buildings, heralding the arrival of hostile company. She could feel the threat in the air that accompanied their appearance. Invisible eyes bored a hole in her flesh as the entities waited for a chance to get to her. They hardly mattered though; it was her connection with whatever Braccus was hiding that was important, not the little pests he had sent to keep her from getting to it. Whatever was happening at this moment was not supposed to happen and she could feel a sudden stirring in the back of her mind; a faint protest from a distant Braccus. She shouldn't have been able to get past the safeguards he placed, yet he felt the link that she was forming with the object. Sara's connection with the thing he had so carefully placed out of the reach of Iam and his followers was being detected far too easily. Someone or -thing he couldn't quite identify was helping her and it wasn't Iam, he would have sensed that type of power. First, he had to stop her, and second find her helper. They were both going to pay for the inconvenience they were causing him.

The confidence Braccus had experienced just a short time before was slipping away. The joy he had felt while roaming the earth destroying civilization and killing whatever unlucky creature got in his way, was replaced with a white-hot rage. A rage he expressed by setting fire to every inch of earth within his sight. Cracked and pitted dirt blew about, and flames danced all around Braccus's darkly beautiful form as he walked the surface killing a large group of his own followers standing beside him. He didn't flinch, didn't even spare them a glance as they screamed in agony and turned to ash; he could always make more of them.

The connection must be broken, he was in control now and intended for it to remain that way. He had not been so foolish as to hide all his secrets in one place, but if she found one piece she would be on her way to finding them all. She had found something of his before she died, but he had seen to it that it quietly disappeared again. With all that had happened, his triumph over the Upper Worlds and the wonderful events of Olie and Ferd's death, along with the loss of the other Keepers, not to mention her death (which should have been the end of his troubles) Braccus was sure that he would never have to worry about her finding anything else of his again.

Maybe he should have paid more attention to Iam when he had been babbling about the future, that stupid book he had passed on to Olie had a lot of stuff in it about what those little souls were supposed to do. Braccus had been too busy writing his own version of the fate of the worlds, and it was a much better book; the ending had been in his favor.

In any case, this had to stop right now. While he wasn't at full strength where she was, he had others he could use to get to her, and fully intended to use them. Curling his fingers together, Braccus reached out across the barrier between the dimensions seeking whatever was left of the thread he had created earlier, hoping to make use of it again.

Thomas felt the anger directed at Sara by the occupants of this place. It would have been impossible to miss the threat that they presented. The dead things were screaming so loudly that it would have penetrated the minds of even a less gifted soul. These things he could face quite easily, while a little more vicious than their living counterparts, were still no match for a powerful Keeper, living or dead. It was the other thing he had begun to feel in that last minute or two that had him extremely worried. The presence he sensed reaching out to him was sickly familiar. It just couldn't be! He felt rage, wanting to punish Braccus for even trying to get through to him again. He knew what Braccus wanted; he wanted to make him a puppet again, to use him to destroy Sara's soul. She was getting too close to his secrets and that rotten beast was trying to reconnect and pull on the power cord that had once connected them.

In alarm, Sara turned to Thomas as she saw his pale body turn darker. It was as if the shadows all around them were drawn into him by the call of his anger. His fingers tightened painfully on her own, he gritted his teeth together trying to fight the urges he was having. He wanted to rip out Braccus's throat, but the urge was rapidly being replaced by a need to hurt the girl next to him, a need that was being transported strongly through his head. The madder he got, the stronger his connection to Braccus became, but he couldn't seem to calm down. The frustration he felt at being used against her once again was very strong and hard to control. The more he tried to prevent himself from being used against Sara, the stronger the connection became. It was anger that gave it strength.

This couldn't be happening! He had severed the bond between him and Braccus when he died. He had left behind the body that monster had occupied, and he was free. He shouldn't be able to reach out and pull him back after death. Closing his eyes together with a snap, Thomas forced himself to remember one thing: he was free, and he wasn't going to be sucked back into that sick place he had occupied when he had first lost his battle with Braccus. He tried to get his mind to believe this and fight, even though he felt himself losing to that jerk once again. He could not, would not, let himself be used as a puppet to destroy Sara.

From somewhere near, an intervention was provided by a slight tug on the corner of his brain, as if a child were trying to get his attention while trying to loosen the enemy's grip on his mind. But other than providing a momentary distraction; it didn't loosen his grip even a little. He felt something inside him clawing at her, seeking that bright section that housed her soul. And while a part of him still screamed in protest, another part laughed in triumph as it ruthlessly sought its prey.

Sara winced as she felt the slimy presence search through her mind, slapping and ripping at her brain, tunneling into the gray matter that hid what his controller was seeking. It was truly terrible to feel Thomas's distress, his fear and anger at being used to fuel Braccus's power over him. She was saddened by his pain, and more than a little afraid of what could happen to him if Braccus could not be removed.

Soft lips touched Thomas's as Sara poured her soul into him with complete trust, she didn't break the connection that kept them so closely bound. She could have done this so easily, but she was willing to bet that what they had was far stronger than the faint trail that Braccus was calling up from the past. She was not going to move away, even though, if she had been alive, his grip would have caused her much damage. His fingers were digging so deeply into her skin that they should have bruised, and a few bones broken, but they weren't. No marks appeared on her dead flesh. She could feel James protesting, ready to step in and break up this struggle, but she made him stay back and concentrate on the other enemy waiting to do damage should their leader fail. His failure was what she was counting on, what she was putting all her heart and soul into making sure did happen.

Chapter Twenty-Seven

Finola had been mingling with a few of the underground refugees when the feeling hit her. She and Eric had managed to wander into the larger section of the cave in the company of a group of children they had found shivering in a few small hidey holes in the tunnels. Eric had heard them speaking quietly among themselves. Each whispered word they uttered sounded loudly in his head; he heard them as clearly as if they were right next to him.

Moving carefully, so as not to attract too much attention, he and Finola managed to sneak back into the thin winding underground halls to merge with the groups straggling into the larger central areas. Fortunately for them, the people they had met were all from different cities and towns in this world, so a strange face wouldn't necessarily create any alarm, as long as it was human-looking. Eric's brief stint in the sunshine had changed his skin from pale white to a light peach, and in the dim lighting in the caves, his eyes were more amber than yellow, so he was able to blend in with the people they encountered. Taking charge of the confused wanderers, Eric had guided them outward, encouraging them to move in the right direction while pretending to be as lost as the group they walked with. It was all going so well that he felt it was only a matter of time before they found the special ones and convinced them of who they were. It was much better than either of them expected, maybe this would be the easiest mission they'd ever had; their hope of success was high at this point.

It was shortly after they had settled in with their newfound friends, that Finola suddenly turned to Eric with the saddest look on her face. Something very bad had just happened. Since the connection was still so faint, she couldn't tell exactly what that bad thing was, but it made her heart flutter and ache for a minute before the pain eased and she felt nothing. Following the faint mental trail to her Circle, she felt them moving around, quietly blending in with the inhabitants of the areas they had gone to. They all answered her quiet call, except for Franklin who seemed to be preoccupied then. He was alive, though; the connection to her Circle had not been broken.

Finola was sure that she would have noticed the loss more than that faint nagging dread that left a strange empty feeling in its wake. She felt like something important had happened, something that she should have noticed more than she did right now. She searched her brain for a reason for the sadness she felt, but it just wasn't coming to her.

Eric spoke, having shared the aftershock of the feelings that swept over her. *Are you alright?* He watched her talk and laugh with her new-found companions, the only indication that she had felt anything at all was a slight crease between her eyebrows.

Yes. Maybe it was just more feelings from the plants; they're having a rough time now struggling to survive. Standing up to help the young people around her, Finola hid her unease with a flurry of activity. It had to be the plants. She didn't know if she could face the possibility that it was anything else, because at this time, the only thing she did have control over was the plants. Activity was the best thing; it helped keep her from thinking too much about whatever it was that had made her feel so badly a few minutes ago.

She and Eric helped move rocks and other building materials to a location indicated by the older members of the group they had joined recently. These people had been hidden further in the cave system and had already started building shelters when Eric artfully herded the lost stragglers to them.

172

They were greeted warmly and given chores to do, the first of which was to make houses for themselves. After quick introductions, they were given instructions about finding and using things to settle into their new environment, becoming part of the neighborhood that was forming here.

Eric couldn't help but notice that while the people seemed to accept the youngsters from the outer areas readily enough; they also continued to watch them with suspicious eyes. Makeshift weapons such as sharpened sticks and clubs were kept close at hand. It was all very iffy at the moment, a kind of guarded peace among people who had survived the most horrifying time in their lives.

It was that way in all the worlds: good, caring people looking at strangers with suspicion, ready to do whatever they had to do to anyone that might threaten them and theirs. After what these people had seen on the surface, they were not going to take a chance that any of those evil things would get down here and do the horrible things that had been done to their people. Killing any threat that arose would be so much easier for them now.

He knew Finola had noticed too, and was both saddened and scared by this turn of events. They couldn't leave, that was for sure. They had to feel their way through this mess, not get caught, and be charming at all times. It was terrifying being so afraid of those they came to help, but there was no getting past what they had to do.

Chapter Twenty-Eight

Thomas was crying inside, mentally trying to pry his hand from his girlfriend's arm. Attempting to stop his connection to her from being used through his connection to Braccus. He knew the anger he felt was making this all worse, feeding the evil in the air, but was helpless to control it. How could he be used this way; even his death wasn't good enough for that evil being? Braccus was going to torment both Thomas and Sara for as long as he existed.

It was painful to push back the instincts that Braccus was drawing from, so very difficult to keep the anger out of his head as it burrowed into Sara's, looking for what she was trying to keep hidden. As far as Thomas could see, he was the problem in this situation and the only way to solve it was to tear himself away from the girl he loved and let Braccus have him once again, permanently. Sara felt his resolve, knew he was going to put everything he had into pulling himself away from her once and for all, and she put everything she had in her to prevent this from happening. Turning up her internal light to megawatt levels, she chased away the darkness in him, using every positive thought and feeling she could until his mind was filled with laughter and love.

Thomas felt his fingers loosen on her shoulders and he began to feel so light-hearted he wanted to cry. She had flooded his mind with so many memories of the good things he had accomplished in life, the loving bond he shared with her and James, and the many people he had helped throughout the years, that the rage that had been building was smothered. The darkness moved slowly away, leaving his face relaxed, a small smile of relief that it was over and his connection with Sara stronger than ever. With the anger successfully squashed, the connection between him and Braccus was broken; it had been the only thing that drew the evil to him. Thomas pulled Sara close to him, hugging her tightly while tears of gratitude streamed down his cheeks, and James heaved a sigh of relief as the tense moment passed. He had felt the intruder in Thomas's head and had been unable to force it out; to force Braccus out. The slimy feelings he had when the guy was meddling was unmistakable.

A few minutes of relief was all they were allowed. James and Thomas felt Sara's mind being pulled back to the connection she had with the object she'd been pursuing. She turned back to move in the direction it called her toward, pulling at her with an increasing demand. She moved so fast now that her feet levitated above the ground, no longer hampered by the unevenness of the stones they trod upon.

At this point in time, no matter what was going on around them, she couldn't have stopped to pay attention to the nasty things that watched and waited for a chance to destroy her. She felt them following, knew James was the one keeping them away from their little group, but she could only hope to stay one step ahead of them as she walked toward the feeling. Her body was burning on the inside now, the urgency she felt made her chest thump as if she still had a heart beating within her body.

Thomas tried to keep her calm, stroking her arm as he floated just inches above the surface with her. He pulled her closer to his mind, feeling the pain that the call of the object was placing on her. It would not let itself be ignored, not let her pull away. And while this one presence was asking a lot from her, another force was ripping at her mind, fiercely trying to pull her away from whatever was urging her on. He regretted that she was experiencing this because she had used some of her strength to keep Braccus out of his head.

176

The strength she needed was buried deep inside her but most of it was held back, waiting for a time when it would be let loose on the enemy with unrestrained power. Now was not the time, so weakness plagued her with each new assault on her system.

Visions of death, pain, hatred were thrown at her until she had the feeling she should back off or lose all connection with this wonderful man at her side. Floating loosely in a black void, all alone with no anchor to keep her there, was all she could think of. It was as if the very thing she sought knew her greatest fear was now being without the man she had grown so close to. Her connections to those she loved were so important that she dreaded the loss, if she would just let go of her connection to this other thing, maybe she could keep them with her. Yet, even as she was sent these messages by the opposition, she realized that it was not possible to back off and logically not a good idea for herself or those she loved.

James walked behind his Circle members; he felt the evil things watching them and intensified his command for them to stay back. They cursed him, throwing out words that might have intimidated a lesser man. He simply brushed them off and let them watch from a distance. They stayed back but continued to watch every move the group made. Diandra sidled closer to him, her fear evident in the way she shivered and clutched at his shirtsleeve. The evil things saw this, watching what they knew to be the weakest member of the group; they let her know just how funny she looked moving through their territory like a scared rabbit.

Sensing that she was the only non-Keeper, they did their best to intimidate her, foul names popped into her head as they created a pathway of communication to her. Mocking voices asked how her parents were, making her fear what must be happening to them after she had died. Telling her that her own dead body was being displayed in the village square, hung above the burning town for all the enemy army to throw stones at. Pictures appeared in her head of the scenes they were describing, long hair hung around her slack and rotting face as she hung on a pole before the group of Ornose and Garren and other various mutations roaming freely about the land. Gagging silently, her footsteps slowed while the images had their intended effect. Despair was taking over and she was beginning to feel a fear so intense, she found it difficult to move another step.

James put the evil things in their place, throwing out a command for them to leave her alone. He made them pull back, sending out strong warnings even as he soothed her mind, offering her comfort. While his two Circle mates continued ahead, walking through the creepy looking town, he stopped and turned her toward him. Beautiful violet-colored eyes in a pale white face stared at him with a shocked look. She hadn't experienced hatred like this before and even being a dead girl wasn't making her feel safe. A feeling of intense love came over him. He had never felt so strongly for someone in his life and it just reinforced his belief that there was something beyond this situation; it wasn't the end. Taking her face in his hands, he kissed her, putting all he was, all that he had ever been, into that simple act. It was his way of giving her the strength to go on a little longer.

Diandra responded by calming down and thinking only of the way she was feeling now, safe, and totally loved. But as nice as it was to be distracted in this way, she was made aware once again that they were not alone. Mocking voices sounded all around them, but she noticed that it was from a considerably further distance than before, and they were transmitting their insults with a little less enthusiasm. She was proud of the way he had effortlessly held them back, so caught up in the two of them as they were, it was hard to force herself to move on and follow Sara and Thomas down the bumpy road.

From behind the buildings, dried, scrunchy leaves blew about in the otherwise still atmosphere. Unseen eyes bored a hole in the young woman's back as the inhabitants of this place moved in the shadows, following, always following.

A flashing wave of darkness descended upon the town. A black glow filled the air in muted moonlight. Twisted figures dressed in beautiful gowns and suits began to move past the buildings while watching them with blank white eyes. Due to James's power, they came as close to her as they dared; which was still not very far at all.

Pacing restlessly, searching for a way to break the hold James had on them, they moved from side to side, muttering among themselves in a whiney high-pitched tone he couldn't understand. Regardless, the intent to harm was clear in the way they jerked stiffly from side to side in a clump closest to Sara.

She didn't seem to care about what was happening around her. Eyes rolled back in her head, hand outstretched, she reached out for whatever connected her to the object, demanding that it come to her. She was counting on the fact that the force guiding her toward the object would also help her bring the object to her, so she gave in and pulled it toward her. Whipping up a whirlwind, she clung to Thomas's and James's spirits, hoping that together they could begin to help their friends while the enemy waited for a chance to stop them.

Chapter Twenty-Nine

It was into this type of situation that the new Keepers walked, risking their lives to reach out to the gifted ones, the ones who would convince the crowds that they were to be trusted. All the groups faced suspicion and danger of being captured and hurt by those they sought to help. The young Keepers needed the help of a trusted insider to get the approval of the crowd. As with everything, it was not going to be easy.

For Alice and Randall, it was much the same situation. They had moved through the doorway and toward the noise created by a large gathering, intent on quietly slipping in to blend with the refugees. It took one quick look at the people standing further down the corridor to make her quickly shimmer out of sight. Everyone that she saw in that split-second before they crossed into the lighted area looked exactly like Randall. There was not one person standing inside the central cavern that did not have red hair and fair coloring.

Men, women, and children here all looked enough alike to make this one brown-haired, green-eyed girl stick out like a cat in a room full of dogs. In these times, looking different was definitely not the way to win over the crowd. From the moment they entered, she was in invisible mode, sticking close to Randall as he was greeted warmly by those around him. Alice was using up a lot of energy remaining hidden for so long, but she was afraid to reveal herself and leave Randall's side. When he moved among the people, she stayed close by him at all times, waiting, watching the people that watched Randall. She was getting tired now but felt she needed to stay the way she was, carefully studying those inside the group.

Alice got the impression that these men watched with a purpose, stern faces taking note of all that passed before them. They had begun to whisper among themselves, faces turned in Randall's direction. She couldn't tell if it was him they were looking at or one of the two people next to him. A few days ago, Randall had become quite friendly with two men that had entered the cave shortly after him; they had been the last three people to enter from the outside. While the men had been welcomed openly enough because they were human-looking, they were still being watched very closely by those who were already present.

It wouldn't have been so bad, the watching; it was a natural reaction to what had happened to their world, but Alice, who hadn't had slept in close to two days, was beginning to get a bad feeling about these watchers. The men, five in all, had been listening carefully to the oldest person in their group, an older woman named Isobel. Isobel had lost her entire family to the monsters that had descended upon the upper worlds; she was an angry, grief-stricken and determined woman. That made her dangerous to the three men she didn't recognize. This frightened Alice so badly, she was on high alert, staring at Isobel until her eyes hurt; watching the old woman just as hard as she was watching Randall.

The old woman's small bent form loomed in the background. Red hair laced liberally with grey topped a face that held the saddest green eyes Alice had ever seen. But the sadness was laced with something else, a strong need for revenge. Rage seethed beneath the seemingly calm exterior, the young woman felt it radiate from every pore in Isobel's body, and it was this emotion that motivated her as she directed her small group of followers.

Randall wanted to talk to Alice badly. He had noticed the woman too and was just as disturbed by what he saw. She handled the men around her with ease, saying just enough to arouse their suspicions, playing on their fears. These men were scared but hung on every word she said, and it worried him, because what she seemed to be saying was that she had a strong opinion that they needed to worry about the three men working under their close supervision. The men in question just happened to be Randall and the two men he had befriended.

She had singled the three out because she hadn't seen them around her village before. There were a few places she hadn't been, and it was possible that they were from one of the remote farming communities scattered throughout the land, but she didn't like the fact that they were the last ones to straggle in after her group had been here a day or two. A small part of her also resented the fact that they had made it down here without a scratch while her own people had been brutally murdered. They were three healthy looking men who should have died fighting the enemy, just like her sons had.

It didn't matter that other men had made it safely to this place, she knew those men, had seen them kill to protect those around them. These men were strangers and all about the age her boys had been when she watched them beaten and ripped apart. But her boys were dead and these men weren't, so she had them watched and she waited for a sign, something to justify the dark acts she might ask the men around her to do.

Alice saw the thoughts flickering through the woman's head; darkness clung to every negative thought Isobel had and she been too afraid to take her eyes off that woman and her followers to give herself over to slumber. Instead of sleeping, Alice had watched while Randall slept and concentrated on keeping a shield around him and all the entrances she was supposed to be protecting. It was getting so hard to do it all and she was terrified that she would soon slip up, that her need to rest would make her visible and let down the barriers she had set up to keep evil out.

Randall felt this need and he had to help her. He couldn't stand here and pretend it was all okay; to continue working among these people as if the woman he loved wasn't suffering to keep him safe. Grabbing a bucket, he loudly announced to Steven and Ray, the men he had befriended the past two days, that he was going to get some water from the stream that flowed a few yards away.

Cold and clear, the stream bubbled up from a source far below and flowed just beyond the line of sight of those in the cave. Its crooked course and lack of light made it the best place he could think of to speak to Alice without being directly observed. She looked so bad right now, her beautiful face was puffy, and she had deep lines under eyes so red and irritated from lack of sleep that he just wanted to cry. She was like this because she wasn't going to let her guard down and leave him vulnerable; at the mercy of these strangers. He couldn't let this go on any longer. She needed rest.

Walking slowly, aware that every step he made was being closely watched, Randall covered the short distance to the water source with Alice following closely behind. He knelt to fill the bucket, speaking quietly in her head to urge her to sleep and trust that he would take care of himself while she rested. She reached out carefully and ran her hand over his cheek, wanting so badly to kiss him, but held back, knowing they couldn't let their guard down for one second in this unfriendly atmosphere. She wanted to argue with him, but she was so tired, she doubted that she could force herself to stay awake much longer. Her body would soon take over and give itself the rest it needed so badly. Just a couple of hours and she'd be as good as new, she promised herself.

Tears fell freely down her face as she crawled into the recessed area just five feet from the stream. Protected from the areas around it by several pointy rock formations, it was the perfect place to hide while she got some much-needed sleep. Randall assured her that he would use the time to mingle with the crowd and find the special ones. His assurances earned him a worried glance and a hurried *Please be careful,* from his exhausted girlfriend before she fell into involuntary slumber.

Isobel watched the young stranger's actions with interest. She couldn't quite put her finger on why he drew her eye, but there was something different about him, the way he seemed to be staring at something in front of him that no one else could see. His face shifted in the shadows, so she couldn't see clearly, but she got the impression, for just a second, that he wasn't alone. He seemed to be focusing on an object next to him and his expression changed enough for her to notice that he was upset before returning to the calm mask he wore before.

She now had what she had been waiting for, a reason to be alarmed and to pass it on to those around her. Isobel crooked her finger at one of the men closest to her. With one eye still trained on Randall, she spoke quietly to the battle-scarred companion who had hung on her every word since they had stumbled into this cave with the others. As he followed each thing she said very carefully, she began to discuss what she thought they should do about the young man she had decided to single out as a threat to their safety.

Chapter Thirty

Sara, Thomas, James, and Diandra stood inside the eye of her little tornado watching as the enemy approached from all sides, footsteps sure and steady despite the high winds Sara had unleashed on the morbid little town. The things that moved toward them were absolutely hideous, animated versions of people long dead; it was as if someone had emptied the graveyards of all their corpses. Bloated, gas-filled bodies with paper-thin skin and heads of hair that appeared to be coming off in clumps as they moved, these soul-less puppets ground rotting teeth and waited for an opportunity to move in and get hold of the blonde-haired girl just yards away from them.

These grotesque forms were dressed in shiny silk dresses and black and white tuxedos. The formal attire stuck to their moist decaying forms and leant a feeling of a horror movie zombie feature to the whole situation. The evil around them appeared to be growing in strength but James managed to hold them at bay with great effort now; he had to ask for assistance from Sara, Thomas and, surprisingly enough, Diandra. His girlfriend's presence in his head was now almost as strong as his Circle mates and it shocked him that it could be so, especially after knowing her such a short time.

He hadn't expected that Diandra would have such an influence on his mind; she wasn't a Keeper after all, just a dead girl. A wonderful and special dead girl, but other than having the ability to see certain things, she had never possessed the power to affect things the way he and his Circle had, the way they still could. Why was it then that he felt as if his own powers were working so much better now because of her? He drew strength from Sara and Thomas because of their soul connection, but this girl completed something else in him and he was glad that she hadn't stayed behind in the safe place. Looking at the restless slimy things that stalked them though, he wasn't so glad that she was now in danger, just like the rest of them

The girl in question looked at him and his fellow Keepers and was very much afraid for them. She felt like the weak link, a huge liability that might cost them both time and victory in this messy situation. Present for a reason she wasn't quite aware of, but knowing she couldn't leave, and that something was about to happen, Diandra tried to force herself to see into the future. Visions of puffy white hands grabbing her boyfriend's arms flashed through her head as she moved as close to him as she possibly could. So close now, they were practically standing in the same spot and she could feel the vibration of his voice as he spoke. Caught up in the bad feelings she was having, it took Diandra a moment to make out what James was saying; he was trying to calm her down and make her back off a bit. Sorrier than she could say for making such an idiot of herself, she just shook her head, held on tightly to James, and turned her attention to the girl in front of her.

Sara said words under her breath, her attention clearly on something besides her companions. "Come to me," she muttered, pulling at the thin line that bound her to the thing she was seeking. An image of a faint blurry object burned in her head so strongly that it actually caused pain, but she couldn't stop what she started, not even when James tried to help her squash the impulse that drew her to the thing. Small, shiny, and square-shaped, the object wavered in and out of focus, teasing her with the uncertainty of what it really was. She had to find out, had to know what Braccus was so desperate to keep from her. What was this thing that could bring down a being as evil as he was and what other force was urging her to find it so strongly? It wasn't Iam; she was certain of it.

A force so determined, so strong, urged her to merge with the object and command it to come to her. She pushed harder, drawing it in with everything she had, and it seemed to be working. She felt a shifting inside her as if her blood was moving like a tide with the object firmly attached to the end of an imaginary line. All she had to do was reel it in. She should be happy about this, but it was beginning to make her feel increasingly sick, as if she were voluntarily exposing herself to some kind of deadly disease. Could dead people get ill? Sara felt an uncomfortable longing, a tug at her heart like she was missing an important bit of information that she really needed at this moment, preferably before this thing she called to her so urgently got here. Her only regret about this situation was that her small band of followers was forced to stumble into the unknown with her. Was she bringing disaster to their doorstep?

And they weren't the only ones forced to follow Sara's progress, wherever she went, so did their gross audience. Bare feet slapped against the wet cobblestone, rotting flesh bubbled and squished, tracking her every movement. Diandra winced at the sound the followers made as she stared at their bizarre parade of pursuers. Bunching her hand tightly to James's shirt, she tried to ignore the strange look he was shooting her way because she had no intention of letting go at this moment. Whatever he thought about her actions, she was holding on for him not for herself, just like her instincts told her to. She didn't want to seem like a clingy fool, but she was having one of those visions again, the kind she used to have when she was alive. The horrible, *destined to gain her nothing but misery* vision that she couldn't stop herself from reacting to in a way that no one ever seemed to

189

understand. She knew what she was doing, and it made perfect sense to her but even though she was now in James's mind, she was unable to explain it to him.

James knew Diandra was worried but was a little bit shocked that she would stick so close to him that they were stumbling over each other's feet. He tried to calm her down by whispering comforting words in her head, but she wasn't listening, only clinging tighter and tighter. He wasn't sure what to do about this situation and he cast a concerned look at Sara and Thomas who were too occupied with Sara's vision to deal with his problem.

Diandra knew James was getting awfully irritated with her for sticking so close to him but she couldn't help it. Every instinct she had was to be as much a part of him as she could because he was all that stood between Sara and the dead things. Her boyfriend was making them awfully mad and, of course, this was shifting their focus of attack to him. For now, they were kept at a distance, but they were going to pull something off as soon as they could, she knew this well.

The enemy, knowing they couldn't get close to Sara with James's interference, decided to change the scenery again in order to throw him off balance and gain the upper hand in this fight. This was, after all, their place and they could do what they pleased. But what they chose to do was so cruel it stopped James in his tracks. Stunned and shaken, he stood with his mouth open, unsure of what to do next. That's when Diandra showed him exactly why she had stuck so close to him.

Chapter Thirty-One

Vincent and Franklin followed their captors to a large building located at the center of the cavernous area. From its size, roughly two times larger than the other structures, with elaborate carvings of distinguished big-headed people gracing its outer walls, the young men guessed it was some kind of central meeting place; kind of like a town hall for this new civilized settlement. There was a carving at the very top of the building's entrance that closely resembled the purple-haired man at the front of the procession. That, and given the way the others in the group seemed to follow his every command, gave the two captives the impression that he was, in fact, their leader.

Both Keepers had stopped all conversation, external and internal, as they walked behind the group that had discovered them just minutes before. It was useless to speak privately when their leader seemed to be able to read their minds effortlessly, following their conversations even when they had tried to make it private. He spoke to them on their new mental pathway, indicating that they needed to cooperate, go where they were led, and not make a scene. There was no implied threat in his tone, but they didn't really know these people or what they were capable of, and since Robert told them not to harm any of the refugees, what choice did they have but to go along and see what happened next?

Franklin, don't set fire to anything, and, Vincent, please don't touch anyone. The pink guy had said to them before they were instructed to walk behind him. The strange-looking man knew their names and what they could do. It looked like the only ones caught unaware were the two Keepers. Not a great beginning for their mission!

"My name is Charlie," the pink-eyed man introduced himself in a calm, *I knew you were coming two days ago*, voice, while continuing to walk toward the impressive building ahead of them. Charlie never broke his stride, never looked back; just kept going forward as they followed, surrounded on both sides by the big-headed people.

Franklin cast a surprised look at Vincent when the man introduced himself with such an ordinary name. He wasn't sure what he expected, but it certainly wasn't Charlie. Obrobomowitz, Fagenheim or some other difficult to pronounce but dignified-sounding name maybe. But Charlie? He almost laughed aloud. After all, this guy looked like all the pictures he had ever seen of most people's idea of friendly little angels. A merry cherub dressed in white linen pants and a blue shirt topped with a bright-red vest. He didn't look threatening in the least but both men felt that in this case appearances were deceiving.

Franklin had seen real angels, they were called Artregeans, and this man wasn't even close. Artregeans were much fiercer and ten times more wonderful to behold. No, he wasn't an angel, but he was definitely a force to be reckoned with. But what was he? Vincent was staring at him and he could tell he was trying to figure out their next move. His brows were raised, mouth slightly open, as if he wanted to speak but didn't. He seemed to be waiting for Franklin to tell him what to do next.

Vincent hadn't needed to perfect civilized interaction with other living beings. Except for the shadowy, almost completely forgotten bond he'd had with a person whose existence he began to question recently, the closest he had come to any connection since he was a small child was the friendship he now shared with Franklin. All he knew how to do was watch from a distance and when necessary to kill evil

192

things. It was all he had done for years. Trouble was, he didn't know what this little man was or what he intended to do, so he waited for Franklin to give him a sign, only Franklin seemed to be as clueless as he was, and that scared him to death. If Iam didn't want these beings' dead, what was he supposed to do with them?

Both men looked around nervously as they followed behind, but other than a few curious stares from the men and women working on the structures they passed, the two Keepers' arrival did not generate much excitement. Big-headed men, women and children went steadily about their daily duties with little interruption. This was encouraging. At least they were not angry or frightened. But the lack of emotion could also be very bad. They didn't know anything about these people and it could just mean they didn't show their feelings, or didn't care what happened to them one way or another.

This turn of events was tricky. If things turned ugly, maybe they could fight their way out, but what would be the point of that? They were here to help these people somehow; hurting them wasn't an option. So they walked along quietly just as Charlie knew they would, facing an uncertain fate, hoping that the other Keepers were faring better than they were at that moment. If they should fail here, it would be up to the other Keepers to try and pull the worlds together somehow.

Suddenly fearful, Franklin wanted to reach out to his Circle members and see how they were doing. They could be in just as much as danger as he and Vincent were in now. If he could just check on them, make sure...But he dismissed this line of thought, reminding himself that Charlie could listen to this conversation, and he didn't want to make him aware of his friends' existences. But he already knew so much, did he know about them too, and if he did, could he affect their missions? He tried not to let his fear show. *Just keep walking calmly*, he thought to himself.

The procession remained silent, passing through two large stone doors set into the side of the cavern. The doors, roughly ten feet high and five feet wide, were carved slabs of thick gray stone with glittering swirls of green and orange ore deposits in the center. Operating on a sophisticated pulley system of ropes and metal gears, the doors slid smoothly shut into a carved archway enclosing them in an enormous, brightly lit room. Though very disturbed by being trapped here, in this uncertain situation, both young men couldn't help but admire what the people here had created. The walls surrounding them all boasted finely detailed carvings of animals and trees, streams, and a cheerful representation of the sun as if the artist, or artists, were trying to recreate the surface of this world as they remembered it. A tribute to the beauty of all they had left behind and hoped to see again one day.

The room was set up like a meeting place for with stone benches set in curved rows all facing a lectern fashioned from a natural rock formation that rose upwards from the cavern floor. A stone slab stood behind the platform to give someone of small stature enough height to be seen by those in the seats below.

Wonder who does all the speaking here? Vincent joked in the message he deliberately sent to Franklin. This produced a small smile from Charlie, who had turned to look at his two visitors now that they had reached their destination.

The procession had stopped moving and the big-headed people moved silently out of view, disappearing into doorways cut into the sides of the room, as if obeying some silent command from Charlie. Franklin and Vincent were now alone with him, and the Keepers stared expectantly at the shorter man waiting for whatever came next. The ceiling glittered brightly with light coming from several large glowing objects pressed firmly into the hard surface overhead. The objects provided enough illumination to see everything quite clearly, and James was quite impressed that it was almost as bright as the mini-suns he managed to create for the other underground settlements.

"My people created this light source with technology obtained on our travels," Charlie said aloud, pointing above. "It is not quite as bright as the fire Porfious used to create"- He hesitated, looked and smiled at Franklin, as if remembering something very pleasant.

Shocked, Franklin could only stare at him.

"You knew Porfious?" he asked, after taking a moment to collect himself, startled that Charlie knew the name of the Keeper whose powers he had inherited, the man whose soul had shared his body for many years. He still missed his constant companion, the one he had called upon to guide him when things were bad. True, he hadn't always listened, shutting Porfious out for a while after Sara went away before; but he had always known how to call him up when he needed support. Porfious was gone for good now, but Franklin had been gifted with the Keeper's fiery power, destined to carry on the work of providing for Iam's people.

"Yes, he was a very remarkable man, a powerful Keeper and a wonderful friend. He was one of the first Keepers to be slain defending Olie during Braccus's first revolt. When he was killed, he passed his talents on to you. It was his way of contributing to the defense of the worlds. It was a sad time when the originals began to die in the battle against evil's first uprising, but we knew that it was only a matter of time before the young ones came back into the worlds to protect the people."

Shaking his head to bring himself back to matters at hand, Charlie waved toward a small circle of stone seats to the left of where they were standing. "I'm sorry. I am going about this all wrong. Please have a seat and I'll start from the beginning.

"We never meant to hurt you. In fact, I am so happy to have you with us," he said as Vincent and Franklin sat down. "I told the Marrikans all about you days ago. It was much easier to prepare them for your arrival after they got over the shock of seeing me for the first time. I have only been here for a few months myself," he added, watching the puzzled expressions passing over Vincent and Franklin's faces.

"I am a Surren," he went on, watching them expectantly, a smile of satisfaction appearing on his face as Franklin nodded in recognition. Olie had mentioned the Surren in one of his lectures years ago but he had never exactly described them, so Franklin wouldn't have known what to look for if he saw one. Foolish young boy that he was, he hadn't paid as close attention as he should have during some lectures, treating what he had been told as a fairy tale, not quite believing all he heard. He should have known better. Olie had always taught with a purpose, trying to prepare his students for the ugliness they would have to face later. He went back over the stories in his head, trying to remember what his teacher had said about them.

Living in the exact center of the worlds, the Surren were Iam's watchers. These little creatures had been around almost as long as the Keepers and were charged with monitoring the comings and goings of all forces throughout the hidden portals. They had worked with the Keepers to maintain the balance of good and evil in the worlds; watching

196

and directing the movement of both ally and enemy, making sure that there was more of good than bad in the world they cared for. He had been told that these beings were very intelligent, fierce fighters, and one of the few life forms that evil feared.

"Not any longer," said Charlie, pulling that thought out of his head. "I am the only of my kind still living." He grimaced slightly. "When the power shift happened, evil broke through the portals and we weren't able to force them back into the dark places. This is their time in control, so naturally they were stronger than we were."

"My people fought bravely but those that weren't lucky enough to be killed immediately had to face unspeakable torture by Braccus's evil followers. When they did die, the shadowy remains of Braccus's creations, the ones they had killed protecting our fortress, entered their bodies and used them to move around in until they were so decayed they were no longer useful. Their remains were then left to rot in the trash heap that remains of the upper worlds." This last statement, he spat out between his teeth as if enraged.

"I am only here because my brothers forced me to leave in the heat of battle and come to Marrik. They knew the people here would need me to guide them to the underground places and teach them to survive. Sara did a wonderful job of leading most to safety, but some people needed a living form to follow and that was me. I managed to convince them that it was better to hide and fight later. They wanted to stay and fight to the last person; the Marrikans can be like that."

This Charlie said with a hint of admiration in his voice. "This is what makes them work so hard: sheer determination to see things through. Once I could talk to them, they quickly realized that if the enemy could not be defeated at this time, they would have to ensure that they got another chance to kill every last one of them. So here we are building a city and patiently waiting for you two to catch up with us."

"But how did you even know we would be coming here?" Vincent asked, watching Charlie very carefully. He wasn't quite ready to relax with him yet.

"I know many things, and yet it seems also not enough," the Surren stated in a matter-of-fact tone. "Everyone that passed through the portals was basically allowed to do so at our discretion. We have seen you and your friends pass in and out many times. You never saw us, and we never interfered, because as Keepers you were expected to make use of the paths. A stray bit of evil was allowed through but understandably kept to a minimum for the longest time. When Braccus began to move around, we noticed him right away, and though the shift was expected, we thought we'd be ready. We weren't. It happened so fast. The only thing we were ever certain of was that the Keepers would help the people during this difficult time. I watched you two myself up until almost the last minute I was in Sherrin. I knew you would come here. It was one of the last glimpses into the future I was allowed."

"Well, obviously, you have things well under control, but what is it that we are expected to do here?" Franklin asked, noticing Vincent's unease with the situation.

"Yes, we have accomplished quite a bit in the short time we have been here," Charlie replied, stating the obvious, waving a hand at all the miraculous things the caves contained. "But we still need Keepers, Finola especially. We have many things, but food is in short supply. Unless we find a way to start growing things, we will be in trouble in a week or two. I got here just in time to convince them to store a few things away, but they'll run out rather quickly. And there are other things too. We must prepare these people to fight. As hard as

Alice is working to maintain the shields, that too cannot last forever. We will have to learn what works to keep them out of the safe places."

Franklin nodded in agreement, pleased to see Vincent relax and sit further back onto the stone bench, his partner's confidence in their safety for the moment guiding his actions. He still had so many questions to ask but forced himself to focus on the task at hand: keeping the survivors safe.

"Good," said Charlie "There is work to be done. Let's go talk to the Marrikans and plan our next move. After all, we will only have you for so long. You do know that eventually you will be called back to your Circles to prepare for an even bigger battle, don't you?"

Chapter Thirty-Two

Alice woke suddenly, rising so quickly that she scraped the top of her head against the low stone ceiling above her. Wincing at the pain, she rubbed the stinging flesh beneath her hair. Trying to gather her thoughts was difficult. When she had fallen asleep, it had been a deep sleep, with no dreams and no idea what was going on around her. A quick scan of the doorways told her that they were still protected, but she had no idea how she managed to maintain them while she slept.

As she sat still for another few minutes, the events of the past few days played over in her head; it still didn't seem real. In fact, she wasn't quite sure it was real, but the scrape on her head and the rocks that surrounded her seemed to indicate that she hadn't been dreaming about the things that were coming back to her consciousness. Her thinking had cleared enough at this point to know that the shields needed to come down soon; it was draining her strength badly to keep them up. Having no idea how long this war for the surface was going to last, it was ridiculous to think that she could keep an entire army from entering the refugees' caverns indefinitely. Maybe she had used too much of her energy on the shields, maybe that was why she was having such a hard time coming back from the sleep she had been in. Vague details were slow to develop, past events much easier to recall than recent ones, her head was still so fuzzy, but she couldn't drop the barriers quite yet.

That old uncomfortable feeling she had when she had overextended her powers was returning. Partly because of the shields and partly because she was putting just as much effort into avoiding the one part of her gift that she dreaded to use: the ability to see into the shadowy places that the dead occupied. Blocking these visions seemed to be taking almost as much energy as defending the portals. Energy she obviously could not afford to use, but she couldn't seem to bring herself to look at another one of those hideous things that dwelled in the in-between places again.

The encounter with the evil thing that had challenged her days ago was still fresh in her mind and it was one she didn't care to repeat. If she hadn't gotten it together at the last moment, that thing would have entered the portal and killed a lot of innocent people. She still felt guilty about falling for its *helpful spirit* routine and was scared to death to repeat that mistake.

Her head still felt groggy; she hadn't slept in a long time and when she had finally passed out from exhaustion, she slept so hard that waking up now was a struggle. Slowly rising to wakefulness, she was a little bit lost, couldn't remember where she was or what she had been doing right before she passed out... Randall! His name suddenly popped into her head as she wiped the sleep fuzz from her eyes. He had hidden her here, insisting she get some rest while he continued to try and blend in with the refugees. When she last talked to him, they still had not found the special ones that would help them get through to the others, but they had heard talk of a few brave men that were scouting out remote areas of the underground places. It was all a bit hard to remember, because she had stayed up far too long at that point and the facts were still so hazy.

How long had she been asleep? She had to check on Randall. Reaching out tentatively, she tried to make contact with her boyfriend, picturing his finely formed face, red hair, and lanky frame, the way he looked at her and made her heart melt. Then she remembered the way that old lady had been looking at him, with hatred and suspicion, and her breath caught in her throat. She just had to know if he was alright. Every action that Isobel had made was screaming danger for Randall, and Alice silently cursed herself for allowing him to talk her into letting down her guard to get some stupid sleep. All the sleep had done was make her duller than ever. Focus, she said to herself, thumping her fist against her thigh. Alice's mind restlessly sought a connection with the young man even as she scrambled out of her little hidey-hole to make her way to his side once again.

Randall, where are you? No answer. She tried again, thinking she may have heard a reply but it was a little faded and hard to make out. Maybe he was busy and just expected her to come to him, but at least he could say something. This wasn't right. She needed to see him, to make sure that her fears were unfounded.

Slipping into invisible mode, Alice moved out into the caverns, checking out the activity around her. Squatting outside the low narrow opening, she tried to get her bearings while watching a few of the red-haired people going about their daily chores. The sound of metal tools hitting stone echoed loudly. Two small children scooped water into wooden buckets from the stream near her sleeping place. A few industrious individuals were hammering into the cave walls, intent on finishing one of the houses. That explained the noise she heard; but other than the sound of a few tools, there wasn't much noise from the villagers she saw milling about.

A group of women and young girls stood around a large kettle, chopping up a few dried roots and nuts to add to a soup they were stirring up for the community meal. None of them talked much, which was unusual to see, she remembered these people as being hopeful and grateful to be alive. They spoke often and tried to keep each other's spirits up with cheerful chatter. They didn't seem so cheerful now. The men that labored around the houses also had little to say today as they moved about, hauling objects to and from construction sites to make these caves a more suitable place for their people to live.

The actions of the villagers were noticeably subdued, each going about their tasks without smiles or conversation, all except for the two young boys gathering water. They seemed to be having quite an animated discussion. Shuffling forward in an odd duckwalk way, brown hair sticking up in a messy post-sleep hairdo, Alice continued forward until she had closed in on the children. Eager to hear what they were saying, she quickened her steps to get as close to them as possible.

Trying not to attract attention, she carefully crossed over the narrow waterway, her footsteps slow and silent as she fell into step behind the little guys now lugging their buckets along. Water sloshed over the sides and hit the ground, masking her footfalls. Moving faster, she was able to catch up with them in time to hear them talking excitedly about something that was happening in one of the distant corridors.

"Did you see the way they took that guy and dragged him out of here?" the taller of the two boys said, gesturing to an opening just behind her.

"Yeah, what was that all about? My parents wouldn't let me follow," his companion answered, slightly out of breath as he put his buckets down. They now stood in front of a house sixty feet away from the stream and, after looking carefully around to make sure no adults were watching, they plopped down on the ground next to their cargo, taking a break to continue their conversation.

"Do you think they'll kill him?" the first speaker asked in wavering tones.

"I don't know," the other child began to speak again, "What do you think he did...?" The rest of the sentence sounded like blah-blah-blah to their invisible eavesdropper.

Randall, she shouted once again, taking off at full speed as she homed in on the connection she shared with her boyfriend. Alice knocked over one of the buckets as she started running headlong towards the yellowy-blue trail that she recognized as his. Cool water splashed all over the boys who scrambled up to their feet with frightened looks on their faces. They stood shaking and staring at the spot where a strangled cry of alarm came from mid-air. Nothing was there, but they felt a sudden something speed past them, flinging stones up in the direction of the corridor they had been talking about.

Chapter Thirty-Three

After a few days of watching the people she had befriended go hungry, Finola's resolve to blend in with the crowd was weakening. She had a gift that would help them and yet here she was pretending it was okay that she heard little children crying because the food rations they were given were not enough to keep their stomachs from rumbling. She saw parents giving up what little food they had to help keep their little ones full and they were paying the price for this by getting totally run down. It hurt to see sunken cheeks and pale skin as the adults struggled to carry on with their daily duties while starving. The dark, damp caves were not providing the helpless people with what they needed. She was afraid that they would soon see some people die if they were unable to do what they were capable of doing for them. All through this, she and Eric went hungry along with them, waiting and watching each and every person for an indication that they might be the ones to help them transition from fellow starving refugee to Keepers who could help them to survive.

Finola had managed to make a few berry bushes grow near cracks in the ceiling of the cave, conveniently "finding" them when she was moving about helping with daily chores. But it wasn't nearly enough. Eric had made her stop after she created three such bushes. "It looks a bit suspicious that you are the one to find them every time, especially when some of these people have been down here longer than we have." The people were already jumpy and suspicious as it was, they didn't need to bring attention to the fact that he and Finola might be different than those around them and, therefore, dangerous.

Eric was worried about Finola. She tried to act like she was okay with the current situation, but he knew she didn't like dark enclosed areas. This cave may be big, but it was still basically, to her, like one of those places she had been trapped in as a helpless foster child, abused and alone. He put all his heart into keeping her calm and hopeful, and was so proud of her for handling herself so well. Her heart was beating so hard in her chest that it hurt him to feel it, yet there she was smiling and giving encouraging words to those close to her as if nothing were wrong.

He, on the other hand, was perfectly comfortable with dark places. Having spent most of his life in caves, his night vision was marvelous. Eric could move around effortlessly yet stumbled around in the half-light like the rest of them, not wanting to stand out in any way. Trying to fit-in, the young man worked along with the others in the dim light cast by torches set in the cave walls. Acting just like them, he moved slowly about trying to make this moist dingy place more like home.

But it wasn't home, and they ached to start fighting to regain all that they had lost on the surface of the worlds. All this waiting was hard; Eric had to remind himself several times that that they needed to be patient and wait for the right time to help. But it was difficult to convince himself, let alone Finola of this. She seemed to be having the hardest time fighting her urge to do what her gift called her to do: provide and protect.

They're starving, she spoke to him as they sat holding hands after a hard day's work. They were both so tired from working to finish the shelters on what little could be shared from the salvaged food left down here. The food, a large collection of potted meat and jars of preserved fruits and vegetables, had been found one day in a shadowy section of the caves by some of the refugees looking for anything they could use for shelter. If it hadn't been discovered, the people down here would all have begun to starve soon after arriving in this place. At first, the group was puzzled and suspicious, but an old man that many of the others seemed to trust, had told them that the items must have been left over from the time they used to mine these caverns for ore years before. This explanation seemed logical, and so they had all begun to store the food and divide it up amongst the survivors.

This provided an explanation for the odd collection of items they began to find scattered all over the cave: blankets, a few shirts here, a pair of pants there. The two-by-fours and tree stumps were most likely left over from the miners stay here as well as the additional preserved food items which Eric didn't think looked very old. But they had to have been here awhile, the old man assured them, these caves hadn't been used in a long time. This story made sense, and since they were desperate, the people put their finds down to simple good fortune, storing them and sharing everything together. But even using their resources sparingly, they were still running out of staples and there wasn't anything they could do to replenish their supply.

I could help them, Finola said, as he squeezed her hand comfortingly. *I must help them.* She repeated, looking at the people around them settling in for the night. Their worn, thinning faces tore at her heart.

Finola, we have to hold on a little bit longer, Eric said, staring into her sad brown eyes. *There are a few people settled further down the corridors guarding the doorways. I have heard some of the settlers talk about them, but I haven't seen them. I will try to visit them in the morning. Maybe the person we are looking for is among them.*

Finola smiled sadly at his assurances. She was so tired and hungry that she wouldn't have made it this far without him keeping her spirits up. He made her feel better just by being next to her; he regenerated her soul. Reaching down to the dirt and stone floor of the cave, she called up a few stray roots which blossomed quickly at her command, turning into bright red berries. Picking a handful, she held them out for Eric, who looked around the caves nervously, trying to see if anyone else had seen what she had done.

Stop that, he snapped, irritated at her foolishness. Her beautiful doll-like face crumpled at his tone, hand still outstretched in the act of offering him the fruit she grew for him.

He was sorry for hurting her feelings this way, but this was a serious matter. She couldn't just do things like that; this careless display could quickly turn their fellow cave-members against them. Kicking at the roots, he tore the small bush up and threw the pieces into a dark recess behind them. Fortunately, most of the people around the encampment had already turned in for the night so there were very few of them still up and moving around. The ones that were, didn't seem to be paying any attention to the two of them.

"You need to go to bed now," Eric said, as she stood slowly, letting the berries drop to the ground, uneaten. "It will all be better tomorrow, you'll see." He felt like a complete jerk for making her look so sad. He knew her so well, had so many memories of her that came from a time long before he occupied this current sixteen-year-old form. He knew how she thought, and just what to say to get his point across. Sometimes she acted before thinking and this was not the time for that. She had to be reminded to take care. He wanted to say *I love you*, but didn't want to soften on this point. Instead, he just pointed in the direction of the wood and stone hut that she shared with two other girls and said goodnight.

Finola moved slowly towards her shelter, looking back once to find that he had turned away. What she didn't see were the tears welling up in his eyes as he opened a narrow door and went in to bed.

Chapter Thirty-Four

James stood staring in amazement at the thing standing in front of him. The form of a newly dead person grinned at him from just a few feet away; its formerly light brown skin pitted here and there with recent signs of decay. Skin was slowly peeling off the fine narrow nose, all sign of the familiar freckles that had dotted its surface gone. The corpse's lips were loose and peeling, the smile it gave him caused them to flop downward, hiding teeth that he was sure he didn't want to see anyway. Parts of the scalp were visible because the hair had come off in tufts, littering the dead guy's shoulders which were visible underneath the torn fabric of his shirt. He could see strips of skin flaking off underneath the material; a few pieces had fallen down the arm and hung below the level of the sleeve, reminding him of a snake shedding its skin. The young man he was facing had only been dead a couple of days, at most, but the body was decomposing pretty fast. How did he know how long this guy had been dead? Because he recognized his own body as it stared back at him. He knew that the spirits in this place had been using human bodies as their vessels, it seemed to make their movement through the portals easier. But he had no idea how they would have found his. Truth be told, he had no idea where he left his body after he died, but how in the world was it possible for his corpse to be holding the hand of Diandra's dead body? They had not been anywhere near each other in life. From what she had told him she was in an entirely different world than his when she died.

While looking at his own body used as a dead-meat puppet was painful enough, the fact that it held the hand of his new girlfriend was even worse, especially since her body was torn to pieces. The only way he recognized her was by the one side of her face that remained intact. The rest of her was badly damaged, having been ravaged by something that obviously had a deep hatred for young woman.

Diandra's body was torn and smashed, with bones protruding at angles they hadn't been designed to move. And yet, she stood at his side, a smile fixed on the part of her face that was still in one piece. Behind her stood his entire adopted family, their bodies all lined up, his sisters, brothers, and parents. It was as if the evil things had seen everything he cared about, everyone he loved, and were using them against him like pawns on a chessboard. The shadowy wraiths that ran the show here somehow knew the people he loved were keeping him going even after death.

The hope that what he was doing here would keep them alive was what drove him on, kept him from giving up. James was sure they were going to survive him and if he could get through all this somehow, he could return to them and everything would all be okay again. Now he was seeing them all dead and inhabited by enemies that were urging him to give up and surrender his soul because they had already won this game.

A strangled cry came out of his mouth as the gathering of his dead loved ones now moved slowly toward them. They had noticed his weakening concentration, distress at seeing his loved one's bodies used as vehicles for evil spirits. Sweat rolled down his face as the determined enemy moved closer and closer to Sara, casually passing by James who stood with his hands covering his face while Diandra tried to get him to regain focus and push them back.

"James, look at me!" she yelled at him, pulling at his hands until they stood face to face. A quick look back at Sara showed her that the dead things were moving much closer to the woman so caught up in the pursuit of the thing she

214

sought, that she no longer paid any attention to the dangers around her. Thomas was caught up with her, unable to pull away from the connection that bound them so tightly together. He had gone far into her head to understand why she wasn't able to break the chain that bound her to the thing trapped there with her. The object pulled persistently at her until that's all they could see now. James had intended to push the enemy back until whatever was happening to the two of them stopped, or they found the thing, whichever came first. His lack of focus was putting them all in danger. For a moment, Diandra closed her eyes, gritted her teeth, and tried to come up with something that would help her to help him. Stupid visions had haunted her all her life, never coming to her when she wanted them to, and always getting her in trouble with the people around her. She had suffered from this most of her life. Now that she was dead, the least she could expect from this curse was for it to work for her when she needed it the most.

A brief flash of light followed by a popping noise was all she got for her trouble. She opened her eyes once again to find that the dead things had approached Sara and Thomas, reaching out their hands to them. *Come on!* she screamed in her head, looking for anything she could use. The scene in front of her swam in and out of focus and she got her wish. One vision that both made her want to shout for joy and cry at the same time. This vision was clear enough to make her sure of what she needed to do next. "James, open your eyes," she said, dragging his hands away from his face. This strong man had almost been broken by the loss of all that he loved, and she needed to let him know that it was all a lie. "Look carefully at these things in front of you," she spoke softly, trying to hide the tremor in her voice as she glanced back to see that the dead things were trying to pull the light that was Sara and Thomas's souls. Rotting fingers made contact with the flesh of the Keepers, digging inward as they sought the golden brightness that was the essence of Iam's special creations. James responded by shaking his head and staring into her eyes.

"I can't see my family like that, can't see you like that," he mumbled. "Even if we succeed in finding the thing to destroy Braccus, what's left? I'm already dead, so are you and so are they."

"No, James, look at them," she cried, forcing his head in the direction of the hideous things that surrounded his Circle members. She didn't want to tell him everything that she had seen now, things she would have to tell him eventually. It was more important to cling to the hope that they could make a difference because that's what would get him through this. His friends needed him.

James turned toward the ugliness that was left of Diandra and his entire family. Heart in his throat, he opened his eyes to see what she wanted him to see, trusting her but resenting the fact that she was insisting so strongly. He looked at the awful sight, the collection of dead beings surrounding his Circle members, seeing just what he had before: the bodies of his family and Diandra digging their fingers into Sara and Thomas, seeking to remove their souls. He blinked his eyes, trying to come to grips with what he was seeing and what he would have to do to protect his friends. Pushing his anguish down, as Diandra said, "Don't just look at them, James, see them." She repeated over and over until he wanted to scream at her, to just shut up. But her tone was so urgent that he felt compelled to do what she said. James's eyes focused on the mass gathering behind him, and even as he looked at the bodies that had caused him so much pain earlier, he noticed them changing as he stared. What he had seen as Diandra and his family, was just a group of ugly dead bodies, of people he didn't recognize at all.

The dead things were not him and his family; it had all been a trick, an elaborate masquerade to make him give up. They had obviously been here a long time, long enough to watch the living. Obviously, they had seen him and his family when they were still alive, and knowing he was a Keeper, had used images of the people he loved the most to divert his attention from protecting Sara. Standing up like a strong Keeper, his faith restored by Diandra's actions and need to continue what he had started by following Sara into death, James used his gift to push the gruesome jackals away. Regaining control, he sent them visions of daylight and a force so powerfully good that it hurt them to even think. The enemy couldn't concentrate on what they were supposed to do, they just wanted to run away and hide in the darkest part of this dark place until the Keeper took the light away. Screeches of anger and pain filled the air as they slinked off, backing away from the two people still stuck in the trance that was drawing the object to them. James turned to Diandra and hugged her tightly, thanking her over and over for her help while the dead things looked on and waited for another chance to get to them.

Chapter Thirty-Five

Time being of the essence, Alice moved with certainty towards Randall's trail. Popping through the thin layer that separated the sections of space, she moved past patches of light and dark toward the thread that bound her to him. Moving this way was part of her gift that she normally only used against the enemy to send them somewhere ugly and unsafe. She had only used it on herself a couple of times, when she was in danger and just had to get out of some place or be dead. Because traveling this way was extremely draining, she rarely moved in this fashion, especially now when she was much more aware of all the hidden things that hung out in those in-between spaces she had to pass through. This was one of those emergency situations; she had to be where Randall was very quickly.

Alice pushed against the thin current of air surrounding her. Fighting against the resistance it produced, she plunged back through yet another dimensional barrier to arrive on the other side with a loud pop. Dizzy and disoriented, she found herself back in the solid dimension, moving toward a glowing orange light, one of the portals to the nightmarish world of the surface.

She had emerged close to where Randall was, could still see the cord that connected them together. It ran around a bend in the path she had landed on. She couldn't see him, but could hear voices echoing in the tunnel just ahead. The shuffling of feet and angry tones indicated a struggle was going on beyond her field of vision. Fearing for Randall's safety, Alice fought the dizziness that was threatening to overtake her and started to run the last few feet that separated her from her beloved boyfriend. She was stopped by the sound of his voice in her head.

Alice, wait. Isobel's men are now arguing about whether or not to send me to the surface. Maybe, if I can just get them to listen to me, I can stop them.

The surface! she shrieked, lowering her transmission a little when she realized she was yelling at him. *I will send every one of them out there first.* Her tone was deadly serious, and he knew that the group of people in front of him was in a lot of danger even if they didn't realize it now. She was still tired, terrified for his safety, and had passed through several layers of thin air to get to him. This was not a very good combination. Randall was trying very hard to get out of this situation unharmed and he wanted the people he'd come to help to have the same chance. He had to admit, though, that if the situation were reversed and it was Alice in trouble instead, he wouldn't hesitate to electrocute the unlucky jerk that tried to hurt her.

When Randall had first been grabbed by Isobel and her cronies, he had gone quietly enough, afraid to do anything that might to lead them to Alice. His girlfriend had just fallen into a deep sleep and he couldn't have awakened her if he tried. Her body was so worn out she would have been at risk for capture too, and he wasn't going to let that happen.

After he was taken away from the central cavern, they had not headed straight for the doorway. In fact, Isobel seemed to be a little bit confused as to where she should direct her men to go. So the group wandered around the caverns for hours while the old lady asked him several questions about where he was from and why he had been one of the last to enter the caves.

He told her that he had fled from his village, fighting the enemy along the way. The only explanation that he could think of to hide his true identity was to seem like just one of the people that belonged here. Isobel wanted to know why it

220

was that he managed to make it down here alive when so many had not. He tried to explain that he was merely fortunate to have escaped with his life, much like the men that were with her now. His answer did not please the old lady at all. In fact, it infuriated her. She walked up and slapped his face several times before regaining control of herself and instructing her men to keep looking for the exit to the surface.

Her loss of control had an interesting effect on the men; the two that had been holding his arms hesitated for a moment. Their grip loosened, looks of concern on their faces as they watched the woman they had been so convinced had all the answers losing her self-control. Randall had used that time to break free and call out for Alice who he sensed was now awake and reaching out for him. He managed to call out her name before another one of the men more loyal to Isobel slugged him in the head and he blacked out for a while.

When he came to again, Randall was lying in yet another dark section of the cavern where he heard Isobel and her men talking about what they should do now that they had him and couldn't seem to find the portal to rid themselves of him. One of the bolder men, Isobel called him Matthew, suggested they just kill him and be done with it. The two men that had looked worried about Isobel earlier, the ones she had called Hank and Tyler, began to argue with Matthew.

"That is not what we agreed to do," the small and chunky man named Hank said. "We agreed to put him out there with his own kind. If he is one of the enemy's agents, he will have to stay there with them; he won't be able to get back in, right?" His voice wavered as if he didn't believe what he was saying. *This was crazy! How could he have let her convince him that this guy who looked just like all the other people in this land was actually an enemy spy? What had come over him?*

"Yes, they seem to be locked out right now, something is keeping them back. We haven't seen any of the monsters for a while now. He may not be one of us. I mean, I traveled all the villages in this land and I have never seen him, but that doesn't mean that he deserves to die. What if I'm wrong? What if you're wrong? He could just be a stranger from one of the farms on the edge of everything. We can't do this," Tyler added his opinion to the argument.

Encouraged, Randall, had opened his mouth to speak again, to appeal to the two men that were beginning to doubt their leader. Before he could say a word, he was hit over the head from behind by one of the men. When he came to again, he found, to his dismay, that they had found the doorway and were dragging him toward it. That was when he began to struggle and felt Alice close by. He wanted to zap the people off him and run to her, but hesitated in order to keep his promise to Robert. He had to try to get through to them. After all, they were Iam's creations, it was what the Keepers had been created to do.

Alice, stop. Randall spoke her to her silently as he spoke to Isobel aloud. "Please listen to me." He used the softest tone he could to try and sound calm and reasonable even though he was surrounded by people who were determined to hand him over to the enemy. "I don't know why you are doing this, but whatever you think I have done, surely it isn't bad enough to send me back up there."

Randall was trying to appeal to the two men that had stuck up for him earlier, hoping that they would interfere once again. If they provided enough of a distraction, then he could throw out some electricity, enough to stun them while he made his way back to Alice. His eyes sought out his two

222

sympathizers, only to find they were no longer there. He was standing between Isobel and the three unfriendly men, one of them being Matthew, arguing only whether to kill him or not before they threw him through the portal. That was when he made his last attempt to reason with them, hoping that Alice didn't send them all to their deaths. It would be hard to convince the rest of the refugees that they were allies if they killed a prominent member of their little society. Alice was reading Randall thoughts, knowing his situation was critical. Turning the corner as fast as her weakened body would allow, she ran full force towards their connection, only to find the spot where she was sure he was empty.

Chapter Thirty-Six

Eric woke up regretting the events of the night before, wanting only to go to Finola and let her know how sorry he was for the way he'd made her feel. Surely she would have had time to think about why he said what he had to her. They could talk today, and everything would be alright. They would both continue to be safe and would find the special ones that would make the others accept them. Today would be the day that all the good things happened, and they would be able to start doing what Finola had so desperately wanted: help these people survive.

With renewed hope, the young man walked out of his shelter only to stop dead in his tracks, staring in dismay at the sight that greeted him. Eric walked out into the middle of a jungle, everything around him was green; vines clung to the ceiling and dripped down the cave walls to dangle into the center cavern like curtains. Apple trees grew next to pear trees in neat rows in the middle of the large space the survivors had settled in. Dark green grass grew on stone surfaces that under normal circumstances would not have permitted this substance to thrive. Rows of corn, beets, tomatoes, and beans were laid out in empty spots between dwellings. Finola had crammed every spare section of this place with life sustaining plants and in the process brought about a whole bunch of trouble.

The people around him stumbled among the plants in confusion, they didn't know whether to laugh or cry. *What had done this?* Since it was not natural for these things to be growing in the poor lighting of the caves, and overnight growth impossible, nothing about this could be good. This had to be a trick by the evil things that had chased them into the caves. Even though they were hungrier than they had ever been in their entire lives, the people would not touch any of these cursed plants.

Cries of alarm came from those walking out of their houses as they did their best to avoid walking on the grassy areas. Tiptoeing past the plants and turf as if they were made of broken glass, the villagers stood as far away from anything green as they could. People were pointing and talking all at once, voices bounced around the cave walls making a terrific racket, until a man they called Rodney jumped up on a pile of fallen rocks and yelled for them to stop.

It was quite an accomplishment for him to get their attention with all the confused excitement going on. But he did get them to calm down. While he began to speak to the crowd, Eric's eyes scanned the area for signs of Finola. He saw her emerge from her shelter, a panicked look on her face.

I was just thinking about it before I went to sleep. I think I may have dreamed about it, too, she said while she stood watching the refugee's horrified reaction to the gift she had given them. She had never done anything like this before, not without actually trying; but it had been on her mind ever since she had come to the caves. Seeing what was happening to these people had fueled her desire to stop their suffering. She was consumed with a need to provide for them. Maybe that's why her subconscious had taken over and done something to help feed all the hungry refugees, calling up all the green stuff she could think of.

Now that it was done, she couldn't understand why they were so upset. They seemed angry, afraid, and looking for someone to blame, someone to hurt. She listened to the man standing above the others. Looking down, he advised them not to touch the food, telling them to destroy all the growth they saw. It was a trick, he said, magic devised by the enemy to poison them all.

Panicked, they started to do what he said, each villager grabbing whatever they could find and moving carefully to the plants, began hacking and slashing at the precious, life-preserving food. Eric stared in horror as Finola reacted exactly in the way he feared she would. Despite his frantic mental warning for her to remain silent, she began to scream at the top of her lungs. She ran at those who would destroy what she had provided for them.

"Noooooo!" she shrieked, pushing at the startled men busy digging up her tomato plants; their feet covered in red where they had stomped the ripe fruit into the ground. Eric managed to tackle her shortly before one of the men, not thinking it was a mere girl that had attacked him, swung at her head. He missed narrowly, Eric having successfully removed her from the path of his fist. The man saw Finola and Eric lying on the ground and paused for a moment, staring in shock and shame at what had almost happened. The look on his face changed quickly as the man who appeared to be giving all the advice, told them that she must not actually be a girl. The enemy was clever, he said, disguising itself as all kinds of things.

"That's how they work," Rodney bellowed, anger and fear in his every word. "They change their appearance and move in among the rest of us. The young man must be in on it with her; they're together all the time!"

Eric rose quickly and grabbed Finola's arm while the suddenly irrational villagers gathered together and began to form a circle around them, moving closer and closer to try and get hold of the pair that Rodney had decided was now a danger to them all.

At this moment, Eric didn't care what Iam had intended for these people. All he knew was that they were going to hurt Finola if they got their hands on her. She had only done what lam had created them for, using her gift to save their lives. They were not going to hurt the girl he loved. Raising his hand and flicking his wrist created a very painful high-pitched whine that had the attackers backing away with their hands covering their ears.

Eric used this diversion to pull Finola down a dark corridor just beyond the main settled area. This place had not been fully explored yet; it was so dark that the first two times the refugees tried to enter it their torches hadn't provided enough light to safely move around. There were many loud threats shouted at the two young Keepers; idle threats, for now, as those issuing them were too afraid to enter the inky atmosphere they had retreated to.

Darkness wasn't a threat to Eric. In fact, in this moment, it was more of a blessing because it kept their pursuers from coming too far in. He had Finola well down the corridor and in his arms to comfort her while the frightened refugees followed only the first few feet before running back to the central area. Holding the fragile girl closely, he tried to show her what he was seeing around them; soothing her fear of dark places with gentle words while carefully avoiding looking at any of the crawly things that slithered around in the darkness. He had a feeling she would almost rather face the unreasonable anger of those they left behind than stay in here with bugs and other things. Instead of mentioning the six- and eight-legged things that surrounded them; he chose to show her the beauty of the rocks, let her hear the soft trickle of water as it ran in a small waterfall down the cave wall.

He used the sound to drown out the voices of their pursuers, as he continued to hold her close. Drip, drip, drip, each drop sounded loudly in her head as the water made its way through cracks to land finally in a river deep below them. The soft swish of the water flowing even deeper into the cave sounded loudly in her head until it was one of the few things she heard other than Eric's voice.

"It's not your fault," he repeated, reading her thoughts. She was shaking with anger and fear. Eric's mind was working overtime to find a way out for him and Finola before the villagers worked up enough nerve to brave the darkness and come after them.

Chapter Thirty-Seven

Alice woke up alone. The energy she had used to move through the dimensional barriers to reach Randall on relatively little sleep had caused her to pass out. He was in danger and she had not been able to help him. How could she have lost the connection that guided her to him? Her mind was racing as she sought a path to him again, coming up empty at every turn. Shaking with shock and grief, she sat in the distant corridor, light from the portal spilling over her; she was now visible. A detail that she hardly cared about. No one knew she even existed down here and, in this remote section of the caves, it was highly unlikely that anyone would stumble across her. She didn't want to waste any energy on remaining unseen, she just wanted to gather her strength and find Randall.

Alice stared at the portal, trying to get a fix on its energy; she could feel the flow of power it generated and the darkness that lurked beyond it. The shields were still up, but the enemy was waiting for their chance to get through. Pacing back and forth, she felt them searching for a sign that the defenses might be weakening. The way she was now feeling, they might very well get their chance. It was all she could do to keep from having a total nervous breakdown and still provide protection for all the portals while her world crumbled and her loved ones were in danger.

Randall was nowhere to be found, he did not answer her when she called, and she couldn't tell if it was because he was already in the hands of the enemy or dead. Both options she refused to consider. So she went with her instincts which told her to keep looking.

Alice knew that her heart would be shattered into a thousand pieces by such a loss. No. He was still alive and out there somewhere looking for her too. She just couldn't figure out what had caused her to be so mistaken about the trail she had followed; she didn't feel like it was Braccus, the strong feeling of being overwhelmed by something she couldn't control was no longer there. If she wasn't so tired she could figure this out. There had to be a way to reconnect, to find Randall.

Deliberately letting her mind go numb, Alice reached inside for a little something extra to keep her going. Think, think... Wracking her brain for some kind of answer, a way to find the connection she had lost, she realized that she wasn't alone.

A sound reached her ears; a soft hissing sound vibrated in the stillness of the cave. Listening carefully, she froze. Was that breathing she heard? Was Randall here, after all? Eyes were on her, she felt herself being watched. Maybe Randall had escaped his captors and was headed back to her. Alice struggled to rise, ready to greet him, while promising herself never to let him out of her sight again. Looking with hopeful eyes for her wonderful boyfriend, she stopped in mid-movement as she spied them.

Two young men stood in a shadowy corner watching her like they had just won the lottery. Alice stood slowly; ready to protect herself if needed, her shield going up around her like a fine sheet of plastic wrap. She didn't bother to try and go invisible. What would be the point? They had already seen her. She had been sitting in the light cast by the doorway and they were partly in shadow, so she couldn't quite make out who they were, but guessed if they were evil, they could have easily attacked her when she wasn't paying attention. In short, if they had wanted to hurt her, they would have already tried.

Alice studied the men as they continued to gawk at her in that satisfied fashion, almost as if they knew they would find her here. The only people she had expected to see were the ones that had taken Randall, and if they had anything to do with his disappearance, they were in so much trouble.

Eyes wide with wonder, the two men stood in the exact place they knew they should be. At first, Steven thought that his brother had been all wrong. If so, it would have been the first time it had ever happened. In the upper world his big brother Jacob had been a leader, serving as mayor in a small city called Reed, as well as captain of a small militia force that had patrolled the countryside and maintained peace. He and his men had driven away small groups of tall skinny men that had been frequently making trouble in the outer villages just before life on the surface went totally crazy.

Jacob was well-known and respected by most of those that had survived the enemy's attacks; they were grateful because he and his men had been the reason they made it here alive. He warned them because the beautiful young woman had told him before she made the doorways visible for them to escape. He listened because she was one of them, the Keepers. His visions of who and what they were had started months before she had spoken to him. When she had started communicating, he knew exactly what to do. Everything Sara told him to. Sara was the name she had given, and she told him to expect others like her to come and help his people.

Jacob had been successful in his endeavors because he could see things before they happened. It was something he had always been able to do but had shared with only a few of his closest friends and brother, of course. It was Jacob who had warned as many people as he could that something bad was going to happen days before it had. He had also seen that

233

once they made it to the caverns, help would come for the people, and that help would be here in the evening on this day. Jacob's group had kept careful count of the days on makeshift calendars since they had arrived in the caves, waiting for the event their leader had seen. But, after sitting here for several hours, they had not seen a thing until she appeared out of thin air. A dark-haired girl with green eyes shimmered into view just yards away from where they were hiding. She was lovely, magical, and everything that they would have expected from what Jacob had told them of the saviors they should expect to see.

Since he had arrived in the caves, Jacob had kept away from the main crowd, sending Steven and Ray in to mingle with refugees. They had been sure that the young man they had met while moving through the corridors toward the main settlement was the one they were looking for. This young man had been named Randall and he was different to the rest of the villagers. They were certain that he would be the one and had gone back to Jacob with the news that they were sure that they had found him. When they returned for their friend, he was gone, taken away by the grief crazed woman named Isobel and her stupid followers. The worried men followed where the villagers had said they'd gone, hoping to catch up with them before any harm had been done.

They had arrived to find this place empty, and so they had stopped to wait for something to happen. Maybe this is where Randall and his captors would be and that's why they were sent here. They waited so long they had almost given up, and then there she was. Her dramatic appearance was very impressive. They hadn't seen her walk in, though the light had been more than adequate to see a short way down the path. She hadn't made a sound, appearing from nothing in a mere blink of an eye, looking like she had just woken from a bad dream.

Alice stared at the two men who seemed too afraid to move towards her, standing rooted to their spot like scared rabbits, before it dawned on her foggy brain that she knew them. These were the men that Randall had befriended. She saw the way they had interacted with him and not once did she feel that they were a threat to him. But why were they here? Walking hesitatingly forward, she kept her shield in place even though she was still so incredibly tired. "Steven, where is Randall?" she asked.

The young man's face paled at the sound of his name being spoken by the magical girl. How did she know who he was? The look on her face that told him she would gladly unleash whatever powers she had on him if his answer was not to her liking. She was here to help them; Jacob had said so. If Randall was with her it meant that Steven had been right about that young man being what Jacob had called a Keeper. Afraid of making her angry by telling her something she didn't want to hear; it took him a moment to gather his wits before he was able to answer.

Chapter Thirty-Eight

Sara and Thomas hung on to the object they sought, urged on by an entity that seemed far more familiar with it than they were. The connection stood out so clearly in their heads, it was all they could think of. Nothing else mattered, not even when the dead ones surrounded them, touching them with the slick puffy hands of their rotting hosts. The air popped and crackled with energy and it took a moment to notice they were fading a bit inside, like something was pulling at their very essence. But they were so caught up in the search for whatever Braccus had hidden, they were unable to do anything about it.

Whatever was guiding them was so driven by its need to expose Braccus's secret, it had lost regard for the safety of its own instruments of detection. It was lucky for them that James regained control of their attackers in time to stop their souls from being taken and tossed into permanent darkness. The image of what they sought got stronger and stronger: small, square, and vaguely familiar, it floated teasingly in their minds. A memory, not theirs, of course, played an event back for them and they were mesmerized by what they saw. The object was sitting next to a bubbling black stream, its owner glancing anxiously over his shoulder as he pounded it into the ground with his fist. A few thumps of his clenched hand drove the object far deeper into the soil than should have been humanly possible. Then again, Braccus had never been truly human. The location burned itself into Sara and Thomas's heads as they saw it from high above, staring with interest at the actions he had taken thousands of years before.

The object quivered from its spot deep in the molten rock that formed this land, trying to maintain its place. But the command from Sara's mouth was so strong it seemed to be having a hard time resisting her summons. Somehow, she had memories of the thing, and it had memories of her. The object strained at the dirt covering it, wanting to reconnect with a time before it had been hidden, a time when this very spot had been so different, and it had been familiar with a particular being.

This place had once been darkly beautiful, with trees of silver and gold highlighted with a pale green light cast by its constantly hanging moon; the sun had never shown here. Streams filled with black water that glowed with a fine silver sheen running over stones of deep red. Heated by the very core of the earth, the stones did not cool in the air, glowing hot and bright. The hot rocks made the air quite steamy and comfortable for its creator. Braccus loved what he had made from nothing, his pride in all that surrounded him here, its darkness a perfect opposite to Iam's lightness was felt by Sara and Thomas.

Braccus's creations had always been the opposite of Iam's and in the beginning, were not always twisted. This dimension had been one of Braccus's early experiments, the place he could get away from the perfectness of Iam and his group of *oohing and ahhing* children, to just be himself. Created at a time when he was just beginning to release his greatness, and before he had decided that Iam was too foolish to listen to reason; this had been a refuge of sweet, calm tranquility for Braccus. Even then, darkness had been his choice, it defined all that he really felt, and hid so much that he didn't want to see or to be seen by others. The land here had been carpeted with a thick brownish-black grass that thrived in the pale twilight he had designed for the sky. He had come here many times, allowing his mind to run free, to plan all he wanted to accomplish in the other worlds.

238

His secret hope of bringing Iam around to see things the way he did and the desire to have a certain life-force here with him some day, burned strongly in him. He would reveal this place once it was understood by all that he was their superior and, of course, Iam's equal. Then she would know how truly great he was. He had it all planned out until his carefully arranged sequence of events were changed in a single day. The day he had brought her here.

He wasn't aware that he had done so, but the very things he sought to hide from her drew her to follow him. Shalsar had been one of the less powerful Keepers when she came into being, but even so, she had seen what no one else had, and was compelled to pursue it. Braccus knew she was fascinated by him from the very start. In his arrogance, he assumed that she would never dare invade his privacy the way she had. He hadn't thought it possible and hadn't noticed the intrusion until it was too late. By then, his secret had been revealed and his thoughts had become bitter and twisted, taking on a life of their own.

The thoughts shifted and became shadows; the shadows that manipulated this place now. The shadows festered, taking away any beauty that once existed, filling it with the filth and sickness of Braccus's deep-seated hate for everything he had once sought to be a part of. Enjoying their new-found freedom, the shadows drifted around his former refuge, at first just content to be out in the open. Then they began to get a strong yearning to be in the outer dimension, searching for a way to take solid form so they could move out into the areas they wished to dominate.

Shalsar had run from him when she learned what he was doing behind Iam's back. She hadn't stopped to let him explain himself, to give his side of the story. He had been so angry with her, which only fed the shadows more. She had fought him then and continued fighting him with all she had for the rest of her existence. When she died, she had passed on that need to the one who had inherited her powers.

It was pain and rage that had made him hide the object in the first place. She shouldn't have seen him here; he hadn't been ready for that. Shalsar had given her life fighting to resist his taking his rightful place as master of all that existed. She met him on the field of battle and when he had defeated her, sent her spirit to Sara; the girl who haunted his thoughts because of what she carried around inside her.

Shalsar was still fighting him through that girl even though he had spared her a second time after her death. He actually had her in his possession when Sara was in her four-year dream state. Shalsar had stayed so close to the place Olie had made for the girl that he was able to trap her and take her back to his own ugly version of the dreamlands. He kept her for as long as he could, but she would still not give in to him and there wasn't enough of her spirit left outside of Sara's body for him to fully control her, so he contented himself with making her suffer; torturing what little spirit she had left on the outside. Shalsar was so tightly connected to the girl that separating them at this point was just not possible and he both hated and longed for them because of it.

It was his strongest wish to regain what he had lost and so much more. Shalsar's memories were growing stronger and stronger inside Sara, giving her the advantage of seeing things she had never experienced. And that, combined with what was already inside her, would make dealing with her truly challenging. Presently, Sara was caught up in a situation that she didn't quite understand and Braccus was going to use the confusion to keep what was hidden stay that way.

His secret was going to remain just that: a secret. While standing just outside one of the underground entrances in the outer worlds, he had felt the connection he had with Shalsar being used to find his object. Face purple with rage, he felt them defying him from beyond the grave, both of them, one long dead and one just recently so. Anger made his skin burn brightly, he dug his fingernails into his arm and tore the flesh away with such great force that his boiling blood spurted out and burned the already barren ground. Bit by bit, he tore away the surface of his sheltering flesh until all that was visible was a thick red form of muscle and tissue. His rage was making him strip away all pretense of humanity, exposing the beast underneath for all to see.

Stupid, blundering spirits! He had provided them with bodies to move about in and this was how they showed him their appreciation! *They couldn't even finish what they had started!* He wanted her soul; it was all he had left to take from her. If he could just get hold of that last part of her then it would be a start to make things right for him. He would have things his way, and once he took away every last thing Iam cherished, he would use that precious soul and bend it to his will. The fact that Shalsar's soul was blended so artfully with Sara's made it a prize worth capturing, despite all the inconvenience he'd had to endure so far.

Braccus's strong voice boomed out in the air, as he moved with incredible speed through several dimensions, back through the barrier between life and death. He cut through the edge of the clean and beautiful area the Keepers had created, not caring to encounter the light. He hated the light. As soon as he killed the rest of the Keepers, this place would have to go. Despite this confident declaration to himself, he still turned his eyes away from the brightness that dwelled here and hurried to pass through as fast as he could.

No longer resembling anything human, the burning form moved to stand in the circle of fire that had transported it to this dimension in search of the girl causing him all this misery. He should have ended this quite some time ago, but her powers were stronger then. She had almost gotten hold of what lay below the surface, using just enough of it to make him weak and diminished. But his time in power was now and he intended to make sure it stayed that way.

The teardrop stone she had cast years ago to make him into that weak and pathetic version of himself was just a prop, given to her by Iam to make her think she had some kind of magical fallback to get rid of the monster. No, it was all her, driven by her need to save her friends she had tapped into her internal light. And they hadn't told her. Instead of letting her know how strong she was, they kept her as a child, believing that they knew how to best handle this untapped talent. He had gotten his revenge, though. All those years she missed, spent in slumber because Olie hadn't been able to remove his spell from her, had been very satisfying because he had taken away her childhood. Now he was going to take what was rightfully his. Her spirit would be his biggest trophy.

Braccus quickly followed the thin wavering line engraved in his memory from a time long before Iam had populated the worlds. The trail wound down between wisps of black clouds and gnarled, rotten trees toward an area just out of his sight. He sped on, anxious to reach Sara and end this situation, once and for all. Heart beating faster and faster, Braccus prepared to take control of everything he had ever desired.

Chapter Thirty-Nine

Vincent listened to Franklin interact with Charlie, preferring to let his friend do all the talking as they planned the defenses for the underground city. That was the only way to describe this place. So much work had been done to the formerly bleak surroundings that it was now quite an organized civilization. Buildings had gone up so fast since their arrival two weeks ago, that soon, there were several neighborhoods lining the main area. The houses faced well defined streets with lighting provided both by Franklin's mini-sun and the glowing rock things Charlie had brought with him. Small stockades were set up on the edge of the huge central cavern housing all manner of livestock to be found in the winding corridors that led deep into the mountainside around them. Charlie had managed to get several of the citizens to round up the creatures they had managed to hide underground and bring them here.

Rabbits, deer, sheep, and remarkably, a few cows had been found roaming in a panic around the dark trails along with one or two dogs and half-a-dozen cats, who were finding comfort in the arms of some of the settlement's children. Gathering up the animals had given the people something to do and helped create unity by giving them all purpose. Naturally hard-working people, the Marrikans had been glad for the chance to be useful, it gave them hope, when at first, they felt they had none. So, day after day, they went out and looked for more, bringing back a new animal each time. Today, ten more bunnies and a gopher found their way into a smaller corral that was being used as a petting zoo. The smaller animals were being cared for very well by three of the older children. Cleaning and feeding them little pieces of shrubs while making sure that they stayed in the fenced-in area was a great way for them to pass the time. It hadn't entered their minds to use any of the animals for food, even though food supplies were getting low. Right now, it was more important to keep these living things safe and healthy. Before Vincent and Franklin arrived, Charlie had won the people's trust by providing them with everything he possibly could for their survival. By using their strong work ethic and higher than average intelligence, he showed them how to create comfortable homes furnished with objects found scattered throughout the far edges of the cavern, close to the portals that had once provided access to this place. Charlie had greeted his old friend Robert, one of the original Keepers, here several times as he dropped off much-needed supplies. He had sadly said goodbye to the Keeper, watching him lumber away in the form of a large rodent, after promising not to tell the people where the items had come from. It was all happening as he had known it should and he was doing what little he could to maintain order until the young ones arrived. Thank goodness, they had. He had begun to worry about keeping the people down here alive for much longer without them.

The modern dwellings were heated on the inside as well as being lit. Heating was provided by a warm thermal current that came from the core of the planet. The Marrikans had managed to drill holes in the areas he specified and channel the air through the housing units, fighting off the natural coolness of the caves and making it a more comfortable temperature inside at all times. The warm air also served to dry off all the clothing washed in the streams. With all the other conveniences provided, this was a pretty nice set up for the refugees in this world.

But for all that Charlie could provide them, there was still a lot that he could not. That was why they needed the Keepers to come and channel their collective gifts to all the worlds. These modern surroundings would be a nice place to starve if they didn't get Finola's gift here soon and Alice was, of course, guarding the doorways at present. Randall, Eric, Vincent, and Franklin were all familiar with the enemy and would be valuable in teaching the people how to protect themselves in this crazy time.

Charlie had made sure the young men were welcomed by the survivors of this land and, despite Vincent's gift and the fact that all the refugees had to be warned not to touch or even come near him, they seemed to truly appreciate the fact that he was here with them. For Vincent, it was strange to feel appreciated like this. For the first time since he could remember, he felt almost like a part of the crowd. Well, at least he wasn't being pushed back into a corner and feared. They looked at him with a kind of admiration, at least he thought it was admiration, he hadn't really seen that look aimed at him before. This whole experience was strange but exhilarating, he almost felt... normal. This wasn't like the reluctant acceptance of his fellow Keepers, with the exception of Franklin, of course. It was awe-filled respect. Franklin shared Vincent's thoughts and was happy for his friend, glad that he had the chance to have this experience. It was strange. This enjoyable and almost too easy entry into what they had anticipated to be a very difficult situation. Sometimes you should go with your first instinct. None of this was in their minds when they called out to their fellow Keepers, trying to arrange a connection to share their gifts with the collective worlds, but it probably should have been.

Chapter Forty

Alice spoke to the men, demanding they answer her. Her nerves were stretched so thin right now she wasn't sure how she would handle any answer other than the one she wanted to hear. Her eyes stared at Steven as if looking into his very soul, wanting so badly to believe that he wouldn't let her down, that he would tell her the truth. *Please don't lie to me.* The young man watched her hesitantly, trying to gauge her response to what he told her. If she were indeed one of the special ones, then that meant that she had to be good. If she was good, then it was a sure bet that she would never purposefully hurt one of the people she was meant to protect. He spoke to the girl who could appear out of thin air, trusting his instincts about her.

"I don't know,' he answered truthfully. "I heard that Isobel and her people had taken Randall. When I arrived right where Jacob said they would be to try and rescue him, I found you here instead." Steven stepped back a bit as her face got darker. He was beginning to wonder if he had misjudged her horribly. Green eyes sparkled with an intense anger, and she didn't look very reasonable. Right now, right or wrong, all she wanted to do was go through them to find Randall. Alice didn't want to hurt them, but she wasn't going to let Randall die. This man was going to tell her something. He was going to tell her what she wanted to know. *Please do not lie to me.*

"Who is Jacob?" she said, visualizing a very hot, rundown place to send this guy and his friend if they had anything to do with Randall's disappearance. Steven was scared; she picked that up right away. His eyes got wider, watching every movement she made, hands raised to defend himself. Alice took note of that and the fact that his companion moved back a bit, stepping carefully to the side as if he might be thinking of moving behind her. Why would they do that? Fear or guilt? She may be tired, but she had seen her share of battles and her senses were on high alert as she tried to keep both men in her sights.

Not going to happen, boys. Her shield flared a bright pink color, snapping and hissing as she made it known that they were messing with something way beyond their ability to deal with. She didn't want to show them that she was scared to death and didn't want them to come any closer. Going head-to-head with dead scary things was one thing but having to fight one of Iam's creations was absolutely terrifying to her. He felt strongly about his creations and hurting them was not what she was made for. If, on the other hand, these guys had somehow harmed Randall, she wouldn't be able to control herself. *Please don't lie to me,* she whispered silently. It would be so nice to have a little help right now as she was still exhausted and lost. *Talk and don't lie.*

Steven didn't answer her right away, as he considered how best to present his brother's ability to see the future. His mind was working overtime, trying to reassure her when his friend made a very unwise move.

Ray had been watching the girl with interest as Steven took center stage in the conversation, doing his best to convince her to go with them. This was ridiculous! They needed her help so badly and she needed to know that. If she were indeed all that special, then she should know they were the good guys. Instead of greeting them with open arms, she was treating them like she didn't trust them, like maybe she thought they were bad, too. She had to understand that she was supposed to help them; they had been promised that it would be so.

Years of doing battle had taught Ray to study his opponents closely, and he could tell that this powerful girl was nervous, edgy, and not being very reasonable. Maybe he could get into position and corner her, get her to listen. He was going to test her defenses. Maybe if he surprised her, Steven would be able to capture her and bring her to Jacob. When she was calmer she would see that they were on the same side and would forgive him for what he had to do. He continued to circle around the slim girl who stood perfectly still, eyes trained on his friend. He was so close to the pink light that clung to her body. What could it do? he wondered as he reached out a finger to touch the filmy covering. With a yelp of surprise, Ray jerked back as he received a nasty shock upon contact with the substance.

The sound of the young man's pain startled Alice, who instinctively protected herself. Hand raised, she aimed at the man immediately behind her, and Ray shimmered in and out of view. A startled gasp escaped the young man's lips as he hung in-between dimensions, seeing things hidden there that terrified him. How was she doing that? The ugliness he saw was far worse than the horrifying monsters he had seen in battle.

"Stop it!" Steven yelled, getting Alice's attention, making her pull back and return Ray to his solid state. She let him loose and soothed his mind, erasing some but not all the things he had seen; wanting him to remember enough to keep him from trying to get at her again. Shaking uncontrollably, she stood with her back to the cave wall, staring at both men in horror. Afraid of them, afraid of herself, she was ashamed both by what she had done to him and the fact that she would do it again in a heartbeat if it would lead her to Randall. She wasn't going to allow him to get away with hiding what he knew. *Don't lie to me.*

Alice stared at Steven, waiting to hear what he had to tell her, to hear where Randall had been taken. Her head hurt and all she wanted to do was find the man she loved. These two strangers had been hanging around him, had been aware that Isobel and her men were after Randall. They had to know something. Why had they not been around to stop those people from taking Randall? Had they helped them, even? Whose side were they really on?

"Who is Jacob?" Stress was causing her eyes to blur; desperation making her act impulsively. Wherever Randall was, he was running out of time and she needed to find him soon. If these men could lead her to him, then she was willing to do whatever she needed to in order to save him. But that might mean doing something horrible. Maybe she wouldn't be able to pull back next time. Sheer rage and anxiety might make her leave one of these men in a truly rotten place. She might regret it later. She wasn't sure, but she didn't want them to make her have to do it.

Steven answered quickly this time, unnerved by the slightly unfocused look on the young woman's face. He tried to appeal to her sense as a caretaker of the ungifted. "Jacob is my brother. He told me to tell you when I met you that he is one of the gifted ones. He knows why you are here and what you can do. He tells me that you, and others like you, are the reason that our people will survive. He wants to meet you, to introduce you into the population properly. The people need to meet you as the special being that you are." He stood with his hands raised in the universal *I'm totally harmless, please don't hurt me* gesture while looking anxiously at his friend. Ray was shaken but otherwise unharmed. He didn't speak, just backed up to the cave wall, touching it to reassure himself that he was whole and real once again. How could someone so young, beautiful, and frail-looking also be so powerful and intimidating? He wanted to give her a hug and hide from her at the same time; a strange sensation.

The last thing Steven wanted was to make her any angrier, she didn't look very stable; her lovely face was a bit drawn, with dark rings appearing underneath her eyes. She obviously wasn't rested. He didn't know where she had been hiding all this time, but she clearly hadn't taken care of herself. She seemed upset and a little unbalanced, a dangerous combination for someone that powerful. At this moment, she was scarier than if she had come at him with snakes growing out of her head and fire shooting from her eyes. He needed to appeal to her sense of duty; his brother was counting on him to make contact. He also had a feeling that Randall needed their help soon.

"Is Randall one of your kind?" Steven asked softly, watching closely as she nodded her head and choked back a sob. Steven thought he understood her behavior; she obviously cared for Randall and was scared that he was missing. He had felt that way about someone who had disappeared years ago. It was at the time when he had first started patrolling the villages with his brother, when the first slightly disturbing incidents had made the men gather together and watch what was going on around them.

A few raids in isolated areas were followed by a disappearance here and a disappearance there. Mari was one of those who went missing. He had searched for her for the longest time, exhausting all avenues until she was just a haunting memory that he couldn't forget, conquer. So he had fought with his brother and the other men to pass the time in his life when he missed her so much. He didn't know what else to do with himself, except save the rest of the population. He was going to help her; they were going to help each other because she needed them, and they needed her.

"It's alright; we aren't out to get you. I understand why you're upset. Ray and I can help you if you let us." Steven lowered his hands and sat on the ground to begin the conversation. "What's your name?"

"Alice," she whispered, letting her shield down because she finally knew, finally felt what she had been waiting to feel. These men had not been behind Randall's abduction, she was reading them the way a mother might read a child that she had raised. These men were about her age, but she was so much older inside and when she set her mind to it, she could see almost everything. So why couldn't she see Randall? They were her best hope of finding him. For some reason, her connection to him had been compromised and she had to rest to find it again.

Yes, rest would be nice, but she didn't have the luxury of that. She was going to take what they offered: help.

"Wherever they took Randall, it wasn't out there." Alice pointed to the doorway. He was being held somewhere; she didn't feel empty like he was completely gone, just a faint tingling interference like she needed to find the connection once again. She had thought she was beyond this, that she had learned her lesson in her last encounter with Braccus and his dead servants. There was something still missing, and it had to do with the thing she had been avoiding.

Taking a deep breath, she listened to Steven talking to her softly, explaining about his brother again, telling her that he and Ray would use their skills in tracking the group that had taken Randall because both she and Randall were important to the people here. She smiled. She knew that she would only see results by doing the one thing she didn't really want to do. Carefully slipping a shield around the two men sitting

across from her, Alice reached out and drew on the
connection she had with the dead.

Chapter Forty-One

Maryann and Robert walked slowly through the tunnels, leaving Rianna's burial place. Her husband was heartbroken by the loss of his old friend. He was trying not to show it, trying to be strong for her and the others, but she could feel him crying on the inside. They had managed to break through the stony ground and dig a grave big enough to house the coffin. Small, simple, and made from scrap wood he had brought to the caves weeks ago, this final resting place was all he could offer, and he felt so ashamed of not being able to give Rianna more.

It had been so hard to place his fellow Keeper's body in such a plain resting place, when he knew she should have been transported to the perfect place with Iam. She had given up that right willingly to seek out Sara and save her from Braccus. This wonderful woman had taken him on, merging with the evil entity in order to hold him back, making him weaker than he would have been on his own. She had done all this knowing what it would cost her dearly and he was sad for all that she had lost, loving her even more for it.

Robert had never seen a Keeper's body remain earthbound after death. He was aware of what had happened to Olie and Ferd, but he hadn't been there to witness their slaughter and didn't want to imagine it. Seeing her lifeless body lying there had suddenly made him realize just how much things had changed and how vulnerable they all were now.

He had dug her grave himself in the form of an extra-large Mole, using his huge claws to burrow into the unyielding earth, placing her gently in the box and covering it with soil. Maryann watched from the other side of the small cavern they had chosen for her resting place, quietly offering him support as he performed this painful task.

Switching form when he needed more strength, he transformed into a good-sized Orangutan. Grabbing hold of a boulder it might have taken a few big men to move, he pulled it over the grave to serve both as a marker and to protect her body from being disturbed in any way. Muscles straining beneath the thin layer of red hair, he settled the heavy rock in place with a thump, a small groan escaping the lips of the animal as he carried out the task. A tear dripped slowly down the animal's brown leathery cheek, the only indication of how Robert was feeling at this moment.

Maryann wanted to reach out to him so badly, but waited as the animal became her husband once again, standing to walk back to her side. He turned to her and closed his eyes, sharing his grief quietly, mind to mind. They stood there in a silence broken only by the sobs of the small group of mourners who had gathered around the grave site to say goodbye to the Keeper they had loved so much.

Villagers who had grown up knowing Rianna's kindness had followed his progress silently, waiting for him to finish before they gathered in front of the grave to ask Iam for mercy for this Keeper. They too had never been able to remember a time when they had to witness the burial of a Keeper and while they had never been sure of what happened to them after they ceased to be in the world, they were pretty sure this was an unusual event. Therefore, they asked for whatever had gone wrong for this lovely woman to be set right. With bowed heads, they issued a united silent plea for understanding and forgiveness for Rianna. Robert and Maryann felt their request and it made them smile despite their sorrow.

It wasn't only the kind and thoughtful gesture made by their people; it was the result that their actions brought. Robert felt the presence of two very familiar spirits hovering close by, their connection to him so strong and loving that an even bigger smile formed on his lips. He couldn't help it, couldn't stop it from happening, a feeling of joy so intense that he wanted to burst out in laughter. Just minutes before he didn't know how he was going to deal with the loss of yet another of his loved ones, now he knew they were here with him. Olie and Ferd appeared so clearly in his head that he didn't want to open his eyes. Because right now, they were standing right next to Rianna's grave and holding their hands out to the pile of rocks covering it.

Maryann saw them too and she squeezed Robert's hand tightly as a thin wavering grey light snaked out of the ground and wound its way between the cracks in the rocks to appear in the air above. At first thin and shady, it gradually became thicker until a shape formed and Rianna stood on the ground next to Olie and Ferd. More beautiful than he had seen her, the Keeper stood next to her companions with a smile that lit up their hearts.

They understood that she would be with the others who had given up eternal rest, doing what they wanted more than anything, caring for their people. They were content with their lot, not resting in peace, but together and productive in their own way. This was enough for them now. With a brief but well understood message that all was well, and they would always be as close as they could, the three spirits left the cave. A feeling of well-being and rest stayed even as they departed to do what they could in the other worlds.

Opening their eyes, Maryann and Robert exchanged hugs as they led their people away from the grave site and back toward the central cavern that was now their home. As they walked, Maryann was receiving more information from the young Keepers. She didn't want to share what she was seeing, but it was coming through anyway. Visions showed that things weren't working out all that well.

Finola was sobbing, terrified of the dark place she and Eric were hiding in. Tall thorny hedges provided a protective barrier against the persistent angry, frightened refugees trying to get to them. Eric was sharing his ability to see in the dark with the girl, but her fear of dark places was getting the better of her and she was fighting panic by concentrating on keeping the thorny barrier intact. To say that their mission had not worked out the way they intended was a major understatement. If they didn't get help soon, they would be in deeper trouble than ever. As it was, it would take a minor miracle for them to gain the trust of these people now that they knew these two were different in a major way. Maryann couldn't reach out to them, she was forced to watch the sad scene until it faded and was replaced by another.

Alice was sitting across from the two young men she had seen working with Randall, but there was no Randall. They were talking, but she could tell Alice was concentrating on something other than the conversation. She looked exhausted and sad, but also very determined. Maryann couldn't tell what she was about to do, but she was concerned by the darkness that was hovering around her. She was scared for the girl and couldn't do anything to help her. She hated the fact that she couldn't see very much. She was obviously missing a lot, and to make matters worse, she lost that vision too, being unable to maintain contact with any of them for very long. What had happened to Randall? Why were they separated? There was no answer as she was shown yet another vision.

Vincent and Franklin became visible, in a scene much more pleasant than the others. They were talking to what Robert told her was a Surren, and that was a good thing. He had been their introduction to the people of this world. They had been accepted now and could begin to help them as they had been intended to. It was the only bright spot in the otherwise bleak storyline the others were facing, and she was glad to see that they were successful.

But their success was just one part of a bigger picture. For this all to work as it should, they would need to have all the worlds connected. There were seven worlds in all, so while they had arrived in three of them, they still had so much ground to cover. With the condition of the other teams being in less than desirable states, it was necessary to get things under control as soon as possible.

Vincent and Franklin needed to find a way to reach out to their friends and help them find a way to get through their own bad situations. They needed the skills of all the Keepers to provide their unique abilities to the worlds and seal up the doorways for good. In order to make sure the enemy could not enter the underground refuges, access to the upper worlds had to be completely shut off for now. It would take them working as a complete team to do that, well, as complete a team as they could be without Vincent's other half.

As Maryann thought about what she had seen, discussing with Robert the possibility of reaching out to them to help, he shook his head sadly. They would have to fix this themselves and do it before the shields went down. He could sense that Alice was tiring; she couldn't possibly guard all the doorways for much longer. It was draining her much too quickly. He felt so useless not being able to leave and rescue them but his appearing among the already panicked people would serve no purpose other than make a bad situation worse. Maybe Olie, Ferd and Rianna could reach out to them, if they couldn't help physically, maybe they could make enough of a connection to guide them in the right direction. Robert forced himself to think only of success for the young Keepers as he joined with Maryann, diverting her attention from the fading visions to concentrate on issues with the people they were living with now. They spoke to the villagers of managing the food supplies, and of occupying them with chores as they struggled with the day-to-day issues of staying alive here. There was nothing else to be done for the others. It was useless to torture themselves with thoughts of things they could not control. He pushed his dark thoughts aside and concentrated on living.

Chapter Forty-Two

Braccus arrived at the place he had felt her so long ago. The other two were with her, he could tell, but he wasn't interested in them. He reached out for the connection he refused to let go of, because with her, as always, was Shalsar. The cord that bound them together despite everything she had done to try and block him out, drew him directly to her. The trail wound past the rotted and corrupt landscape of his once beautiful refuge. He rather enjoyed the atmosphere now; it matched how he felt. The destruction and pain that this dimension had undergone was exhilarating to him. Where once he had a brief moment filled with the need to create on Iam's level, now he craved the ending of all. Wanting everything to look as wild and angry as he was inside.

Her essence pulled him in, making his whole being tingle as he got closer and closer to her. There was no escaping him; he owned it all now and was going to be merciless. Braccus almost drooled in anticipation of all he would do when his reign officially began with total control of both dimensions. The only rules that would apply anywhere would be the ones he made, and they would change constantly so that he would be able to punish anyone and everyone in any way he chose. Of course, now that he was about to take over, he would have to do some major redecorating. As wasted as the surface of the worlds were, he wouldn't have to do much to them, but he would have to completely wipe out any trace of Iam's influence on the underworlds. He would have access to them as soon as he wiped out the rest of the Keepers.

Only after he got rid of them would he be able to create all kinds of wonderful new plants and animals. He was confident that he could do a much better job at covering the surface with useful and interesting things than the pretender to the throne that currently hid from this struggle. Tucked away in his perfect place with those useless guardians the Artregeans, Iam had refused to answer his challenge, letting his lesser creations do all the fighting for him. It was an insult he wanted to avenge in person.

The only thing that would make his victory complete would be to have Iam crawling and begging at his feet. He would get to him soon enough. For now, it was more than enough to know that Iam would be watching when he destroyed what was left of his pitiful creations. He would also be watching when he took the soul of what Braccus was sure was his last great hope to save the worlds: Sara, his pet Keeper.

He could see her now, just below him as he raced in a mist-like form to reach the dead girl. Faster and faster he pushed himself toward her, anxious to begin absorbing her power, wanting to watch her strength and light disappear into his darkness. With a thud, his feet touched familiar ground. He smiled with anticipation at the thought of the fear she must be experiencing upon his arrival. He was not as she remembered him from before, not the wasted old man, not the rotting corpse form she had seen when she confronted him the first time, but as a strong awesome being who had come into his own greatness.

Tall and confident, he walked toward her, a true representation of what he was, glowing body radiating with heat that would have melted everything around him in the natural world. But here, he merely moved through the darkness, having no effect on the ground around him, because here really wasn't here. Here was what he made it, here was his place, and he was the supreme being of it all. He liked the way the molten lava of his body looked against the darkness, the slickness of his fleshless muscles flexing as he moved. It was all working out so perfectly; the final battle was on his turf and he was as he should be: truly master of it all.

Braccus moved at a deliberate slow and steady pace so she could see him approach and shiver in fear at what was about to happen. He ignored her companions, standing closely at her side. They were of no consequence to him. He just wanted to see her blue eyes opened so wide with terror that the whites glared against her pale skin. He craved her reaction. He sought only her face wanting that last intimate connection as their eyes met and he took her soul for his own.

He watched her face closely with each step waiting for a good clear view before he made his first move, but as she became more and more visible he was startled to see, not terror but smug amusement looking back at him. Sara faced him with a big satisfied smile on her face. She was laughing at him! He heard the sound even as he denied the possibility, and she wasn't laughing alone, the three other dead ones with her were laughing, too. How dare they! Didn't they know he had the upper hand? He had arrived in time to prevent them from obtaining part of his secret. They had lost, and he had won. They weren't supposed to be laughing. Rage made him act faster than intended. While before, Braccus had wanted to draw out the moment, all he wanted to do now was destroy that troublesome girl. Raising a bloody red arm, the evil being twisted his hand and beckoned the blonde girl toward him. Her body responded. Her head snapped downward, golden hair spilling across her face as he commanded her to move while he waited. What happened next was equally unexpected. Instead of jerking forward as he intended, Sara recovered her balance, raised her head and her arms, and pulled him directly toward her. To his unpleasant surprise, he was forced to go where she commanded. *What was happening?*

When she had first felt him arrive in this place, Sara's heart had plummeted. After all, she was in his secret place, the place he had made to his specifications. The other part of the afterworld wasn't his and he was vulnerable; but this place, like most every other area that existed, belonged to him.

That should mean that they were in serious trouble. There should be nothing they could do to stop him from taking what little power they had left. But for some reason, when he finally did appear, when she actually saw him touch down on the surface, she felt calm; there was no fear at all.

Sara felt his confidence, his total conviction that he was master of all that surrounded him; it flowed from his being as he strutted his grotesque skinless form toward them like an overstuffed rooster. She should know that this was truly the end.

She should be scared witless now, but a flip switched somewhere inside and there was clarity instead of panic. Then a thought popped into her head that came from nowhere logical and she knew; they all knew, what they were supposed to do: the last thing he would have expected. Gathering together as a single mental unit, they invited him in and used Braccus against himself.

For the first time since he had crawled into her head, seeking to gain entry into her soul, she stopped fighting whatever it was that drew them together and pulled on it. They called on the power and wisdom that dwelled inside of her group of three, the parts of them that knew things that they as humans had never fully accessed while they were alive.

The power was there, the knowledge was there; it flared to the front of their brains and flowed into Sara's outstretched hand. The slight tug of his initial command had moved her a little but when she knew that she was indeed able to resist it, she used it against him and gave a sharp tug back. Braccus's shocked expression was priceless, replacing the smug smile of seconds before. This unexpected result brought a feeling of joy over the three as they watched their enemy's body jolt forward and laughter bubbled up from their lips at the discovery of what they could accomplish. The fact that it made him furious was just an extra bonus for the way they were feeling right now.

Unsteady on his feet, Braccus stood with twisted lips and aimed an assault at Sara. He focused on the strongest soul in the group as they were all gathered together in her. Grabbing onto the connection that he had used to get to her in the first place, he struck back. A sharp push with his hand stopped the laughter and sent them reeling backwards onto the slick and oozy surface he created beneath them. It stopped the laughter but had no other lasting effect on their abilities.

Sara and her friends quickly got back on their feet, fighting the pull of the wet thick goo beneath them. The swampy surface was like trying to stand in a bowl of oatmeal with extra oats. Sara froze it enough for them to crack it with their feet and stand upright once more.

James, Thomas, and Sara then circled around Diandra to provide protection as they maintained their position inside Sara's head. They knew what he was thinking, and they had no intention of allowing him to get to the only non-Keeper here.

A blast of darkness in the shape of a lightning bolt struck at Braccus, slicing through his body with deadly accuracy. A meaty red arm dropped onto the soupy ground to be swallowed rapidly by the blackness before being replaced by another one at Braccus's command. A new arm shot out from his shoulder socket like a quick growing weed, taking

265

form so fast that it was almost like it had never been lost. He contained his blood, the attack, though a direct hit; never caused a single drop to hit the ground. It clung to him like plastic coursing through his very visible veins. Whatever he was, he wasn't dead, just changed in form enough to suit his need. He couldn't afford to lose any of his precious fluid to the blood hungry soil here, so he contained it by using his supreme powers.

Brushing back the fine black hair that still clung to his red skull, Braccus turned back to the group. Eager to vent his anger on the members of the circle, he raised an arm and sent a volley of sharp sticks and snakes at them. All these failed to make their mark and would have no lasting effect anyway. They were no longer alive and didn't have the same concern about their bodies that he did. Braccus needed to be a lot closer to them to do the amount of damage he intended.

Back and forth the blows were exchanged from a distance, Braccus changing his focus to the only member of Sara's group that had no ability to protect herself: Diandra. He called her to him, fully intending to use her weakness against the others. But he failed as Sara deflected every attempt he made with a strong defense of her own, keeping the girl safely behind her and the others.

Braccus was disturbed to see that his dead things were kept away at James's command. They should be far more afraid of him then that gangly young man. Blow after blow was sent, each side giving as good as they got, having no major effect, but making Braccus angrier by the minute as he failed to gain any ground while they stood against him.

Seeking to make some headway, Braccus swiped his hand downward in one quick motion with the image of Sara firmly placed in his head. The result was a bloody trail of tears in her face while she stood her ground just feet away from him. He had done it as a reminder that he could still get to her, if not fatally yet. Jumping slightly at the contact, she was surprised to find that it hurt a lot, and what she felt Thomas and James did also. Rage flared into Thomas and James's heads as they saw what Braccus had done, thoughts of making him pay dearly for this assault flaring into their heads.

His tactic to break their ring of control almost worked, the sight of Sara standing next to him with deep fingernail scratches marring her otherwise flawless smooth face made Thomas falter for a second, his eyes blurred red with anger, making it hard for him to see. James was refocused by Diandra, his temper kept in check by her reminder that Sara could take care of herself and he was needed to keep the dead things back.

Thomas, on the other hand, wanted to launch himself at the guy that looked like a walking pile of meat sauce, and rip what was left of him into tiny little pieces. Sara scolded him sternly as he almost pulled back to check her injuries, reminding him that she was dead, and this was merely an illusion, no real harm could come to a dead body. It was their souls they needed to watch out for. Sara drew on Thomas's anger. For the first time since they had been together she encouraged the one part of him that had troubled him since he was a young boy. His temper had always brought out the worst in him and bound him closely to Braccus. As such, it could be used against Braccus also. In fact, for some reason, what may have been a liability for them in the living worlds, seemed to be working well for them in Braccus's play-ground.

They could use this; they all realized that at the same time. Raising their arms together, the three companions with the symbol of the moon binding them together, tore up a good section of otherworldly ground beneath Braccus and watched as he fell straight down. A smile of satisfaction curved up the edges of Sara's lips as she watched him being sucked into the muck; the deep red marks on her face fading as her happiness radiated outward.

The battle they were fighting had gone on for hours and Braccus had to admit, at least to himself, that there was no winning for either side now. She could not leave here, she was dead, but he could; he intended to depart and make her pay in as many ways as he could by getting to whatever she loved that was still alive in the worlds. Yes, he was going, but before he went, the evil entity did the only thing he could think of to turn this situation in his favor. He had to remove the thing that she could use against him. Closing his eyes and summoning the vision she had stopped calling to herself, he brought the silver box to mind. He saw it suddenly in his hand and then he was gone.

As soon as he shimmered out of view, Sara knew this was not good. She felt him moving away, gloating as he took what he knew she had been looking for. So sure in himself as his thoughts returned to revenge, of making her pay for all that she had put him through. She could not stop him from leaving, she was aware of that, but she could not allow him to get away with the object. It was the reason she was dead in the first place.

As sickening as every contact she had to make with him was, Sara reached out again and, casting out her partners, she put herself in his body. Her thin filmy soul raced after him and slipped easily into the sickness and decay that was his brain. Moving into his mind, she used the connection to gain access much in the same way he had stayed with her all those years when she was asleep and forced to roam around in dreamland. Together yet separate, aware of each other but not fully connecting, she read his thoughts and became an interested observer. Only this time, he was the helpless one, for a whole second or two.

As he moved, she stayed with him, guards up enough to prevent being totally absorbed into his being. She hung on, molding her form beneath his, not letting the fact that he was trying to get out of here as fast as possible deter her from doing what she intended. He felt her there, fully determined to leave here with her soul on board, she was guarded enough to not let him gain complete control, but if he could just keep her inside him long enough, he could make it through the portal and escape with the one thing he truly wanted. He was winning, after all.

She stayed put, reading his intentions easily and feeling the strong presence of Thomas as he sped after her. He was screaming in protest while Braccus was laughing inside. She burrowed into his mind, making his limbs move, loosening his grasp on the object she refused to let him remove from this place. Just a moment more, she felt her brain popping and humming with the effort of keeping her position in his head without letting him take her over or throw her out. She loosened his fingers one by one. Braccus sped toward the exit using her determination to stick with him as a way to get her out of here with him.

So, so close to the exit, just a second or two more... Braccus moved faster as he felt his fingers uncurl from the box. His foot touched the portal and she was still in there, he was grinning despite the fact that his object was now falling to the filmy ground. It mattered so little that the object stayed if she were trapped inside of him to be at his mercy once they crossed over into the solid world.

269

"No!!!!!!" a man's voice screamed, breaking the eerie silence as Braccus's entire being passed through the door which slammed shut behind him, sealing it with a sharp electric snap. The entrance to the afterworld was sealed; nothing could enter or exit now. What was on either side would stay there. Only one entity, angry beyond all reason now, was going to make sure that this situation was reversed as soon as he could manage it.

Chapter Forty-Three

The scream was so loud and unexpected that it shook the underground inhabitants of the worlds. The wail radiated all around, penetrating all ears that could hear. It was an angry sound, a mournful sound, seeming to come from nowhere but everywhere at the same time. Maryann huddled closer to Robert when they heard it; whoever had issued the scream was obviously very angry and out to make someone pay for their pain. They looked at each other and tried to carry on with their daily routine, but it was hard to concentrate when all contact had been broken with the Keepers. Maryann could no longer see what was happening. This disturbed her greatly. The last thing she had seen from most of them had not been good. The young people were in trouble and there was nothing they could do to help them, she couldn't even check in to see if things were getting better.

She and Robert had told themselves that they would concentrate on getting their people through this until the Keepers could get back to them, but it was so hard to carry on when they didn't know for sure what was happening. Then there had been that horrible screaming. *Who was that?* Comforting the frightened villagers around them, they downplayed the incident by telling them that it was just another of the enemy's tricks designed to scare them. But they both knew that something significant had happened and that it would affect either their side or Braccus's eventually. It was horrible not to know which and in what way.

Far away in another cave, Finola nervously watched the darkened areas around her with the aid of Eric's excellent night vision eyes. Holding his hand, she waited for another horrible scream to break the silence, but it didn't happen. They did, however, hear the refugees on the other side of her thorny wall of vines. They were scared, both of her, Eric, and the frightening noise that had come from thin air.

There were loud voices all speaking at once, demanding that the two of them come back to face them and explain what they had been up to while hiding among the normal, "good" people in the caves.

"Come back and be judged," a loud voice yelled, boldly demanding that they come back into the central area and turn themselves over to him. They also heard other voices; some seemed to be arguing with the loud person and others seemed to be encouraging him to continue yelling. Scuffling feet and more arguing could be heard before Eric hit the mute button to comfort the girl he loved. She was trying so hard to not show her fear, to smile bravely and not complain. He could also tell she regretted revealing their secret to the people here; he couldn't let her beat herself up about it any longer.

"I love you," Eric repeated over and over again, until all she heard were his words. He spoke about what they were going to do when they got out of here and how they could spend time going over all the memories they shared. Ever since they found out what they truly were, the history of their time before they inhabited these bodies was becoming easier to remember. Shutting out all the fear, they shared beautiful visions of a time long before this scary one.

Finola focused on these memories, trying to take her mind off the fact that she was in the dark surrounded by creepy-crawly things, and in a lot of trouble with the angry refugees. She held his hand tightly, enjoying the distraction while they waited for something good to happen.

Far away in another world, Alice sat focusing on a spot beyond her two young companions, jolted from her attempt to reach for the dead things by the terrifying scream that had

torn through the air a few minutes before. The three newly
introduced occupants of the dark passageway shared a
frightened glance as the eerie sound faded away, leaving an
uncomfortable silence behind it. *Who or what was that?*
Alice prayed with all her might that it had nothing to do with
Randall and the people that held him captive. If it did, she
would not be able to stop herself from reacting in a very bad
way. After checking to see that both young men were still
protected, she let herself slip into that dangerous place. A
place that she dreaded to go, but knew was necessary to find
her boyfriend.

While Alice made her difficult choice, Vincent and Franklin
were standing with Charlie in front of a group of Marrikan's.
The scream startled them and left Charlie with a troubled
look on his face. Vincent got the impression that this
mysterious event was not so mysterious to the little man. But
when asked about it, the Surren simply shook his head and
denied that he had any idea of its meaning.

Maybe the little man wasn't telling them everything because
he was uncertain about the outcome or he was trying not to
upset them, but Vincent now felt, more than ever, that he
needed to watch Charlie more closely. Seeds of suspicion had
been planted in his mind and, once settled there, he could
not kill their growth. This place was not as perfect as it
seemed. Maybe they still had things to worry about. He kept
the thought that he was going to stick closer to Franklin than
ever. Vincent was going to watch his fellow Keeper's back,
and if it became necessary to take his side over all the other
people in this cave; then he was with his friend one hundred
percent, no matter what their original mission. He was
rewarded with the same silent thought from Franklin who
was now acting as the spokesperson for the Keepers in this
world. They would be helpful but always on their guard.

Vincent listened as Franklin spoke to him and the refugees about defending themselves against an enemy that lacked not only a conscience but any form of mercy for those they faced in battle. Trying to convince a basically decent and good group of people that they needed to fight dirty was not easy. It wasn't their first instinct to fight to kill, hoping rather to drive the enemy back and away from all they loved. Hurting them just enough to want to leave the area was their original plan; it hadn't worked very well for them so far.

It would not be enough at this point to make life uncomfortable for the enemy. The people here had to know that the Keepers were willing to do what had to be done when the time came for the next face off with the monsters that had driven them down here. Guilt must be taken away from the equation. While they were required to show mercy, it was, after all, a part of them that Iam cherished most and encouraged, they also had to be willing to destroy the evil ones if it were called for.

It was all a natural part of the balance that both sides face each other repeatedly until there was more of one than the other. The creator must come out the victor, his will dictated that it be so. This struggle would be a wake-up call to his people that free will and courage were called for when life became difficult and that he had created a fierce group of beings more than capable of rising to the challenge.

They spoke of joining forces with the other Keepers, trying to give the people around them hope that they could turn this situation into a new beginning for their world. Vincent let Franklin talk to his small audience, while they both had the same thought that they were terrified, that they might not be up to the task they were faced with. They had lost contact with their partners a day or two ago, as they had all tried to blend into their surroundings and not give away the fact that they were different. Both young men were thinking of reaching out again, especially after that weird screaming sound they had heard, but were afraid that doing so might put their friends in danger. They were all waiting for a sign that it was safe before using their mental abilities.

Putting off contact a little bit longer, Vincent and Franklin tried to keep positive for the people they were here to help. It was the same all around as each group, isolated as they were, did their best to do what Iam had sent them to do. With the outcome so uncertain, the Keepers dug deeper into their souls to find the strength to continue with the job of saving Iam's people, if they would only allow them to.

This is the beginning of the struggles. We pause as time continues without us to rejoin our heroes at another time in their lives.

The End

www.ingramcontent.com/pod-product-compliance
Lightning Source LLC
Chambersburg PA
CBHW051419170626
46809CB00006B/2236